Praise for the novels of
#1 *New York Times* bestselling author
Debbie Macomber

"Debbie Macomber tells women's stories in a way no one else does."

—*BookPage*

"Macomber is a skilled storyteller."

—*Publishers Weekly*

"With first-class author Debbie Macomber, it's quite simple—she gives readers an exceptional, unforgettable story every time, and her books are always, always keepers!"

—*ReadertoReader.com*

"Macomber's storytelling sometimes yields a tear, at other times a smile."

—*Newport News Daily Press*

"It's clear that Debbie Macomber cares deeply about her fully realized characters and their families, friends and loves, along with their hopes and dreams. She also makes her readers care about them."

—*Bookreporter.com*

"No one writes stories of love and forgiveness like Macomber."

—*RT Book Reviews*

"Virtually guaranteed to please."

—*Publishers Weekly*

DEBBIE MACOMBER

Their Perfect Match

mira

mira

ISBN-13: 978-0-7783-0887-4

Recycling programs for this product may not exist in your area.

Their Perfect Match

Also available from Debbie Macomber and MIRA Books

Midnight Sons

Alaska Skies
 (Brides for Brothers and
 The Marriage Risk)
Alaska Nights
 (Daddy's Little Helper and
 Because of the Baby)
Alaska Home
 (Falling for Him,
 Ending in Marriage and
 Midnight Sons and Daughters)

This Matter of Marriage
Montana
Thursdays at Eight
Between Friends
Changing Habits
Married in Seattle
 (First Comes Marriage and
 Wanted: Perfect Partner)
Right Next Door
 (Father's Day and
 The Courtship of Carol Sommars)
Wyoming Brides
 (Denim and Diamonds and
 The Wyoming Kid)
Fairy Tale Weddings
 (Cindy and the Prince and
 Some Kind of Wonderful)
The Man You'll Marry
 (The First Man You Meet and
 The Man You'll Marry)
Orchard Valley Grooms
 (Valerie and Stephanie)
Orchard Valley Brides
 (Norah and Lone Star Lovin')
The Sooner the Better
An Engagement in Seattle
 (Groom Wanted and
 Bride Wanted)
Out of the Rain
 (Marriage Wanted and
 Laughter in the Rain)
Learning to Love
 (Sugar and Spice and
 Love by Degree)

You…Again
 (Baby Blessed and
 Yesterday Once More)
The Unexpected Husband
 (Jury of His Peers and
 Any Sunday)
Three Brides, No Groom
Love in Plain Sight
 (Love 'n' Marriage and
 Almost an Angel)
I Left My Heart
 (A Friend or Two and
 No Competition)
Marriage Between Friends
 (White Lace and Promises and
 Friends—And Then Some)
A Man's Heart
 (The Way to a Man's Heart and
 Hasty Wedding)
North to Alaska
 (That Wintry Feeling and
 Borrowed Dreams)
On a Clear Day
 (Starlight and
 Promise Me Forever)
To Love and Protect
 (Shadow Chasing and
 For All My Tomorrows)
Home in Seattle
 (The Playboy and the Widow
 and Fallen Angel)
Together Again
 (The Trouble with Caasi and
 Reflections of Yesterday)
The Reluctant Groom
 (All Things Considered and
 Almost Paradise)
A Real Prince
 (The Bachelor Prince and
 Yesterday's Hero)
Private Paradise
 (in That Summer Place)

Debbie Macomber's
 Cedar Cove Cookbook
Debbie Macomber's
 Christmas Cookbook

CONTENTS

PROMISE ME FOREVER

To Aunt Betty and Uncle Lavern,
Aunt Lois and Uncle Lyn. This one's for you.

One

Joy Nielsen brushed a dark strand of curly hair away from her face and straightened her shoulders. She stood in front of the closed door, strengthening her resolve. She'd been told what to expect. Absently her hand smoothed the pants of the uniform she wore as a physical therapist. This was a new case, and she couldn't help feeling apprehensive after listening to Dr. Phelps.

Determined, she forced a smile and opened the door. Quickly her brown eyes scanned the interior. Although the sun was shining, the drapes were closed and the room was filled with dark shadows. A solitary figure in a wheelchair stared silently into the distance.

With purpose-filled strides, Joy walked into the room.

"Good morning, Mr. Whittaker. I'm your physical therpist, Miss Nielsen. I believe Dr. Phelps mentioned I was coming."

Silence.

Undeterred, Joy pulled open the drapes and paused

momentarily to take in the beauty of the California coast. Huge waves crashed against the beach. The sky was the bluest of blue and not a cloud was in sight. Joy sighed with appreciation.

"Close the drapes." The harshly whispered words were barely audible.

Joy ignored him. No one had mentioned her patient was so young, mid-thirties at most. His hair was dark and needed to be trimmed, his eyes were like that of a caged lion—fierce, and at the same time hopeless and angry. It wasn't difficult to see that this man had once been vital and proud. But he was close to being broken. That was the reason she'd been hired.

"It's a beautiful morning. I was up at dawn and saw the sunrise."

"I said close the drapes." There was no doubting the command a second time. He squinted against the light.

"I'll be bringing in breakfast in just a few minutes, if you'd like to get ready."

His mouth thinned. His two large hands rotated the chair to her side.

"Would you like to eat on the deck?" she asked.

Ignoring her, he leaned forward, grabbed the drapes' pulley, and tugged them closed.

Expelling a frustrated sigh, Joy turned to him, hands on her hips. No, she wouldn't let this man get the better of her. It would be best for them both if he recognized early on that she wasn't like the others.

The room was again dim, with only a minimum of soft light. Dragging a chair to the double glass doors, she unhooked the pulley, opened the drapes, and tossed the cord so that it caught on the valance.

"If you prefer to have the drapes closed, then do it yourself."

His eyes seemed to spit fire at her, but he said nothing. Although his face was covered with at least a day old beard, Joy could see the nerve twitch in his jaw.

"I'll be back in five minutes with your breakfast," she told him. She closed the door on her way out and paused to inhale a deep breath. Dr. Phelps hadn't understated the situation; Sloan Whittaker could easily be her most difficult case.

The white-haired woman Joy had been introduced to earlier that morning glanced up expectantly when Joy entered the large, modern kitchen.

"How'd it go?" Clara Barnes asked.

"Fine," Joy assured the older woman.

As Clara chuckled, a network of wrinkles broke out across her weathered face. "I've been working for Mr. Whittaker too many years to accept that. Odds are you won't last the week." The cheery tone carried a note of challenge.

"I'll last," Joy said as she poured a glass of juice and set it on the tray.

A brow flicked upward approvingly. "I said to Mr. Whittaker's mother the minute I saw you that you'd be the one to help Mr. Whittaker be his ol' self again."

"He has to help himself. There's only so much you or me or anyone can do," Joy explained, and lifted the breakfast tray from the kitchen counter. She didn't mean to sound rude or discouraging, but it was best to set the other woman straight. She wasn't a miracle worker.

"Mr. Whittaker's mother will be here this afternoon. I know she'll want to talk to you."

"Let me know when she arrives." The swinging kitchen door opened with a push of her shoulder.

Sloan had wheeled across his room. He glanced up when she entered. His look was hard and unwelcoming. "I'm not hungry."

"No, I don't imagine you work up much of an appetite sitting in the chair, do you?"

His eyes narrowed menacingly.

"Well, if you're not hungry, I am." Joy walked onto the verandah and set the tray on the table. She made a small production of lifting the silver-domed food warmer. A thick slice of ham, two fried eggs, and hashbrowns filled the plate. An order of toast was wrapped in a white linen cloth and set to the side. Joy deliberately slid the knife across the ham and lifted the first bite to her mouth. "Delicious," she murmured with closed eyes.

Twice she felt his gaze on her, but she said nothing. When she had finished, she stood and walked to the far side of the long deck. The view was fantastic. Sloan Whittaker must be more than bitter to block this beauty from his life. But then, she knew what it was to be immune to the lovelier things of life.

"I'll take the tray back to the kitchen and send Paul in to help you bathe."

He ignored the comment. "You didn't drink the orange juice." He reached up and lifted it from the tray. There was a suppressed violence about the way he handled the glass—as if he wanted to hurl it at her. "The hired help eat in the kitchen. Remember that."

She shouldn't have smiled. Joy realized that too late. Without warning he emptied the contents of the glass on her uniform. An involuntary gasp escaped as the cold liquid ran down her front. Calmly she set the tray aside. Their eyes clashed and held as she struggled to maintain control of her temper. "I'm sure that was an accident, Mr. Whittaker."

"And I assure you it wasn't." His hard gaze held hers.

"That's unfortunate," Joy returned, and without a backward glance she emptied the remains of her luke-warm coffee in his lap. Not waiting for his reaction, she took the tray. "I'll send Paul in," she announced crisply, and left.

Her hands were trembling when she came into the kitchen. Sloan Whittaker's arrogant pride was definitely going to be a challenge. But he'd learn soon enough. The display of temper pleased her. He hadn't lost the will to fight. That was good; in fact it was very good.

Clara looked up from the sink, his eyes widening as she noted the juice stain.

Joy laid the tray on the counter and smiled wryly. "I had a small accident," she explained.

"Sure you did," Clara muttered with a dry laugh, and lifted the empty plate from the tray. "Well, I'll be. Mr. Whittaker ate his breakfast," she cried in open astonishment. "First time in six months that he's cleaned his plate. You are a miracle, girl. What did you do?"

Joy couldn't put a damper on the woman's enthusiasm. "I'm afraid that's a professional secret, but I promise to let you in on it before I leave."

Smacking her lips, Clara beamed a brilliant smile. "I always said that once Mr. Whittaker started eating again he would walk. He won't ever be strong unless he eats."

"I couldn't agree with you more," Joy replied with a soft sigh. "But after such a large breakfast you should keep his lunch light. Nothing more than broth, but do me a favor and cook his favorite meal tonight."

"I will, miss, that I will."

Pleased with herself, Joy walked down the hall to her room. She understood Sloan's frustration. His story was a familiar one. His car had skidded on a rain-slick road and smashed into a tree. The bare facts had been related by Dr. Phelps. Only when Joy pried further did she learn he had lain in the twisted wreck for hours in an agony beyond description before anyone found him. The initial surgery had saved his life, but in his weakened condition the operation to relieve the pressure on his spinal column had to be delayed. Months passed before he was strong enough to endure the next difficult surgery. Now there were no guarantees. Dr. Phelps told her there was feeling in Sloan Whittaker's legs, but the pain remained intense, and Sloan had decided to accept the wheelchair rather than endure the agony of learning to walk again.

Joy didn't need to be a psychologist to know that a man who resigned himself to a wheelchair had far more reason than pain. Something had happened to make him lose the will to use his legs. She'd know what it was before finishing this assignment.

After six months, the bitterness had built a thick wall around him. It wouldn't be easy to crack that granite fortress, but Joy was determined. She wanted to be the one to help him.

Entering her bedroom, she paused again to take in the expensive decor. The room was decorated in a powder-blue color scheme: the wallpaper contained tiny blue-bells, the azure carpet was lush and full. The flowered bedspread matched the walls and drapes. Joy had seen pictures in magazines of rooms like this, but she'd never imagined she would be sleeping in one.

Money could buy a lot of things, and in Sloan's case it had bought him the privilege of choosing life in a de-luxe model wheelchair.

Opening her closet, she took out and changed into a fresh uniform. She rinsed out the juice stain in the pri-vate bath off the bedroom. Once she'd turned off the water, she could hear the angry words coming from the room next to hers. Apparently Sloan wasn't in any better mood.

Paul had seemed the perfect type to deal with Sloan. He was an easygoing, laid-back sort of person who rec-ognized a good thing when he saw one. His job entailed helping Sloan bathe and dress each morning, stimulat-ing his leg muscles with massage, and lifting weights. Paul Weston was a body man, and he had been given free use of the equipment in the room off the kitchen—equipment Sloan had once used.

Now that she was here, she'd see to it that Paul's du-ties were increased. She was going to need his help. One of the first things she planned to do was get Sloan

Whittaker into his swimming pool whether he wanted to go or not. And for a time she was going to need Paul to get him there.

She had finished reading over the medical reports kept by the previous therpists when Clara came to tell her Mrs. Whittaker had arrived.

Glancing at her watch, Joy raised a speculative brow. "She's early."

"Mrs. Whittaker's anxious to meet you," Clara explained unnecessarily.

The older woman, seated on a long white sofa, was the picture of grace and charm. She was delicate and fine-boned, her hair silver and stylish. She glanced up when Joy entered the room. Joy watched as the smile died on her lips.

"Miss Nielsen, I can't tell you how pleased I am to meet you," she said with a frown.

"Is something the matter?"

"It's just that I expected someone older," she admitted.

Joy's back remained straight as she sat across from the older woman. "I'm twenty-eight," she said in a deliberate, casual tone.

"But Dr. Phelps explained that…" She let the rejoinder fade into silence.

Joy's eyes held the older woman's. "I can assure you that I'm perfectly qualified for the job."

"Oh, my dear, I didn't mean to imply otherwise. It's just that there is so much resting on you. I'm at my wit's end with that son of mine. I've all but given up hope."

"To do so would be premature."

"Have you met Sloan?" Her eyes were anxious.

"This morning."

"And?" she inquired gently.

"And he's bitter, resentful, in pain, mad as a wet hen at the world and everyone in it."

"His last therpist stayed only one day."

"I may not look like much, Mrs. Whittaker," Joy strived to assure the woman, "but I can guarantee it's going to take far more than a few angry words for me to pack my bags."

The woman looked relieved. "I can't tell you how pleased my husband and I are that you agreed to take this assignment. Dr. Phelps has nothing but good things to say about you, and quite honestly I don't know how much longer my husband can continue managing the company."

"Pardon?"

Margaret Whittaker lifted the china teacup to her lips and took a sip before continuing. "I'm sorry, dear. I assumed Dr. Phelps told you."

"No, I'm afraid he didn't."

Margaret Whittaker sighed, drawing Joy's rich, brown eyes to the carefully disguised age lines that fanned out from the older woman's eyes and mouth. "My husband came out of retirement after Sloan's accident. I'm afraid the pressure is more than Myron can cope with. We'll be forced to sell the business unless Sloan can assume some of the responsibilities soon."

Joy frowned thoughtfully. "I'd like to talk to your husband when it's convenient. I can't make any promises, Mrs. Whittaker, but I would think involving your son in the business again would be in his own best interest."

"Yes, but…" She looked disconcerted, and Joy noted that her hands shook as she replaced the cup to the saucer. "Sloan's convinced he will never walk again. He's given up."

"Mrs. Whittaker, I think you should realize that a man like your son never gives up. Although he wouldn't let you see it, he's fighting. No matter what he says or does."

The silver-haired woman paused, her hands folded primly on her lap. "You're very wise for your years." She regarded Joy thoughtfully. "I apologize for doubting. I can see that you're exactly what Sloan needs."

"I hope I am," she murmured softly, "for your sake and for Sloan's too."

The soft hum of the wheelchair sounded behind them. Sloan's look was hooded as he moved into the room.

"I wasn't aware you'd arrived, Mother." A sarcastic inflection laced his words.

"I was introducing myself to Miss Nielsen. I hope you appreciate how fortunate we are to get her."

"Oh, yes." His light, mirthless laugh was filled with disdain. "About as lucky as I was the night of the accident."

"Sloan." Margaret Whittaker breathed his name in protest. But his dark head had already turned away, effectively cutting off any further discussion. "You'll have to forgive him." Anger trembled from the sharp edge of his mother's voice.

Joy glanced up, surprised. She would have thought Margaret Whittaker was the type of woman who would never lose her poise. The small display of temper showed Joy how desperate the situation had become for Sloan's mother.

"Don't worry, Mrs. Whittaker. I understand."

An hour later Joy wandered into the kitchen. Clara was busy fixing lunch. "Mr. Whittaker's tray's ready. He has all his meals in his room these days."

"I'll take it to him," Joy volunteered. She wouldn't avoid another confrontation.

She knocked once before swinging open the door. "Good afternoon. I imagine you're anxious for this."

"Then you imagined wrong."

"Listen, Sloan, we can do this easy or we can do this hard. The decision is yours."

"Nothing in my life's come easy," he returned sharply.

Joy's laugh was filled with challenge. "You're sitting in this showroom house with people fighting to wait on you, and you want my sympathy? You're looking at the wrong woman."

He tipped his head to one side and glared at her. "Get out—or I'll throw you out."

"If you want me to leave, you'll have to do it physically. That's pretty tough for a person with disabilities."

His nostrils flared. "Don't be so confident."

"Oh, I'm sure." She tossed the words at him flippantly. "I run two miles every morning, and in addition to being in great physical condition, I could flatten you with one swift punch. Look at you," she returned smoothly. "You've been sitting in the wheelchair for six months. Your muscles are weak and limp. I doubt that you could lift your own weight. But if you want to try, don't let the fact I'm a woman stop you."

A muscle jumped along the side of his jaw. With a violent shove, he propelled the wheelchair onto the verandah. For now, Joy recognized, he was running; he didn't know what else to do. But the time was fast approaching when he'd have nowhere to go.

Before she left, Joy set up the meal tray. A satisfied smile spread to her eyes as she regarded the meager contents. She'd bet hard cash Sloan Whittaker was going to eat his lunch.

When she returned she noted that she'd been right. He'd devoured every bit and would probably look forward to dinner.

"I'm taking you outside now," she told him in a silky, smooth voice.

"No, you aren't."

She didn't argue. Instead she stuck her head out the door and called Paul.

Almost immediately the muscle-bound young man stepped into the room.

"I'd like you to take Mr. Whittaker to the beach."

"No," Sloan shouted.

"Do as I say, Paul," Joy encouraged.

"You so much as touch my chair and you're fired." The way he spoke proved that the threat wasn't an idle one.

"She told me you'd say that."

"Don't do it." The thin line of Sloan's mouth was forbidding.

Uncertain, Paul glanced to Joy for assurance. They'd had a long talk and had reached an understanding where Sloan Whittaker was concerned.

"You can't fire either one of us. You realize that, don't you?" she explained in a bored voice.

"Like hell."

"As I understand the situation, it's your family who hired us, and therefore we work for them. Not you."

Joy could have kissed Paul as he effortlessly pushed Sloan out the bedroom door. Only at rare times had she seen such barely restrained rage. Sloan's face was twisted with it as Paul directed the chair out the back door and onto the sheets of plywood they had laid on the sand to help manipulate his chair.

The day was gorgeous, and a gentle breeze ruffled the soft brown curls about her face.

"Is that all?" Paul looked to her and she nodded, indicating he could leave.

Slipping off her shoes, Joy sat on the soft beach and burrowed her feet in the warm sand. Lifting her face to the soothing rays of the sun, she closed her eyes, oblivious to the angry man beside her.

After several minutes of contented peace, she lowered her gaze and turned to Sloan. He sat erect and angry, like a prisoner of war. He *was* a prisoner, she mused.

"Tomorrow we'll start with the therapy."

"What therapy?"

She ignored the censure in his voice. "Your first session will be in the morning with me. I'd thought we'd start in the pool. Later in the afternoon Paul will be helping you tone up the muscles in your arms."

His hands grabbed hold of the arms of his chair in a death grip. "What has my mother told you?" He breathed the question.

Joy let the sand drain out of her closed fist, watching it bounce against the beach. "Plenty."

"I refuse to fall into your schemes."

"We'll see about that." She rose lithely and rolled up the pant legs to her knees. The ocean was several hundred yards away, and she ran down to the water's edge. Her big toe popped the tiny bubbles the surf produced. The sun felt soothing and warm, and she basked in the beauty of the afternoon. When she glanced back she saw that Sloan had somehow managed to turn his chair around and with a determined effort had begun to wheel the chair toward the house.

For now she'd let him escape. His pride demanded as much.

Joy didn't see him again until later that evening. She wasn't surprised when Clara proudly exclaimed that Mr. Whittaker had eaten his dinner.

The sky was pink with the setting sun when she unpacked her flute and stood on the verandah. The music flowed from her unbound and free. There'd been a time Joy had to decide between a musical career and the medical profession. Once the decision had been made she had no regrets. She was a good therpist, and she knew it. Cases like these were her best—and for a reason. Absently she stopped playing and rubbed her thigh.

"Don't quit."

The words surprised her, and she turned around. Sloan had rolled his chair onto the verandah and was only a few feet from her. Foolishly, Joy hadn't realized their adjacent rooms shared the deck.

Wordlessly she lifted the flute to her lips and played her favorite pieces. Lively jigs followed by the sweet soulful sounds of the classics.

"Where did you ever learn to play like that?" he asked in a whisper.

It was the first time she had heard him speak without being angry. "I started as a child. My father was a musician."

His strong profile was illuminated by the darkening sky. Her eyes fell from the powerful face to the chair, and her heart wanted to cry for him. Arrogant, noble, proud—and trapped.

No. Swiftly she jerked her gaze free. The last thing she wanted was to become emotionally attached to a patient. For now Sloan Whittaker needed her, but that would soon change, and he would be free from the chains that bound him. As he became independent to live and love again, he wouldn't want or need her.

Joy had never fooled herself—she wasn't a beauty. Dark hair and equally dark eyes were probably her best features. Her mouth was too small to be sensuous, her nose a little short, her cheekbones too high. The Sloan Whittakers of this world wouldn't be interested in a hundred-pound misfit.

"Good night, Mr. Whittaker," she spoke softly.

"Miss Nielsen." He remained on the deck while Joy turned sharply and entered her room, closing the sliding-glass door after her. Her heart was pounding wildly, and she placed a calming hand over it. What was the matter with her? It would be utter foolishness to become attracted to this man. Two, maybe three months at the most, and she would be leaving.

Joy woke with the alarm early the following morning. The sun hadn't broken the horizon as she pulled open the drapes and stared into the distance. Quickly she dressed in sweatpants and an old gray sweatshirt. She hadn't run on sand before, and wondered about wearing tennis shoes.

The house was quiet and still as she slipped out the kitchen door. A chill ran goose bumps up her arms, and she jiggled them loosely at her sides as she performed the perfunctory warm-up exercises.

An angry gust of wind nearly toppled her along the beach as the surf pounded the shore. Heedless to the blustery force, Joy picked up her heels and ran. The first quarter-mile was always the hardest. Her lungs heaved with the effort. Sand sank in her shoes, making it almost impossible to maintain her usual pace. Soon she discovered it was much easier if she ran close to the water, where the sand was wet.

When she figured she'd gone a mile or more, she turned and headed back. The house was in sight when she spotted a seagull walking along the shore dragging its wing. Slowing her pace, she watched as the poor creature pitifully attempted to fly. After several tries the large bird keeled over, exhausted. Realizing the pain it must be enduring, she stopped running hoping she could find some way to help. When she took a tentative step toward it, the gull struggled to sit upright and flee.

Speaking in soothing tones, she fell to her knees in the sand. "Long John Seagull, what are you doing here?"

The bird hobbled a few steps and fell over.

"It looks like you need a friend," she said softly. "Stay here. I'll be right back." With urgent strides, Joy raced toward the house.

Breathlessly, she stumbled into the kitchen.

"Dear heavens, are you all right?" Clara stood with her back to the sink.

Out of wind, all Joy could do was nod.

"You scared me clean out of my skin."

"Sorry," Joy managed. Not wishing to wake Sloan, she moved quietly down the hall to her room. Only yesterday she'd unpacked several emergency medical supplies. She gathered what she thought she'd need in a large shopping bag, found some tough garden gloves, and hurried out of the room.

"You headed for a fire?" Clara asked as Joy scurried through the kitchen a second time.

"No. I found an injured seagull. I'll be back as soon as I can."

"But, Miss…" Clara called after her.

With the wind beating against her face, Joy returned to her newfound feathered friend.

A half hour later her back ached and her fingers felt swollen and numb with the continued effort of trying to help the bird while not being cut by his powerful beak. As far as she could tell, the wing hadn't been broken, only injured. After carefully applying some antibiotic cream and binding it to his body with a strip of gauze, Joy felt confident the gull would heal.

Long John didn't look pleased when she picked him up and carefully placed him in the sack. A movement out of the corner of her eye captured her attention. She straightened and placed a hand above her eyes to shield them from the glaring sun. She saw that Sloan was on the verandah, watching her. Even from this distance she could see that he was displeased.

"His bark is worse than his bite," Joy informed the bird, who stuck his head out of the sack and looked around. "Don't worry. I know a safe place for you."

Her hair was wet from the shower when Joy came out of her room and closed the door.

"What were you doing this morning?" The question came at her like an arrogant challenge.

"Running," she replied, and rotated to face Sloan.

He glared at her. "I saw you working on something."

"I found an injured seagull. His wing," she added. "Are you ready for breakfast?"

Sloan's gaze hardened and shifted to her eyes. "You like to play the role of the rescuer, don't you? Birds, animals, people. Well, get this straight, little Miss Miracle Worker. I don't need you, and furthermore I don't want you. So get out of my life and stay out."

"My, my, we're in a fine mood this morning," Joy

said cheerfully. "How do you want your coffee? Luke-warm and in your lap, or perhaps over your head?"

In return she saw a hint of a smile. "Would it be too much to ask for it in a cup?"

"That depends entirely upon you," she said softly. "Don't go away. I'll be right back."

A few minutes later she brought in his breakfast tray. "You'll be pleased to know I ate in the kitchen," she said, a mocking reminder of his earlier statement.

Again a near-smile came over him.

"I thought that would please you," she said.

On Joy's instructions Clara had prepared a much lighter meal this morning. A warm croissant was served with butter and homemade strawberry jam. She poured his coffee and set the pot to the side.

"I'll be back in a few minutes with Paul."

"I don't need him this morning," Sloan said stiffly.

"Are you already in your suit?"

"My suit?"

"We're going swimming, remember?"

Sloan laughed coldly. "Not likely."

"It'll probably hurt, so prepare yourself."

"Miss Nielsen," he muttered grimly, "there's no way in God's green earth that you're going to get me in that pool, so kindly accept that and save us both a lot of trouble."

"We'll see," she returned lightly.

The grooves around his mouth deepened with defiance. "Has anyone ever told you that you're a stubborn bi—"

"I do find such language unnecessary." She effectively cut him off by pivoting and walking away.

An hour later, dressed in her one-piece turquoise swimsuit, Joy dived into the deep end of the pool. Her slim body sliced through the water. She surfaced and did a couple of laps, enjoying the feel of the cool water against her skin.

When she paused she found Paul standing outside the pool, looking ill at ease and uncertain.

"Whittaker isn't pleased about this."

"I don't imagine he is. If necessary, bring him down here naked. He's coming in this pool one way or another."

"You're sure?"

"Very," she repeated confidently. "Throw him in, if necessary."

"If that's what you want."

Waiting in the shallow end of the pool, Joy could hear Sloan long before seeing him. An angry torrent of abusive words were followed by the sight of a red-faced Paul.

"Thank you, Paul." She smiled at Paul and then glared at Sloan. "The time has come to separate the men from the boys."

Two

A slow smile spread across Joy's face. "Come on in. The water's fine."

"I could hate you for this," Sloan growled.

"I've been hated by better men than you," Joy informed him cheerfully. She didn't doubt Sloan; her job was to channel some of his angry intensity into the exercises. Clara had told her how much Sloan had loved the pool, swimming laps early every morning. He would again if she had anything to do with it. "Put him in the water, Paul."

She turned and dived into the blue depths, feeling slightly guilty that Paul was left to deal with the abusive end of Sloan's temper. By turning away she offered him the privacy to climb into the water without her seeing Paul lift him. His pride had taken enough of a beating lately, and she didn't want to make this any more difficult than it already was.

When she surfaced at the far end of the pool, Joy

noticed Paul was standing back from the pool's edge, his look unsure.

"That'll be all." Treading water, she raised one hand and waved, indicating she wanted him to leave.

Sloan was sitting on the steps that led from the shallow end, his look foreboding. "Let's get this over with so I can get out of here."

"All right," she agreed, swimming toward him. Her arms cut through the water as she stroked. Because of the distance separating them she couldn't hear the harshly muttered words, which was probably just as well.

He held himself rigid, and one hand gripped the side of the pool.

"I've always loved to swim," she announced, and playfully dipped her head back into the cool, aqua-blue water.

Sloan's dark gaze followed her actions.

"When I was a child, my father was the one who taught me," she said. "I loved those days. We could never afford a pool like this, but summer evenings when Dad got off work, my brother, mother, father, and I went swimming in the pool at the park."

Sloan looked bored.

"It seems ironic to me that my father would drown," she continued. Her unflinching gaze met Sloan's. "For a year afterwards I couldn't go near a pool. In some obscure way I think I wanted to punish the water for taking my father."

Sloan exhaled a short, angry breath.

Joy's mouth formed a humorless smile. It'd been a

mistake to speak of her beloved father. She couldn't understand why she had—especially with Sloan Whittaker.

"For now all I want you to do is familiarize yourself with the pool. Tomorrow I'm going to start you on a series of exercises. I won't try to kid you. These movements are going to hurt, but they're supposed to."

"Do you want me to leap for joy with some pie in the sky dream you have of my walking again?" he said and his eyes snapped fire.

"No, but I'll tell you this. Progress will be slow enough; if you fight me, it'll only take longer."

"In other words, a lot of pain and only a little progress."

"That, Mr. Whittaker, is up to you."

"If it was up to me, you'd get the hell out of my life."

She couldn't hold back her amusement and a smile twitched at the edges of her mouth. "I'll be happy to leave, but when I go that wheelchair will be in the attic."

His fist slammed against the water, spraying it along the pool's tiled edge. "Spare me from optimistic women."

"Starting tomorrow, Paul will be taking you to the whirlpool before our session here. There are several reasons for that, none of which would interest you, I'm sure."

His impassive expression didn't alter.

"You can go for now. I'll see you at lunchtime."

"Don't hurry."

The sun's golden rays bathed his pale features. Joy realized that only a year ago Sloan Whittaker would have been bronze and sun-browned. Once he had been a compellingly handsome man, but pain had chiseled blunted, abrupt lines in his face. His dark eyes seemed to mirror the agony of the past months. Mournful and intense. Joy had seen it before, but never had it affected her like this. In some degree she gave a part of herself to each of her patients. Her greatest fear was that Sloan Whittaker would take her heart. That she couldn't allow.

"I won't hurry," she answered at last. "I'm not any more anxious to see you than you are me."

"At least we understand one another."

Joy called for Paul and swam laps as the young man helped Sloan out of the water. She again offered him privacy to salvage his pride.

Later when she brought in his lunch he regarded her skeptically. When she delivered the tray to the kitchen, Joy was pleased to note that he had again eaten a decent meal.

That night, after the sun set, she picked up her flute and stood on the balcony to play. A gentle breeze stirred her hair and felt like a whispered caress against her smooth skin. The sounds of the Beatles' classic, "Yesterday," filled the silence. She loved the song.

Joy paused when she finished, noting that Sloan had rolled onto the balcony and was staring into the still night.

"You can't bring back the past," he said. The words were filled with regret.

"No," she agreed softly, "you can't. Today, this minute. Now, is all that matters."

Again she played the songs she loved best. Michael Bublé and Josh Groban, mellow sounds that produced a tranquil mood within her.

She sighed as she lowered the musical instrument. The day had been full, and she was exhausted. "Is there anything I can get you before I go inside?" she asked softly, not wanting words to destroy the mood.

At first it didn't appear that he'd heard her. He rotated the wheelchair so that he faced her. "How about new legs, Miss Miracle Worker?"

"I'm fresh out of those," she replied evenly. "I'm afraid you'll have to make do with the ones you've got."

Joy heard him exhale and knew her comment hadn't pleased him. After a moment, she turned away. "Good night, Mr. Whittaker."

He didn't reply, and Joy guessed that he wasn't wishing her anything good.

The next week was miserable, an unceasing confrontation of wills. Sloan fought her every step of the way. Several times it was all she could do not to retaliate out of her own frustration.

She hadn't minced words when she told him the exercises were going to cause him pain, although he never indicated that she was hurting him. He worked with her because he had no choice, and although he didn't resist her as she manipulated his legs, he didn't aid her, either. Some mornings after their session Joy noticed how ashen his face was as he struggled to disguise the pain. The lines of strain were deeply etched about his mouth. He rarely spoke to her, seeming to prefer sullen silence to open confrontation. Apparently he'd learned early that the biting, sarcastic comments rolled off her as easily as the pool water, that she could give as well as she took. In some ways a mutual respect was beginning to blossom, but it didn't lessen the intense dislike he felt for her or the frustration she experienced knowing she wasn't reaching him or gaining his trust. Although getting him in the pool and exercising his legs was good, she'd failed in the most important area.

Sloan came onto the balcony at night as if waiting for her music. Rarely did he comment, silently wheeling back into his room when she'd finished.

On Saturday Joy rose and dressed at the usual time. Her heart felt weighted, and she wasn't sure why. The crisp morning air felt cool as she slipped out the back door. First she checked Long John, the seagull she'd found and was nursing. He didn't like the confines of the fenced portion of the yard, but like Sloan he was trapped and unable to flee. The bird squawked and hobbled to the side of the yard when she opened the gate. Several times he had lashed out at her hand, once drawing blood. He didn't trust her, again like Sloan.

For six days she had worked with them both and had failed to earn more than a grudging respect. At least the bird wanted his freedom. But Sloan had no will to walk or reenter the mainstream of life. What would make a man content to sit in a chair? Perhaps this was all another battle of their wills, in which he was determined to prove he didn't need her.

Long John squawked, and Joy focused her attention on the bird. "Good morning, fellow," she whispered. "Are you glad to see me?"

The gull stared at her blankly.

"Don't worry, I'm not any more popular with the master, either." She yearned to reach out and comfort her winged friend. She wanted his trust, as she wanted Sloan's, at least enough so that the bird would allow her close enough to touch him. But he wasn't confident enough yet. Moving slowly, she placed a bowl of cut-up fish and high-protein gruel on the ground and filled his bowl with fresh water. On her knees, she held herself motionless for several moments, hoping he would be hungry enough to overcome his natural reserve. It didn't take her long to realize that the bird wouldn't eat as long as she remained in the yard.

Releasing the latch, Joy let herself out of the gate and locked it. For a time she stayed and watched, but Long John defiantly remained where he was. The pungent scent of the ocean greeted her as she walked along the shore. A gentle mist wet her face and hair, and she ran a hand along both sides of her cheeks. Tonight she would go out, do something special. She needed a few hours of escape. An evening away would help her perspective.

As she turned and headed back for the house, a solitary figure on the balcony caught her attention. She hesitated, hands thrust deep into jeans pockets. It seemed Sloan Whittaker was watching her. Maybe he was hoping she'd leave and never return.

The morning followed its usual routine. Joy brought him his breakfast.

"Good morning," she greeted with a smile. "You were up bright and early this morning."

His response was muffled and gruff.

"Long John seemed to be in an identical mood when I brought him his meal."

"Long John what?"

"The seagull," she explained as she set the tray on the desk.

"Good grief, don't tell me you've still got that poor creature."

"He's improving, which is more than I can say…" She let the rest of what she was going to say fade when Clara appeared in the doorway.

"Mr. Whittaker's here to see you."

"Bring him in, Clara," Sloan instructed briskly.

The older woman shifted from one foot to the other. "Mr. Whittaker said he wanted to talk to Miss Nielsen."

Sloan's gaze swiveled to Joy for a long, considering look. "What could my father possibly have to say to Miss Nielsen?" he demanded.

"I'll take notes, if you'd like," Joy volunteered.

"Don't bother."

Joy felt his gaze burning into her shoulder blades as she stepped out of the room.

Even Clara seemed puzzled that the senior Whittaker had sought out Joy. The question was in the older woman's eyes as Joy took a left turn into the living room.

"Miss Nielsen." Myron Whittaker stood and extended his hand. He was tall and as large as Margaret Whittaker was petite. His shoulders were as broad as a wrestler's, his hair white and receding from a wide forehead. Joy's hand met his and was clasped firmly.

"My wife mentioned that you would like to speak to me."

"As a matter of fact, yes. I'm glad you've come." She sat in the large modern chair across from the distinguished-looking man. It wasn't hard to tell where Sloan got his compelling features. Father and son were a lot alike.

"It's only fair to tell you how pleased my wife and I are that you've agreed to take on Sloan's case."

"I think I'm the lucky one. I've never had the pleasure of working in such elegant surroundings."

"Yes, well…" The older man cleared his throat. "We want you to know we appreciate what you've done."

"I haven't done anything yet," Joy admitted wryly. "But part of your son's recovery will depend on you."

"Anything." He rubbed a hand across his face, his eyes tired.

"Part of Sloan's therapy will be mental as well as physical. He's got to be brought back into life, given responsibilities." She hesitated and leaned forward slightly so that her elbows rested on her knees. "Your wife mentioned that you've assumed Sloan's job in the company since the accident. In some ways this is good, but the time has come for you to return those duties to your son."

"How do you mean?"

"Decision-making, paperwork. These are things that can be done from the house. At least come to Sloan when a decision needs to be made. Part of the problem with your son is that he feels useless. Prove to him he's needed."

"He is," Myron returned forcefully.

"Don't overpower him," she suggested. "Start with updates and reports that will keep him in tune with what's happening. Then gradually lead into the other matters. I don't know that much about your business, but I'm sure you'll know how to approach this." Dr. Phelps had told her that the Whittakers owned a ski equipment company. Joy had never skied, but from Sloan's home and lifestyle it was easy to see the business had been a profitable one.

Myron Whittaker looked down, but not before his dark eyes conveyed the toll of the last months. "I'm not sure of anything anymore."

"Your son's going to be fine, Mr. Whittaker." She leaned forward and gave the elder Whittaker's clenched fist a reassuring pat. "He's strong-willed and determined."

Tears glistened in the proud man's gaze. He closed his eyes and gripped her hand with his own.

"My, my, isn't this a touching scene." Sloan wheeled into the room. "My physical therpist? Honestly, Father, I think you're lowering your standards unnecessarily."

Myron Whittaker sprang to his feet, his face twisted with rage. "You will apologize for that remark."

Joy's gaze swiveled from father to son. Sloan's hands gripped the wheels of his chair until his knuckles were white. His mouth was slanted and scornful.

"Wheelchair or no wheelchair, I won't have a son of mine make that kind of suggestion."

"Mr. Whittaker, please." Joy could feel the hot color explode in her face. "This isn't necessary."

"It most certainly is," he barked.

How often Joy had heard that same tone of voice. Father and son shared more than looks.

Sloan's hard gaze hadn't relented. "I regret the implication," he managed between clenched teeth.

"If you'll excuse me." Joy hurriedly left the room. Her heart felt as if she'd completed a marathon as she let herself into her quarters. Her hands shook as she slipped into the swimsuit. The decision this morning to get out, go to a movie, anything, had been a good one. Sloan Whittaker was getting to her. Keeping a cool head with this man was essential to success.

When she slipped out of her room and into the hall, she could hear the angry exchange between Sloan and his father. Joy wanted to shout at them both. Arguing would solve nothing. She bit into her bottom lip tightly and moved outside.

Paul was lounging in a chair by the pool when she came out. "Morning," he said. "How's it going?"

Joy rolled her eyes expressively, and Paul laughed. "He's really something, isn't he?"

"You can say that." Her relationship with the other staff members had relaxed considerably. Almost everyone called her Joy. Since she and Paul worked directly with Sloan she felt a certain camaraderie with him, although they rarely had time to talk for more than a few minutes at a time. "How are the afternoon sessions coming?"

Paul shrugged. "Better, I guess. At least he's stopped yelling."

"In other words, he submits, and that's about it."

Paul nodded.

"The good news is that when he yells we know he's involved." Absently Joy slipped off her sandal and dipped her foot in the water. "This lackadaisical attitude concerns me."

"He's all but given up."

"I refuse to accept that," Joy murmured. "A man like Sloan Whittaker isn't a quitter. I think he's afraid to show he cares simply because he cares so much." Joy felt Paul's gaze and glanced up.

"I think you're right."

Joy was glad Paul agreed. "I'm betting on it."

Clara ambled toward them, wiping her hands on the ever present apron. "Mr. Whittaker told me to say he's ready for you now."

"I'll be right there." Paul sat up and stretched his arms high above his blond head. "See you in a few minutes."

"I'll be ready." Joy waited until he was out of view before dropping the terry-cloth cover and stepping into the water. It gently lapped against her waist. Lowering her lashes, she lay back, paddling her hands at her side to keep afloat. Even with her ears in the water she heard the approach of Sloan's chair. But she remained with her back to him until she was certain Sloan was in the water.

As she straightened, their eyes met and clashed across the distance of the pool. Her attention was diverted by Paul, who waved.

"See you later, Joy."

"Joy?" Sloan spit out the word distastefully. "Your name is Joy?"

She wouldn't rise to the barbed comment.

"Talk about irony." His laugh lacked warmth. "A torturer named Joy. It's almost hysterical."

Little he could say or do would intimidate her. She'd done verbal battle with him far too often to fall prey to another needless confrontation.

"Are you ready?"

"No." He held himself stiffly against the side of the pool. One elbow was elevated onto the tile rim, supporting his weight.

Undeterred, Joy swam to his side. Viciously he lunged for her, his fingers gripping hold of her upper arm.

She attempted to shrug free, but his grasp was surprisingly strong.

"I hope it hurts," he said cruelly.

"Let go."

"What do you know of pain?" he sneered. "How can you possibly know what it is to lie in a hospital and pray to God you'll die just so the agony stops?"

With her jaw clenched, Joy tried to pry his fingers loose. Already she could imagine a bruise forming.

Sloan tightened his grip. "What could you know of pitying looks and lost dreams?"

She struggled, and demanded a second time, "Let me go."

"Does it hurt? Good, it's supposed to." His eyes darkened with emotion. "Be objective about it. Isn't that what you said to me? Your turn, Miss Miracle Worker."

Boldly she met his gaze, and to her horror tears welled, blurring her vision. His hand relaxed, setting her free. As she pulled away she heard him utter a frustrated groan. Twisting her upper torso, she dived under the surface. The water felt cool against the flushed skin of her face. When she thought her lungs would burst, she surfaced and found herself at the far end of the pool. An angry bruise had turned her skin black-and-blue. Her arm throbbed.

"Paul," Sloan shouted. The muscle-bound man appeared almost immediately. "Get me out of here," he muttered thickly.

Paul glanced at Joy, who nodded and turned her back to the pair. Sloan had asked her what did she know about pain? It was funny enough to make her want to laugh.

Purposely she avoided Sloan at lunchtime. Clara took his meal in to him and returned with a worried frown. "Didn't so much as touch it. His favorite soup, mind you."

Alone at the kitchen table, Joy released a broken sigh.

"And you're no better," Clara accused. "You've done nothing more than rearrange the food on your plate. What's going on around here?"

"I guess it's an off day. Everyone's entitled to those now and then."

"Off day?" Clara clucked. "The air around here feels like an electrical storm passed through. And Mr. Whittaker and his son fighting? I don't know when that's happened." She wiped a hand across her brow, and her face narrowed. "And you look like you've lost your best friend."

Joy gave the older woman a weak smile. "You're right," she said with determination. "I need a change of pace. Don't fix dinner for me tonight. I'm going out."

"I'd say it's about time." Clara nodded approvingly. "Pretty young thing like you should be out having fun every night."

Joy laughed. Young she couldn't deny, but pretty was something else again.

She wouldn't be able to avoid Sloan forever, but she gladly relinquished her duties that afternoon. Without explanation, Paul seemed to know she needed the break. When she took part of the day off to go shopping, no one questioned her. At the time she was hired, the Whittakers had told her to set her own hours.

Although Joy browsed around several shops, she didn't buy anything. It felt good to get away, if only for a few hours. She checked the newspaper and drank coffee in a small café. A movie she wanted to see was playing, and Joy decided to take one in later.

Clara was busy in the kitchen peeling apples when Joy returned.

"Did you enjoy yourself?"

"It was nice," Joy admitted, and handed the woman one long-stemmed rose. "This is for you."

"Joy." She took the flower and sniffed it appreciatively. "What are you doing buying me flowers?"

"Well, actually, I didn't buy it," Joy admitted grudgingly. "I picked it from the bush outside."

Clara laughed and gave her a spontaneous hug. "I knew the minute I saw you what a dear girl you are."

Joy sat on the countertop, dangling her feet over the edge and talking to Clara for several minutes. She had the impression Clara wouldn't allow many the privilege of invading her home territory so freely. She stayed in the kitchen until dinner was almost ready.

Luxuriating in a bubble bath, she hoped to wash away some of the unpleasantness of the day. A smile came to her. Could one ever wash away hurts and pains? Dear heavens, she was becoming philosophical.

The sky was painted a bold shade of pink, and Joy paused to admire the vibrant color as she slipped a full-length silk robe on and tied the sash.

How could the night be so beautiful when the day had been so ugly? Joy mused. Without thought, she wandered onto the balcony. The palms of her hands rested against the painted rail.

"Lovely, isn't it?"

Joy froze.

"Sometimes when I sit here and stare into the sunset, I can almost forget." The whispered words were spoken so softly that Joy had to strain to hear.

The sound of Sloan's chair told her he was coming toward her. She didn't move.

A finger traced the pattern of the ugly bruise on her arm. "Did I do that?"

"Yes," she answered without turning.

"Dear sweet heaven," he muttered, his voice suddenly thick. "You must hate me."

"No," she replied softly, and turned her face to him. "I don't."

Again he ran his index finger along the bruise. His touch was gentle, almost a caress, as if he wanted to blot out the pain he had caused.

"I'm going out for a while tonight," she announced.

He dropped his hand. "A date?"

"No." She shook her head. "Just a movie. I'm going alone."

His hands rolled the chair back a couple of feet, then swiveled it around, presenting her a view of his back. "Have a good time, Joy."

A frown creased her brow. She found it hard to understand this man. "Thank you."

He hesitated a second before wheeling into his room.

Joy watched him go. Sloan regretted the incident that morning with his father and later with her in the pool. He was a man driven to the limits of his endurance. Mentally, Joy pictured him standing at a crossroads. He would either choose life or a living death. Unconsciously she brushed the hair off her forehead as a smile came to her. Interestingly, she had viewed him standing, and not in a wheelchair. Why such a nonsensical thing should lighten her spirits she didn't know.

Joy was whistling on her way out the front door. She hadn't been hungry and had skipped dinner. All of a sudden she felt ravenous. There wasn't time to stop and get something before the movie, so she decided to wait until after.

The show was a light comedy that made her laugh, and heaven knew she needed a reason to smile.

On the way down the coast highway, Joy pulled off at a fast-food restaurant. She hadn't paid much attention to the kind of food until she stepped out of the car. Fish. The tantalizing aroma of deep-fried fish and crisp French fries filled the air.

Joy read over the menu and absently wondered if

Sloan knew about this place. He would have, of course, since it was only a few miles from the house. But how long had it been since he'd tasted something like this?

"Can I help you?" An eager-faced youth leaned half-way out the order window.

"Yes." Joy's eyes didn't leave the menu that was painted in bold-faced letters over the grill. "I'd like a double order of fish-and-chips. And a Pepsi."

"Will that be all?"

"No, make that two orders," she added impulsively.

"To go?"

"Pardon?" Joy's puzzled gaze found the girl's.

"Do you want to eat here or take out?" she asked in an impatient breath.

"Take out."

Even as she paid for the meal, Joy wondered what had possessed her to do anything so foolish. No use lying to herself—she'd bought the second fish order for Sloan.

The lights to his room weren't visible from the front of the house. Joy carried the grease-stained white sack into her bedroom and immediately went out onto the balcony.

His drapes were open, but the room was dark. He often sat alone with the lights off. Sometimes she thought he preferred it like that. He could hide in the shadows, but not in the light.

Tentatively she knocked on the sliding-glass door and opened it just a crack.

Silence.

"Are you awake?" She whispered the question, not

wishing to disturb him if he happened to be asleep. Her eyes adjusted to the dim interior and searched the room. He sat in the corner, his chin propped up by his fist.

"How was the movie?"

"Great."

His chuckle was filled with quiet humor. "Why are we whispering?"

"I don't know." She slid open the door. "I didn't have dinner, so I stopped off at a fish-and-chips place up the road."

"Not Mobey Jake's?"

"I didn't notice the name, but it had a neon whale flashing off and on."

"That's the one. The food's terrific."

"I brought you an order back too."

An uncomfortable pause followed her announcement. "Isn't that fraternizing with the enemy?"

"Could be," she agreed with a secret smile. "But my mother once told me I'd catch a lot more flies with honey than vinegar. But then, my mother never met you."

Three

A contented feeling moved through Joy as she sat up in bed and stretched. Linking her fingers high above her head, she arched her back and released a long, drawn-out yawn.

She couldn't remember an evening she enjoyed more than the one spent with Sloan. He had chuckled when she relayed the movie plot and the antics of the characters. It was the first time Joy had heard the sound of his laughter. The feeling it had produced was warm and pleasant. She had seen him grit his teeth and muffle groans as she manipulated his legs, but never his amusement. How much more she preferred dark eyes that crinkled with laugh lines to ones that struggled to disguise pain.

She dressed in jeans and a loose-fitting T-shirt. Some of the fish fillets had been left over, and she wanted to see if Long John would eat out of her hand. Great strides seemed to have been made with Sloan, and she was eager to see if the injured gull was willing to accept her as his friend.

"Good morning, L.J.," she greeted as she let herself into the yard. The gate latched behind her as she stepped to the food bowl and bent down extending her hand. "See what I've got here? Fish," she answered her own question in reassuring tones. "And I happen to know gulls are particularly fond of fish. I'm not so sure about fried fish, but I think you ought to give it a try."

With an ambling gait that reminded her of Clara Barnes, the bird took a step in her direction.

"Obviously you've got keen eyesight," Joy encouraged her feathered friend.

When the bird was only a few inches away, she edged closer, wanting him to take the fish from her. Almost immediately Joy realized her mistake. The razor-sharp beak sliced into the back of her hand instead of the food. Blood gushed from the open cut. Inhaling a sharp breath, Joy dropped the fish and jerked upright. In a protective movement she held her hand to her body and hurried out the gate. Blood seemed to be everywhere. The gull had apparently cut a vein. The pain was sharp as she quickly stepped back into the house. Clara wasn't in the kitchen. Joy was grateful she didn't have to make unnecessary explanations. From the flow of blood, it looked as if she might need a suture or two.

Intent on escaping unseen into her bedroom, Joy nearly stumbled over Sloan, who was wheeling down the wide hallway.

"Joy, why the rush?"

"I'm sorry," she mumbled, pressing her hand to her shirt. "I didn't mean to startle you."

"You're hurt."

Sloan's pallor became sickly. He swallowed and narrowed his gaze on her hand.

"I'm fine."

"You need a doctor."

"What I need is to see how deep this is."

Stepping into her room, she moved directly to the bathroom sink and held her cut hand under a slow faucet. In the background she could hear Sloan yelling for Clara. Within moments the red-faced cook came rushing into the room.

"I got cut. It's no major catastrophe. Darn, it looks like it may need to be sewn up." Angry at herself for her own stupidity, Joy felt like stamping her foot. Didn't she know better than to rush something as delicate as trust? As an injured bird, she would have probably reacted the same way.

"I'll get Paul to drive you to urgent care." With agitated, worried movements, Clara rushed out of the room.

The fuss everyone was making didn't lessen Joy's feelings of self-reproach. A small towel was wrapped around her fist and held protectively against her stomach. Joy grabbed her purse off the dresser, fumbled with the clasp, and took out her car keys.

Sloan was gone, but she could hear him speaking to someone on the phone. His voice was angry and urgent. Footsteps could be heard rushing up the stairs.

"What happened?" Paul directed the question to Joy.

"I got cut. It's my own stupid fault. But it looks like I'm going to need a few stitches. A vein's been sliced."

A pale Sloan rolled his chair from his room. "Dr. Phelps is on his way."

"Dr. Phelps," Joy repeated, aghast. "You didn't call him, did you?" The whole situation was quickly becoming ridiculous. "You don't ask a noted surgeon to make a house call for a few stitches," she shouted sharply.

"Paul," Sloan shouted, no less calm, "get her into my room."

With a supportive hand under her elbow, Paul led her into Sloan's quarters.

"This is ridiculous," she hissed under her breath.

Sloan wheeled in after her. "Sit her in my chair."

"I might get blood on it," she protested.

"For once, just once," Sloan ground out between clenched teeth, "will you do as I ask?"

Pinching her mouth tightly shut, Joy plopped down on the expensive leather recliner. Paul hovered over her and Sloan rolled his chair back and forth across the room.

"For heaven's sake, you two look like you expect me to keel over dead any minute." Her wit didn't please Sloan, who tossed her a fiery glare. "Look at you." She directed her words to Sloan. "You're absolutely pale. Do you mean to tell me that after everything you've gone through you can't stand the sight of blood?"

"Shut up, Nielsen." The authority in his voice brooked no resistance.

"Well, for heaven's sake, would you stop doing that. You're making me nervous."

"Doing what?"

"That." She pointed her finger at his chair. "You've got to be the only man in the world who paces in a wheelchair."

Paul chuckled, and she tipped her head back and rolled her eyes expressively. "How could you have phoned Dr. Phelps?" she asked, and groaned with embarrassment.

"You've lost a lot of blood." His voice pounded like thunder around the room.

"I'm fine," she nearly shouted, and bounded to her feet, stalking to the far side of the room. Her angry glare met Sloan's as they stared at one another, the distance of the room separating them.

"How'd it happen?" Paul inserted, apparently in an attempt to cool tempers.

"It was my own stupid fault." She watched as Sloan's hands tightened around the arms of his chair in a strangling hold. "I tried to get L.J. to eat out of my hand…"

"L.J.?" Sloan interrupted.

"The seagull I found."

"She named him Long John," Paul explained with a trace of humor. "Rather appropriate, I thought."

"I didn't ask what you thought." Sloan's mouth twisted sarcastically. "I want that bird destroyed."

"No." Joy's voice trembled with rage. "You can't kill something because it was protecting itself. I told you, the whole thing was my fault."

"I don't want the seagull around," Sloan shouted.

"Then I'll find someplace else."

The air between them was as cold as an arctic blast.

Paul moved to the center of the room. "Interestingly enough, I happened to read the other day that there aren't such things as seagulls. Kittiwakes, black-backed gulls, and herring gulls, but technically there are no seagulls."

Speechless, Joy stared blankly at her muscular friend until she recognized that he was placing himself between her and Sloan, granting them each the space to cool their tempers.

Clara could be heard fussing in the hall. "This way, Dr. Phelps."

Everyone's attention was centered on the door as the tall, dark-haired doctor entered the room.

"Dr. Phelps," Joy began, "I'm so embarrassed."

"Anyone that lets a stupid bird slash their hand in two deserves to be," Sloan inserted dryly.

Joy darted him a warning glance.

"Now that I'm here, I might as well have a look." Professional and calm, Dr. Phelps set his bag on the desk and hung his light coat over the back of the chair.

"And since you're here, you might as well check Mr. Whittaker," Joy suggested. "I'm sure he's due for an enema or something."

The good doctor chuckled as he removed the towel from her hand. A fresh supply of blood oozed from the laceration as he pried it gently with his fingers. "Nothing a couple of stitches won't cure," he murmured.

"I have most of the supplies you'll need in my room," she told him, and stood, leading the way.

The necessary equipment was laid out across the small tabletop as Dr. Phelps injected the topical anesthetic. Nonplussed, Joy watched him work. Having seen this so many times in the past, it amazed her how unaffected she could remain when it was her own hand.

The dull ache continued after he bandaged the hand in white gauze.

"How's it going with Sloan?" he asked as he worked. They'd only talked briefly one time since she'd taken over the assignment.

"I'm not sure," she answered honestly. "I'm beginning to think some progress is being made, but it's too soon to tell."

"I don't know of anyone else who could reach him." His compassionate gray eyes searched hers. "Have you told him yet?"

"No, but he'll see soon enough."

The dark head bobbed in agreement. "If you have any problems, don't hesitate to call me."

"I won't."

"And listen, it might not be a bad idea to keep this hand out of the water for a few days."

She laughed softly. "Sloan will love that."

"Speaking of the man, I'll check him, since I'm here." He discarded the items he'd used and closed his bag. "I'll give you a call later in the week."

"Thank you, Doctor."

"I'm glad to finally be in your debt. You're the one who continues to save me." The good-natured smile left him as he noted her hand. "Go ahead and remove those sutures yourself in a week or so. Use your own judgment."

Dr. Phelps left a few moments later and Joy lay back

against her pillow, intent on resting her eyes for a bit. Before she was aware of it, it was afternoon and she'd been asleep for hours.

A blanket had been laid over her, and she recognized it as one from Sloan's room. How had he gotten in? The door to his quarters had been widened to accommodate the wheelchair, but hers hadn't. A gentle breeze ruffled the closed drapes, and she realized the sliding-glass door had been left open.

What a puzzling man Sloan Whittaker was. Rubbing the sleep from her eyes, Joy sat up and swung her short legs off the mattress. Already, half the day had been wasted.

Someone knocked softly on her bedroom door.

"Come in," Joy called.

Clara opened the door and came in carrying a large tray. "I thought you might like something to eat."

"But you didn't need to bring it to me," Joy protested. "I'm not incapacitated, you know."

"Mr. Whittaker insisted that you take the rest of the day off. You rest and I'll bring in your meals."

"But, Clara, that's ridiculous."

"Mr. Whittaker was real worried about you. I can't remember a time he acted like this."

Leaning against the pillows the cook had fluffed up against the headboard, Joy laughed. "For all his bark, our Mr. Whittaker is a marshmallow. Did you see how pale he got when he saw the blood on my shirt? For a minute I was afraid he was going to pass out."

Clara's look was thoughtful. "Mr. Whittaker doesn't like the sight of blood. At least not since the accident."

The humor drained out of Joy's eyes. She was being callous. Of course seeing all that blood had bothered him, especially since he'd lain helplessly in a pool of his own.

The lack of sensitivity robbed Joy of her appetite. She made a token attempt to eat so as not to arouse Clara's suspicions and tucked a few items inside a napkin to give L.J.

After changing into a clean blouse for the third time that day, Joy carried the half-empty tray into the kitchen. "Thanks, Clara. Lunch was delicious."

"Since you're up, I think Mr. Whittaker would like to talk to you. He's in his room."

"Sure," she agreed, and swallowed tightly.

With the blanket clenched to her breast, Joy tapped lightly on Sloan's door and waited for his answer before entering.

They eyed one another warily. "You wanted to see me?"

"Not particularly," Sloan snapped.

Shrugging off his gruff welcome, she laid the blanket at the foot of the bed. "I'll see you later. By the way…" She hesitated, her back to him. "Thank you for putting the blanket over me."

"I didn't."

Joy frowned curiously. He was lying, and she didn't know why. Later, as she walked along the windswept shore, Joy guessed that he didn't want her to know he was concerned.

Paul saw her and waved as she climbed atop a sand dune. Joy raised her good hand and returned the gesture. It was another gorgeous April afternoon. How quickly she was coming to love this beach, this house, this... Her mind refused to form "man." So much of herself was tied up with this case: her skill, her ego, the almost desperate desire to help lift him from the mire of self-pity. The dangers were clear, but as long as she was aware and protected herself, she would be safe.

With long-legged strides, Paul raced to her, feet kicking up sand as he ran.

"How do you feel?" she queried.

"Great."

"Feel up to another confrontation with the master?" she asked in a teasing voice.

"Naw, it's much more fun watching you two argue. But since you're a bit under the weather, what would you like?"

"You've still got that plywood around, haven't you? Let's get him down here on the beach."

"He isn't going to like it," Paul warned.

"Heavens, so what's new? Sloan Whittaker doesn't like anything."

Together they laid down the thick boards of wood. Paul insisted on wheeling Sloan down, and Joy didn't argue. She didn't feel like arguing with Sloan, not today. Her hand throbbed; foolishly she'd refused anything for pain when Dr. Phelps asked. Sitting and soaking up the sun sounded far more appealing than a verbal battle with Sloan.

"I suppose this was your idea, Nielsen," Sloan ground out as Paul pushed the chair down the wooden planks.

She pretended the wind had blown the words away by cupping a hand over her ear.

"You heard me."

"Could be."

Paul glanced from one to the other and chuckled. "He's all yours. Let me know when you need me."

"Thanks, Paul." She watched as her friend headed back to the house.

"You enjoy doing this, don't you?"

"Doing what?"

"This kind of garbage!" He hurled the words at her harshly, as if venting his anger would lessen his confusion. "You seem to have the mistaken impression that once thrust into the beauty of nature I'll forget all my troubles and thank God for the gift of life."

"No." She sat in the sand beside him, her bare toes burrowing under the granules. "I thought a little sun might add color to your face."

"You're lying."

"If you say so," she agreed pleasantly, tilting her face upward and coveting the golden rays. "You know, Whittaker, if you didn't work so hard at disliking this, you could come to enjoy it."

"Never."

"Want me to bury your feet in the sand?"

"No," he hissed.

"Then be quiet. You're destroying my peace."

"Good. I haven't had a peaceful moment from the day you arrived."

She ignored him, pretending not to hear his movements.

"Nielsen."

Opening her eyes, she quirked her head inquiringly. Sloan dumped his sweater over her head. "That's what I think of your loony ideas."

"For a person with disabilities, you're mighty brave."

"And you're a sad excuse for a woman. Don't you wear anything but pants? What's the matter, are you afraid to let a man see your legs?"

"Legs," she cried dramatically. "You want legs, I'll give you legs." Rolling to her feet, she pulled up her pants to her knees and pranced around like a restless filly. The sight of Paul escorting a tall blonde halted Joy in midstride. Stopping completely, her hands fell lifelessly to her side and she took a huge breath. "It looks like you've got company."

"Company?" Sloan barked. "I don't want to see anyone. Send them away."

"It's too late for that." Joy studied the other woman. She would have killed for a figure like this blonde's. Tall. Willowy. Every brick stacked in the right place. And a face that would stop traffic.

As the two drew closer, the woman's pace increased. "Oh, my darling, Sloan. No one told me. Oh, Sloan." She fell to her knees and buried her perfectly shaped head in his lap. The delicate shoulders shook with sobs.

Sloan's hand lifted, hesitated, then finally patted the blonde's back.

Joy took a step in retreat, not wishing to be a witness to this scene. Sloan's eyes found Joy's and cast her an unmistakable look of appeal.

"I'll leave you two alone."

"No," Sloan barked, silently demanding that she stay.

"Maybe you'd enjoy some iced tea? I'll be back in a jiffy."

"Nielsen?" Sloan's low voice threatened.

"I'll be right back." Wickedly she fluttered her long lashes at him.

Paul carried a lounge chair for her while Joy managed the tray with two tall glasses of fresh iced tea each with a slice of lemon attached to the side.

Apparently the blonde had composed herself. Dabbing her eyes with a waded tissue, she stood at Sloan's side, her blue eyes filled with compassion and sweetness.

"I'm afraid Chantelle can't stay," Sloan announced, and his gaze narrowed menacingly on Joy. "Paul, would you kindly escort her to her car?"

In true gentlemanly fashion, Paul placed his arm around the blonde's shoulders and whispered comforting words to her as he walked her toward the house.

"Nielsen, you do that to me again and I'll—"

"Do what?" she inquired innocently.

His hand sliced the air dramatically. "Couldn't you have done something? I thought you were my self-appointed rescuer. Well, rescue me! The minute I really need you—off you fly with the excuse of getting iced tea."

"What in the Sam Hill did you expect me to do?"

"I don't know. That's your job, isn't it?"

"No," she snapped back, then started to laugh.

"What's so funny?" he demanded.

"You! Think about it. It's a sad commentary on your

life when you want me to rescue you from the arms of a beautiful woman."

A poor facsimile of a smile came and went. "Couldn't you see she was throwing herself all over me, oozing pity?"

"Women like to cry," she explained patiently, and sat down in the sand cross-legged. She took a tall glass and handed him the other. "It gives us a reason to appear feminine."

"And Chantelle knows how good she looks with tears clinging to her lashes. Her big, blue eyes staring into mine."

"You sound like you've made lots of women cry."

"Hundreds," he returned sarcastically.

"I wouldn't doubt it." Joy laughed lightly.

"What about you?"

"I don't know of any women who've cried over me," she teased, the wind blowing her soft brown curls across her high cheekbones.

"You know what I mean."

Staring in her tea, she shrugged lightly. "Only one."

"Who?"

Joy swallowed around the tight lump that formed in her throat. "My father."

They were silent after that.

"Tell me about your family," Sloan said after a long time.

"My father was a senior high music teacher and band director, my mother was a stay-at-home mom. There's only my brother. He's two years older, lives in Santa Barbara, has a wife and two children."

"Is he as gutsy as you?"

"Doug? Yes, only in a different way. He's a policeman."

"You said your father drowned." The words were issued softly. His voice inflection made it a question.

Arms wrapped around her knees, she stared out at the waves gently lapping the shore. "He died in Mexico, three summers ago. Mom and Dad flew down to celebrate their anniversary. Two little boys, about eight and ten, tourists from Texas, got trapped in the undertow." She paused, reliving the horror of that summer again. "Dad managed to save one. He died with his arms around the ten-year-old. My mother looked on from the beach helpless." Even blandly stating the facts brought tears to her eyes, and she touched her forehead to her knee, not wishing him to witness her distress. Once her breathing had returned to normal, she lifted her head. "My father was a wonderful man."

"I already knew that," Sloan murmured, and, reaching out a hand, lightly stroked her hair. His touch was gentle. Joy hadn't expected his comfort and expelled a whispering sigh at the warm sensation that cascaded over her from the touch of his hand to her head.

"What about you?" she asked to purposely change the subject.

"There's only me. I think my parents wanted a larger family, but mother had a difficult pregnancy and the doctors advised her not to get pregnant a second time."

"Were you always…"

"Rich?" he finished for her.

"That's not the word I would have used, but yes."

"The company's been in the family for three generations. This summer house is a new acquisition."

"This is your summer home?" Her gaze flew over her shoulder to the magnificent structure behind her. The idea that it was a summer home shocked her. This was the sort of place anyone would dream about living in all year long.

"Usually I live in a condo in Palm Springs, but I have apartments in Switzerland and New York. Had," he corrected on a bitter note.

Her mouth dropped open and she widened her eyes and swallowed. "Oh."

"For heaven's sake, don't go all goo-goo-eyed on me."

Joy forced her mouth closed.

"Actually, this house belongs to my parents. Does that make you feel any less intimidated?"

"Yes." She gestured weakly with her hand. "Sure."

"Does that shocked look mean I'm going to get a little respect?"

"No." She shook her head emphatically. "It means I'm asking for a raise. I hope you realize I'm still paying off a government loan for my college education."

He chuckled then. The rich, clear sounds were carried with the wind. Joy tossed her head back and smiled at him. This moment was one she would treasure when it came time for her to go; Joy was sure of it. The sun. The sand. The sea. And the sound of Sloan's full laugh.

Jumping to her feet, she took off toward the sea.

"Hey, where are you going?" he called after her, his brow creased in thick lines.

"To look for seashells." Swinging her hands high at her side, she walked backward, taunting him. "Want to come?"

"Yes!" he shouted, surprising her. "Bring one of those pieces of wood forward. Once the chair gets on wet sand, you can push me."

"Push you?" Her laugh was musical. "Wheel yourself, bub."

His dark eyes sparkled. "All right, lazy. I'll do the heavy work."

Joy did as he suggested, dragging the wood around until they managed to manipulate the chair close to the shore.

"Come on, I'll race you."

Sloan quirked his mouth to one side. "Trying to take advantage of a person with disabilities, are you?"

"I was going to even the odds," she added with an offended look.

"Sure you were."

"No, honest." She crossed her heart with her index finger and burst into peals of laughter at the look on his face. "Okay, okay, I'll run backwards."

"And hop on one foot?"

"No. That's too much."

"All right. On your mark, get ready, go," Sloan shouted.

Joy paused, hands on her hips, looking on helplessly. His arms worked furiously as he rotated the large wheels.

"Hey, I wasn't ready," she shouted at him.

"Tough." The wind brought the lone word back to

her. She watched as the muscles of his upper arms flexed with the effort.

Serious now, Joy turned around and began to jog backward. Within a minute she was even with him. "Let's negotiate," she protested, gasping for breath.

"Do you concede?"

"Anything."

Sloan stopped and swiveled the chair around so that he faced her.

Soft laughter rose within her, and until she regained her breath Joy leaned forward and rested her good hand on her knee. "You cheated," she chided him. "I wasn't ready."

"You looked ready to me."

Her back was to the ocean, and she heard Sloan's shout of warning just as the wave crashed against her legs, hitting the back of her thighs.

Sloan dissolved into fits of laughter at the shocked look that came over her.

"You did that on purpose," she gasped in outrage.

"I didn't, I swear it."

Flinging her hand forward, she managed to catch enough water to spatter him with a few drops. Not to be deterred, she waited until the next big wave came in and scooped as much water as her cupped hand would hold. Giggling and breathless, she ran toward him, stumbled, and fell forward.

In split-second response, Sloan reached out to catch her, breaking the impact of the fall. But to her horror, Joy pulled him out of the wheelchair and took him with her to the ground.

He lay partially on top of her. "Joy." His voice was urgent. "Are you all right?"

"Disgraced, but otherwise unruffled. And you?" Her back was pressed against the rough sand.

He didn't answer her. Their eyes met, and a flood of warmth swept through her. The laughter was gone from his gaze, and she stared back wordlessly, almost afraid to breathe. Joy knew she should break away, do something, anything, to stop what was happening. But the hunger in his look held her motionless. She didn't blink.

Slowly he lowered his head, blocking out the sunlight. Their breaths mingled as his lips hovered a hair's space above her own. No longer could she see his face. Her heart was crying out to him, begging him to stop and at the same time pleading with him to continue and kiss her. It was no use fighting her clamoring sensations, and she closed her eyes.

Very gently, as if in slow motion, Sloan fit his mouth over hers. At first his lips barely skimmed the surface, as if he didn't want this but couldn't help himself.

But when Joy slid her hands around his neck, his mouth crushed hers, forcing her lips to part. Fiercely he wrapped his arms around her, half lifting her from the sand.

Abruptly he released her and rolled to the side so that they lay next to one another on their backs. Joy felt the cold air and kept her eyes closed. She shouldn't have let this happen. It could possibly undermine everything she had struggled to build in this relationship.

"You asked for that," he said bitterly. "You've been

asking for it all day. Are you satisfied now? How does it feel to be kissed by me? Or is this one of the extra services you provide for all your patients?"

Four

"Mr. Whittaker's breakfast is ready," Clara announced as she set the tray on the kitchen counter. The older woman studied Joy. "You want me to take it in to him?"

For a moment the offer was tempting. But Joy couldn't. Sloan would know why, and he must never guess the effect his kiss had had on her. How stupid she'd been to have let it happen. Now she must pay for her foolishness.

"Air's been a mite thick between you two," Clara mumbled as she set a pan in the sink and filled it with tap water.

"What do you mean?" Joy glanced up guiltily.

"I don't suppose you'd think ol' Clara would notice. But things got real quiet after you and Mr. Whittaker were on the beach yesterday. Mr. Whittaker didn't eat dinner, and neither did you. Then later you didn't play that clarinet the way you have most nights."

"Flute," Joy corrected. "You're right. I didn't play. My...my hand was hurting."

Unconcerned, Clara hummed a soft tune. "You want me to take him breakfast?"

"No," she said with a forced smile. "I'll do it."

Balancing the tray on her knee, Joy knocked loudly on Sloan's door twice. Purposely she'd avoided him the remainder of the day, hoping that if she put some distance between them after what had happened on the beach they could both look at it with perspective. But the nagging questions persisted. How could anything that felt so good, so right, be a mistake?

"Come in," Sloan growled.

Forcing a smile, Joy opened the door. "I can see you're in your usual good mood this morning."

"What's so good about it?" Sloan demanded, and pivoted his chair around so that he faced her. "It's just like any other morning for a person with disabilities."

"You're not a person with disabilities." Her eyes focused away from him as she placed the tray on the desk.

His laugh was short and derisive. "But isn't that what you're so fond of calling me?"

Joy inhaled a calming breath. "I call you one to get a rise out of you. You're a smart man; I'd have thought you had that figured out by now."

"Not many men I know roll around in one of these things," he challenged, and his hand patted the large wheel of his chair.

"It's true that you and that chair are constant companions." Joy wasn't going to argue with him. "But in your mind you're running free."

"How do you know what's in my mind?" he protested, his eyes darkening.

"It's not so difficult," she returned thoughtfully, her back to him.

"Oh?" Again his voice was thick with challenge.

"What is this? An interrogation?" Joy whirled around and leaned against the desk, her hands behind her. "Remember, it's Monday morning. You'll have to make allowances for me on Mondays. It takes my heart ten minutes to start beating once I crawl out of bed."

"You ran this morning."

Joy turned around and lifted the silver warming dome off the breakfast plate and set it aside. "How'd you know that?"

"I watched you."

"Oh." It was crazy, the effect the information had on her. Joy's hands felt clammy and her face warm. She didn't want him invading her thought life this way. When the time came for her to leave, it would only make matters more difficult. And when she left, Joy vowed, she would walk away from Sloan Whittaker intact. Whole. She wouldn't leave this man her heart.

"What's that?" Sloan's words cut into her musings.

"What's what?"

"That." He pointed to the breakfast tray.

"Oatmeal, toast, and juice." She looked at him with a blank stare.

"I hate oatmeal."

"Rolled oats are good for you," she countered with a smile.

"Yes, but have you ever asked yourself what they rolled them with?"

"No," she admitted with a small laugh, "I can't say that I have. Do you want me to have Clara cook you something else?"

He looked up at her, his eyes wide and disbelieving. "Nielsen, you're mellowing."

Joy's nerves suddenly felt threadbare. The need to escape was overpowering. "Maybe I am," she agreed. "But don't count on it," she murmured, and made her exit from the room.

Her hands were trembling as she leaned against the wall in the hallway. She needed its support. With a determined lift of her chin, she straightened and returned to the kitchen. This wasn't like her, but there seemed to be a lot of things she didn't understand about herself anymore.

"Problems?" Clara questioned, her large brown eyes watching Joy with concern.

"None. Why?"

Clara's look was disconcerting. The older woman was too observant not to notice the high color of Joy's flushed cheeks.

"You need to talk to ol' Clara?"

"No, I'm fine," Joy dismissed the offer. "But thanks anyway."

"Anytime."

The sounds of Clara humming followed Joy down the hallway to her room. The door clicked, and she walked across the room to stand in front of the mirror. She forced herself to do an assessment of herself. Twenty-eight, never been married. Not unattractive, but certainly not beautiful. She wasn't another Chantelle, the blonde who looked gorgeous with damp lashes. Joy's hair was cut short and curly. With so many hours in the pool every day, it was the most practical style.

Turning sideways, she placed her hands on the underside of her breasts and lifted them. They were probably her best feature. If it weren't for those, most people would think she was a young boy. That was the problem with being so short. Petite, her mother claimed. Joy called it just plain stubby.

Within seconds Joy had determined she was headed for a lot of heartache if she allowed this awareness for Sloan to continue. In all the years she'd been working, this was the first time she had faced these feelings. A patient was a patient, and she had never allowed herself to forget the code of ethics.

The session with Sloan in the pool didn't go well. Both of them were on edge. The ability to work with one another, although grudgingly, was gone.

Sloan struggled to disguise his pain, and with every wince Joy had to force herself to continue. She didn't need to be reminded that it hurt. She knew.

"Are you going to do the exercises today or not?" Sloan questioned in a vicious tone, angry and impatient.

"What do you think I'm doing?" she shot back. Unconsciously Joy realized that she hadn't been working him as hard, because his pain was affecting her.

When the next series of manipulations had been completed, Sloan was left in little doubt that she was doing her job.

* * *

Later that afternoon, Joy entered the fenced yard to see L.J. The bird hobbled to her, and Joy bent down to talk to her creature friend.

"Hello."

L.J. squawked loudly, and Joy laughed.

"So you can talk. I was beginning to wonder." She held out her bandaged hand. "Did you see what you did?"

The seagull tilted its head at an inquiring angle.

"Well, don't worry. I know it was an accident. But it was a good lesson for us both." She crumbled up bits of fish and some other leftovers in his dish, then stepped back. Almost immediately L.J. began to eat. Joy stayed with him until he'd finished.

That evening she watched television with Paul, but a half hour later she couldn't have told anyone what she'd seen.

When she returned to her room, Joy couldn't decide if she should play her flute or not. But music was a basic part of her life, and she didn't know if she could go without it two nights running. Playing had always calmed her spirit and soothed her.

Her options were few. If she stayed in her room, she would be depriving Sloan of the pleasure he received when she played. It seemed almost petty to put her desire for solitude above what little enjoyment he received from life.

Dusk had cast a purple shadow across the horizon when Joy stepped onto the verandah. She paused to inhale the fresh scent of the sea and closed her eyes. The winds were whispering and gentle when she raised the musical instrument to her lips.

As always, the music flowed naturally. But tonight it was dark and deep, unlike the mellow tunes she normally enjoyed.

"You practicing for someone's funeral?" Sloan asked in a bitter tone.

Joy paused and lowered her flute. She'd been so caught up in the music she hadn't noticed he'd come outside. He stayed several feet away, his profile illuminated by the setting sun.

She shook her head. "No."

"Could have fooled me."

Ignoring him, she played again, forcing out a lively, popular tune. Before realizing what had happened, she slipped into the intense mournful music a second time. When she recognized what she'd done, she stopped mid-measure.

"Will you play at mine?" Sloan asked, his voice a mere whisper.

"Play at your what?" She didn't look at him, her gaze focusing on the tumbling waves that broke against the beach.

"My funeral."

"That's a morbid thought. You're not going to die," she said seriously, her own voice a soft murmur. "I won't let you."

His light laugh couldn't hide the pain.

"Do you want something?" She didn't need to explain what. When it came to painkilling drugs, Sloan was sensible. He never took anything unless the pain became unbearable. The fear of becoming addicted to the medication was always present, and he seemed well aware of the dangers.

He expelled a harsh breath before answering. "What I need is for you to kiss me better." His voice was low and seductive.

Joy didn't breathe; the oxygen was trapped in her lungs. Her hand tightly clenched the railing as she closed her eyes. The battle to alleviate the pain from his eyes with a gentle brush of her mouth over his was almost overpowering. The knowledge that one kiss would never be enough was the only thing that stopped her.

"Want me to call Chantelle?" A fingernail broke against the freshly painted surface of the railing on the verandah. Still she didn't move.

"No." The word was released in an angry rush.

With her back to Sloan, she heard him return to his room.

Joy breathed again.

The following morning Joy walked into the modern-style living room. "Good morning, Mr. Whittaker."

Myron Whittaker placed the coffee cup in the saucer and stood. "Morning."

"You asked to see me?"

"Yes, I did. Sit down, please." He motioned with his hand to the chair opposite him.

Joy sat on the edge of the leather cushion and primly folded her hands in her lap. The Whittakers were wonderful people who loved their son and were willing to do whatever was necessary to help him return to a normal life again. "How's Sloan?" his father began.

"There's been some improvement. I imagine within a few weeks he'll be able to start work on the mats and the parallel bars. From there it will only be a matter of time before he can advance to the walker and then the cane."

The older man lowered his gaze. "Yes, the cane."

Joy didn't need to be told what Sloan's father was thinking. "From what I can tell, your son will always have a limp. The cane will be necessary."

Myron Whittaker glanced up, and Joy had the funny sensation that although he was looking at her, he wasn't seeing her. "That's not it," he admitted absently, and shook his head. "I was remembering…thinking…" He let the rest of the sentence ebb away. "We used to play tennis, Sloan and me. Twice a week."

Joy could see no use in dwelling on things past. "It's unlikely that your son will play a decent game of tennis again."

He lifted the coffee cup to his mouth, and Joy noted that it shook slightly.

"I've done as you suggested and brought some work from the office. Heaven knows I'm not able to keep up with it all."

"I think bringing Sloan back into the mainstream of the business can only help," Joy murmured.

"I was hoping to go over a few of the things with you."

"With me?" Her gaze shot to him. "Surely you don't expect me to discuss the business with your son?"

"To be honest, I was hoping you would bring up the

subject with him. Sloan and I had a parting of ways on my last visit. At this point I feel it would be better if we didn't see one another for a while."

"You can't mean that."

Myron Whittaker stood and paced across the marble floor. He had his back to her.

"Sloan and I have always been close. Don't misunderstand me. I love my son."

"I'm sure you do."

"It hurts me to see him in that chair. There are so many things I wanted in life for Sloan, and now everything seems impossible." He dropped his foot and turned around. "The last time I saw Sloan we said some bitter, hard things to one another. I don't know if it would be a good idea for me to see him now. We both need time."

"But that's something you don't have," Joy countered, and released a slow breath. "Sloan regrets what happened just as much as you. Clear the air between you, make amends. Then bring up the business aspect of your visit. If you'd like, I could tell him you're here."

The agreeing nod wasn't eager. "If you think I should."

"I do."

Sloan was in his quarters, his head resting against the back of the chair, eyes closed.

When Joy tapped lightly on the open door, he straightened and opened his dark eyes, which narrowed on her.

"Your father's here to see you."

At first Sloan said nothing. "Tell him I'm busy."

"That would be a lie."

"When did you get so righteous?" Sloan tossed the question at her flippantly.

Joy made a show of glancing at her wristwatch. "About five minutes ago."

Sloan ignored the humor. "I don't want to see him."

"He's your father," she reminded him.

"Do you want me to wave a banner?"

Maybe Joy wouldn't have reacted so strongly if her own father was alive. "That comment was unworthy of you, Sloan."

"Listen, Miss Miracle Worker. This is between my father and me. I'd advise you to keep out of it."

"No."

The barely controlled anger showed in the tight set of his mouth. His eyes were afire. "Stay out of this; it's none of your business. You seem to think you've got me wrapped around your finger. You're wrong. I refuse to allow you to dictate to me my personal affairs. Is that understood?" His voice gained volume with each word until the room seemed to shake with the sound. "Get out, Joy," he warned in a dangerous tone. "Get out, before I say something I'll regret."

She took a step in retreat, then stood her ground.

Sloan advanced his chair across the room until he was directly in front of her.

"He's your father," she murmured. "Don't do this to him. Don't do this to yourself."

"Stay out of it, Nielsen," Sloan ground out between clenched teeth.

In the past Joy had found ways around Sloan's pride.

Now, facing his steel-hard resolve, she felt defenseless. There was nothing she could say or do.

Sloan's father stood when she entered the living room.

"I can tell by your face what he said. Don't bother to explain."

"I'm sorry, Mr. Whittaker," she added in a weak voice. "I feel terrible."

"Don't." He looked away as though assessing his visit and then reached for his coat.

"I shouldn't have forced the issue."

He snapped the briefcase closed, his back to her. "Give me a call when you think…" Again he let the rest of the sentence trail away.

"I will." Joy walked with him to the front door. "I'm sure everything will work out fine."

Gravely he shook his head. Not for the first time, Joy noted the tired, hurt look in his eyes.

She stood on the front steps until his car rounded the bend in the road. Without questioning the wisdom of her actions, she marched through the house and into Sloan's room.

"That was a despicable thing to do."

"I told you to stay out of it," he stormed back.

"I won't."

Sloan escaped onto the verandah.

"You can't do this to your own father. He loves you. Seeing you like this is tearing him apart."

"You're right, it is," Sloan shouted, appearing in the doorway that led outside. "Don't you think I can see the pity in his eyes? He's no different from anyone else. I

don't want his sympathy. I can't stand to see him stare
at me that way."

Some of the intense anger drained out of her. "I'd
give anything to have my father look any way at me,"
she whispered.

"Don't confuse the issue with sentimentality."

"Oh, Sloan," she moaned, and exhaled a wistful sigh.
"Can't you see what you're doing? You're driving everyone who loves you out of your life."

"That's my choice," he returned bitterly. "I can see
and do as I please."

"But you can't play tennis with your father."

The color fled from his face as his eyes hardened
into cutting diamond chips. Fierce anger shot out from
him. "You're right about that, Miss Miracle Worker. I'm
not going to play tennis with my father. But then, I'll
never play much of anything physical again, will I? So
what's the difference?"

The urge to fall to her knees and hold him was so
strong that it was all Joy could do to turn and walk
away.

To say Joy was miserable was a gross understate-
ment. Paul attempted to lighten her mood by taking
her out to dinner.

"I blew it." They sat at an umbrella table at Mobey
Jake's. The neon whale flashed directly above them.

"Don't be so hard on yourself, kid."

Joy nearly choked on a French fry. "Kid?" she repeated. "How old do you think I am?"

The muscular shoulders lifted with a heavy shrug. "Twenty, maybe."

"Thanks." Joy laughed.

Paul laid his fish on a napkin and looked up thoughtfully. "You should laugh more often."

One corner of Joy's mouth lifted in a bittersweet smile. "There's not much excuse to laugh in this business. I wish my patients could understand that it hurts me as much as them."

"One patient, you mean," Paul inserted.

Joy looked out over the coastline instead of directly at Paul. "One patient," she agreed.

"Are you falling for this guy?" A frown marred his forehead.

Paul was nothing if not blunt. Joy felt the heavy thud of her heart. It beat so loud and strong that it seemed someone was pounding on her with a hammer. She reacted that way when someone spoke candidly.

"I hope not," she replied truthfully. "I've enough problems handling Sloan Whittaker without involving my emotions."

"If you need a shoulder to lean on, let me know."

"Thanks, Paul." Joy meant that sincerely. She'd never worked with nicer people than Paul and Clara.

It was dark by the time they returned to the house. Since Clara had the day off, Joy had cooked Sloan's dinner, and she was grateful when Paul had delivered it to him. Paul and Joy had decided to eat out.

The porch light was on, but the house was dark. As Joy let herself into her room she noticed there were no lights on in Sloan's. Apparently he'd opted for an early night.

Not wishing to wake him, Joy carried her flute down to the beach. She stopped long enough to check L.J. and give him the leftover fish. The bird seemed to want out, and when Joy held open the gate, L.J. hobbled after her.

The two found a log not far from the house. Joy sat, buried her bare feet in the sand, and began to play. For a while L.J. stayed close to her side, but it didn't take much time for him to stray. As long as she could see him, Joy let him wander. The difficulty came when it was time to return to the house. L.J. enjoyed his taste of freedom and wasn't willing to go back to the small fenced area. Joy had to round him up like a sheepdog herding a stray lamb.

Laughing and breathless, she let herself into the house.

"What were you doing out there?"

Sloan.

"What are you doing up?" Joy had never known Sloan to come into the kitchen.

"I asked you first." The room remained dark.

Joy's eyes soon adjusted to the room's interior. Only a few feet separated her and Sloan.

"I… I was on the beach."

"That much I knew."

"Why are you here?" Her hand gripped the knob behind her.

"I heard you playing."

"I'm sorry if I woke you," she interrupted. "I didn't mean to."

Sloan wiped a hand over his brow. "I couldn't sleep. Did you and Paul have a good time?"

"Yes. We went to Mobey Jake's."

"Bring me anything this time?"

"No, sorry. I didn't."

He dismissed her apology with a wan smile. "What took you so long coming inside? I was worried."

Sloan concerned about her? After this afternoon he had all the more reason to want her out of his life. In her eagerness to mend the rift between father and son, she had only done harm. Sloan was right; it wasn't any of her affair.

"Joy?" He seemed to be waiting for her answer.

"I was bringing L.J. home."

"You and that bird." His mirthless laugh was filled with irony. "I was ready to call out the National Guard."

"I'm sorry—for everything," she muttered.

Her apology produced a stunned silence.

"Did I hear you right? Joy Nielsen, gutsy Miracle Worker, actually admitting to a fault? Are you feeling well? Do you need a doctor?"

"I'm fine," she said with a shaky laugh. "Sloan, I feel terrible about today. You were right. I should never have stuck my nose where it doesn't belong."

The amusement drained from his eyes. He extended a hand to her, palm open.

Scooting out a kitchen chair, Joy sat so that their gazes were level. With appreciation for his accepting her apology, she placed her hand in his.

"Friends?" he questioned.

Joy nodded. "I prefer it to being enemies."

His hand closed tightly over hers, his thumb sensuously rotating against the inside of her wrist. "I do too." His eyes holding hers, he lifted her fingers to his mouth.

Joy tugged, and immediately Sloan released her hand. The potential for danger was powerful and strong. If she let Sloan kiss her fingers, it wouldn't be enough; she'd want to taste his mouth over hers. She couldn't risk weeks of hard work for something as fleeting as physical attraction.

Awkwardly she stood and backed away. "Good night, Sloan. Sleep well."

Somehow Joy managed to keep from running into her room. By the time she closed the bedroom door, she was trembling. Covering her face with both hands, she paced the carpet, her heart pounding like a trapped fledgling. Either she came to her senses or resigned from this case. The matter was simple. She was a professional therapist, sensible and proficient. She knew better than to nurture this powerful physical attraction. In the end she would leave the patient, not Sloan. But just as she recognized she must rein in her feelings, she knew she couldn't bear to leave him now.

The next morning, Joy was in the pool doing laps when Paul brought Sloan to the water's edge. Once placed on the side of the pool, Sloan could lower himself into the blue depths.

Treading water at the deep end, Joy waved. "I'll be right there."

"Don't hurry on my account," he shouted back.

A smile flashed from her eyes, and with even strokes Joy swam toward him.

"You look bright and cheerful this morning." Sloan had been up, dressed, and eating breakfast by the time Joy returned from her run. Normally he delayed starting the day as long as possible. Joy remembered the first few days after she'd arrived the struggle she had had just to keep his drapes open. Sometimes she forgot how far they'd come. But seeing him now, she was reminded how much farther they yet had to travel.

Clara hurried onto the patio. "Sorry to bother you, but Mr. Whittaker Senior is here."

A hardness stole over Sloan's face. "Who does he want to see this time?" The question was barely civil.

Joy bit into her lip to restrain an angry response.

Clara wiped her hands on her apron, obviously flustered. "Mr. Whittaker says he wants to talk to you." She directed her answer to Sloan.

"Tell him I'm busy."

"We can do this later," Joy inserted eagerly. "I'll come back…"

"No." His angry shout shut her off.

"Sloan, please," she whispered.

"Do as I say, Clara." He directed his attention to the housekeeper, his dismissal final.

With a quick bob of her head, Clara turned and hurried toward the house.

His narrowed gaze swung to Joy. "Was this brilliant idea yours?"

Joy returned his stare speechlessly. Was Sloan implying that she had sent for his father?

"Is it?" he shouted.

"Of course not. What are you suggesting?"

"I saw the two of you together," he hissed. "I'm not stupid. You two have something up your sleeves. Let it be known right now. I don't want any part of it. Is that understood?" The last words were shouted.

"Something up our sleeves?" Joy echoed incredulously. "Your father is half killing himself to maintain the business. *Your* company, I might add. He's dying in stages. In case you'd forgotten, your father's retired." Joy paused to draw in a breath. "Are you so self-absorbed that you haven't stopped to think what his life has been like since your accident? Not only is he worried sick about you, but he's taken over your position in the company—with all the stress and worries. But you, Mr. High and Mighty, you're so caught up in self-pity, all you see is yourself."

Sloan's face became sickeningly pale. "You don't know what you're talking about."

"Are you accusing me of lying now, too?"

"What can you expect me to think? My parents told me Harrison was in charge of the company."

"Have you looked at your father lately, Sloan, really looked? Can't you see what's happening to him?"

Sloan went completely still, like a lion alert before the attack. "If what you say is true, it's Dad's own fault. He should have given everything over to Harrison the way he said he was."

"Are you really so uncaring?" His lack of concern shocked her.

His blistering hot gaze swept over her contemptuously. "What do you know of any of this?" he shouted. "Safe and warm in your secure little world, it must be easy to sit in judgment of something you'll never comprehend." A muscle worked convulsively along the line of his jaw.

The desire to tell him was overpowering. "What do I know?" She repeated his question with a half laugh. "Maybe it's time you found out exactly what I do." She swam to the steps that led out of the pool. "You asked me once about pain. Believe me when I tell you I'm well acquainted with it." She stood and placed one foot on the painted step. "You told me once you'd lain in a hospital bed wanting to die. I did more than want. I begged."

She turned to him then, the hideous scars that marked her thighs in full view. When she glanced at him she was prepared for the shocked look, even the repulsion he couldn't hide. She'd viewed it before when others saw her scars.

"Paul," she yelled, and hurriedly donned her terry-cloth wrap. "Mr. Whittaker wants out of the water." Unable to bear another minute in Sloan's presence, Joy turned and ran into the house.

Five

"Joy," Sloan called after her, but Joy only increased her pace.

Paul met her halfway to the house. He stuck out a hand and stopped her. "You okay?" His finger brushed a tear from her cheek.

"Fine," she lied. "I'm fine."

Clara gave her a funny look as Joy came through the kitchen, but she didn't stop to explain.

Once in the privacy of her room, Joy slumped into a chair and covered her eyes with one hand. She'd only been sixteen at the time of the accident. A school cheerleader. But she would never be again. The scars were cleverly disguised with the proper clothing, so that no one need ever know. But their ugliness affected her more mentally than physically. She ran, she swam, she played tennis, could, in fact, do almost as much as before the accident. She had her father to thank for that, but even he couldn't force the look of shock and revulsion from people's eyes when they saw her misshapen thighs for the first time.

Joy changed back into her uniform and held a cool washcloth over her eyes, hoping the cold water would take away the redness. Tears were the last thing she wanted Sloan to see. He held enough aces in his hand as it was.

Clara was stirring something at the stove when Joy entered the kitchen. "Mr. Whittaker's been saying lots of things he doesn't mean lately," she commented, her back to Joy.

"Mr. Whittaker didn't say anything to upset me, so don't blame him for something he didn't do. He's confused enough without all of us turning on him." It would be unfair to have the others think Sloan had caused her to cry.

"I still think Mr. Whittaker had better take a good, long look at himself."

Joy pretended not to hear. "Do you mind if I take some of these leftovers to L.J.?"

"Isn't that bird well yet?"

"No. It'll be a long time before his wing heals completely."

"Go ahead, then."

"Thanks, Clara." She took out bits and pieces of meat and fish she knew the gull would eat.

Joy spent a good portion of a half hour with L.J. He allowed her to touch him freely now—a small victory, but one that encouraged her.

When she came back into the kitchen, Sloan's lunch tray was ready.

"Take it in to him while it's hot."

Joy hesitated. She'd rather not see Sloan. He was sure to ask her questions she'd prefer not to answer.

"Go on," Clara ordered.

The door was open, and Sloan appeared to watch her anxiously. Joy was sure a niggling uncertainty showed in her eyes.

"Set the tray outside today," Sloan ordered. "I feel like looking at the ocean."

Still and silent, Joy did as he asked. He joined her at the round, enameled table on the verandah. He examined his lunch, lifting the warming dome and unrolling his silverware from the linen napkin. "Did Clara forget the pepper?"

Briefly Joy's eyes scanned the tray. She was sure she'd seen it earlier. "Would you like me to bring it to you?"

"Please."

With obvious reluctance, Joy returned to the kitchen.

Sloan's eyes followed her as she came onto the deck. "Will you have your lunch with me?"

She focused her gaze on the view of the sky and the sea. A light breeze ruffled the silky, soft curls. Absently she smoothed the hair from her face.

"Joy?" he prompted.

She blinked, forcing herself to look at him. "Not today."

"Tonight then?"

Joy felt drained. "Why?"

"I think we should talk."

"About what?"

Sloan expelled an impatient sigh. "There's no need to be obtuse."

She turned around to face him then, hands clenched so tight that her long nails cut into her palms. "Like everyone else who's seen my disfigurement, you're dying of curiosity. What happened? How long ago? Whose fault was it? I'm not a morbid sideshow."

"I wasn't thinking that," he said tautly.

"Don't lie to me. You're no different. Did you think you could hide the revulsion? Don't you realize I've seen abhorrence often enough to recognize it?" she accused in a choked voice.

"That's not true."

"Oh, for heaven's sake, spare me." Joy shook her head, not wanting to argue. She retrieved the pepper shaker and pointedly placed it on the table and left.

As she walked away, Joy could almost feel the dagger penetrate her back. Sloan was angry. She had watched as he struggled to control his temper. For the first time in her memory, he'd succeeded.

Joy waited until Paul came for Sloan after lunch before she returned his tray to the kitchen. He'd hardly touched his lunch. But then, neither had she.

Adjusting a wide-brimmed straw hat on her head, she took a well constructed straw basket and headed for the beach. On several occasions she'd wanted to go beach-walking to look for seashells, but had yet to bring back more than one or two. The need to explore, to escape, to get away, was stronger today than ever.

When she stopped to check L.J. she noted he was quickly finding his protective home a prison and she decided to bring him with her. Readily the bird hobbled behind her when she opened the fence gate.

Her first find was an unbroken sand dollar, and she bent over to retrieve it from the wet shore. As she did, L.J. came to her side. He pecked away at grass, eating bugs and things she decided she'd prefer not to know. The two of them were content and happy. Two against the wind, two against the sea. Two people against the world.

The day was perfect as only a California spring-time could be, and when Joy turned back to return to the house, she noticed the figure in a wheelchair coming toward her.

She paused, her feelings undecided. One half of her was demanding that she run the other way. Avoid him as much as possible, cast his curiosity and pity away. But the other half of her yearned for the comfort and understanding that could only come from another facing like circumstances.

There was irony here. None of her other patients had ever known. But she had never worked with anyone like Sloan Whittaker. His effect upon her was far more powerful than anyone else's, which made him dangerous in ways she still hadn't fully comprehended.

With L.J. hobbling behind her, Joy slowly sauntered toward Sloan.

"How'd you get out here?" she questioned when they met. Her eyes refused to meet his.

"You're a smart girl. Figure it out."

Hoping to display a lack of concern, she lightly shrugged her shoulders.

"Is it so dark and horrible that you can't tell me?" The question was issued so softly that for a moment Joy wasn't sure he'd spoken.

"It happened a long time ago. Some things are best forgotten."

"What you mean is the painful memories."

"I'm not going to argue, if that's what you want."

"It's not."

She stood stiffly at his side.

"Show me what you found?" he requested gently.

Joy didn't know how to deal with him when he was kind or tender. She felt far more comfortable dealing with his pride and anger.

When she didn't immediately respond, Sloan took the basket out of her hand and fingered the assortment of shells and rocks she'd collected. He lifted his eyes and his frowning gaze studied her. "You didn't want me to know, did you?"

"No," she quipped.

"You would never have told me if it hadn't been for my fight with my father."

Joy's eyes met his. Was that pain she heard in his voice? "Probably not."

"Why?"

"Why?" She angrily threw the word back at him. "You like perfection, especially in your women. I saw Chantelle. The china-doll face, with the figure a woman like me would die for. She's perfect right down to the mascara on the tips of her lashes and the uniformly shaped fingernails."

Her words seemed to anger him. "You're not like Chantelle."

"That's just what I said," she concurred.

"Not in the ways that matter."

Her voice quivered as she struggled not to reveal the hurt his words inflicted. "I can't tell you how many times kindhearted people with good intentions told me that it didn't matter if I was scarred because it was what was on the inside that counted. I don't need to hear it from you."

"Now you're twisting my words."

She shook her head and pinched her lips together.

"You are the most incredibly beautiful woman I know."

Joy released a short, disgusted sound and stormed away. His rolling laughter stopped her. "What's so funny?" she demanded, swiveling around, hands on her hips, feet spread in a defensive stance.

"You are!" he shouted, the wind carrying his words. "Don't you remember how you said it was a sad commentary on my life if I needed you to rescue me from beautiful women?"

"I remember." She didn't lessen the distance separating them.

"I tell you how beautiful you are and immediately you act like I've given you the biggest insult of your life."

"I am not beautiful," she shouted back.

"Then why do I have to struggle not to kiss you? Why do I lay awake at night and wish you were in bed with me?" The violence in his voice stunned her.

Joy flinched at his words. "You don't know what you're saying."

"You're right. Not only am I weak in the body, but I'm weak in the head."

"You won't get an arguement out of me about that." A gust of wind nearly lifted the hat from her head. Joy caught it just before it flew off. Long John squawked, diverting her attention, and when Joy looked at Sloan he had his back to her and was slowly progressing along the beach.

Unwilling to join him, but equally unwilling to leave him on his own, Joy sat and waited. She lay back in the sand and rested her eyes. Could it be possible that Sloan was attracted to her? The thought was heady enough to cause her heart to beat wildly. Sloan Whittaker was more tempting than any man she had ever known. But she would never fit into his world. Sloan was best left in the hands of women like Chantelle. The two of them belonged together. She was a physical therapist that would pass in and out of his life in short order. A year from now he'd have trouble remembering her name. Joy couldn't afford to lose sight of that.

She must have drifted into sleep. The next thing Joy knew Sloan let out an angry curse, and she sat up, surprised.

"You can call off your attack bird."

"Long John," she yelled. Sloan was sucking the side of his index finger.

"What happened?"

"Nothing."

"And you always suck your finger?"

"I do when it's bleeding."

"Let me see."

"No."

"My, my, aren't we brave," she murmured, coolly aloof.

"If you saw this cut you'd think so in earnest."

"Sloan, please. Did L.J. hurt you?"

"Only my pride. It seems your feathered creature doesn't make friends easily."

Joy gave a frustrated sound and fell to her knees at his side. "For heaven's sake, quit acting like a child and let me have a look at it."

His hand cupped the side of her face, raising her eyes to meet his. A heavy sensual awareness rippled through her, and it was all Joy could do not to place her hand over his and close her eyes. She was tampering with fire, and she knew it.

"It…it doesn't look bad."

"I told you it was only a scratch."

"I wouldn't want…"

"What wouldn't you want?" His voice was low and seductive as his hand cupped the other side of her face. "I can't help this," he whispered huskily. "Hate me later." His mouth gently kissed her chin, her eyes, the end of her nose, and caressed her cheek before softly parting her lips.

She should have stopped him. It wasn't him she'd hate later, but herself. Her arms slid around his neck; her fingers stroked the hair that grew thick there.

Sloan's mouth sought hers, and she moved her face

against his until finally, when their lips met, Joy was beyond coherent thought.

The kiss was hard and demanding and showed an expertise she had only rarely experienced. The tip of his tongue outlined her lips. Joy thought she would die from the pure pleasure as his mouth crashed down over hers.

His hand slid down her nape, his thumb moving in a slow rhythmic circle against her sensitized skin. He pushed the neckline of her dress off one smooth shoulder, his mouth blazing a trail of soft kisses that led to the scented hollow between her breasts. When Joy emitted a small protesting sound, Sloan tightened his hold and raised his mouth to the nape of her neck.

"Don't say it," he ground out in a fierce whisper. "I know what you're thinking."

"You couldn't possibly know."

"For once in your life, don't think. Feel." His mouth was on hers. The kisses became longer, more languorous, as he pressed their upper bodies as close together as possible.

"No...no..." She dragged her mouth from his. Stiffening, she pulled away. At first Sloan didn't want to let her go; Joy could sense as much as he tightened his grip. But after the first sign of struggle he released her.

Joy slumped on the sand beside him.

"Don't say it." The command was whispered harshly.

"I won't," she returned unsteadily. "I... I think we should get back to the house."

"Not yet." His voice was softer. "Sit with me for a while."

Joy's first reaction was to refuse. Together, alone like this, was dangerous for both of them.

She brought her knees up and circled them with her arms. For a long time they sat in silence. When she felt Sloan's gaze on her she turned to face him. Their eyes met. Hers, she was sure, were soft, lambent, the effect of his kisses evident; his tired, strained.

Joy looked away. "I was only sixteen." Her voice was barely above a weak whisper. "I was a cheerleader on the way home from a Friday night game when the school bus was hit by a train. I... I don't remember much of the accident. Only the sound of screams and realizing they belonged to my friends...and to me. My father told me I was trapped inside. Everyone told me how lucky I was to be alive." She gave a sad laugh. "For a long time I didn't think so. At least if I was dead the pain would go away."

"I thought the same thing," Sloan added in a gruff whisper. His hand rested on her shoulder as if some contact with her, even the light touch of his hand against her bare skin, was necessary.

"The doctors assured my family I'd never walk again. The damage was too extensive, multiple. My father wouldn't accept that. He insisted on a therapist." She paused and bit into her bottom lip. "It hurt so much I thought I'd die."

"And I had the audacity to ask what you could possibly know about pain." His voice was filled with regret.

"You didn't know. My mother couldn't stand to see me suffer like that. I know it wasn't any easier on Dad, but he was there every session encouraging me, loving me, helping in any way he could. I'd be in a wheelchair today if it wasn't for my father."

"You told me once the only man you'd ever made cry was your father."

Joy nodded. "With the therapist's help, Dad learned the manipulations and assumed some of the exercises. I wanted to give up so many times. But Dad wouldn't let me. He prodded, pried, bribed, and when the pain was the worst he cried with me. But not once in the next two years would he let me quit."

"It took two years for you to walk again?"

"Two of the longest years of my life."

"I can imagine."

"If it weren't for the scars I don't think anyone would guess."

"No. Have you ever considered plastic surgery?"

Joy stiffened defensively. "My medical bills were staggering. My family gave me back my life. The disfigurement can be hidden. No, the thought has never entered my mind."

"I've offended you and I didn't mean to. I'd like to do that for you, Joy. My gift to you for everything you've done for me."

"I haven't done anything."

"How can you say that?"

"Easy. Want me to do it again?"

"Joy." He ground out her name in frustration. "Why is it every time I try with you it backfires? I think you're wonderful just the way you are. The scars don't bother me. Keep them, if you like."

"I like." She stood and brushed the sand from her

dress. "Paul and Clara will be worried. We should head back. Do you want me to push you?"

"No."

Joy had gone several feet, but Sloan didn't follow. When she glanced back expectantly, she saw that he hadn't moved, his gaze resting on the rough ocean. "You coming?" she called.

He turned toward her and nodded, but it was several long moments before he did so.

By midnight the house was as quiet as a funeral parlor. Joy remained in her room reading, or at least made the pretense of involving herself with a best-selling mystery plot.

The light tap against the sliding-glass door that led to the verandah startled her. She threw back the covers and quickly donned her housecoat.

"I couldn't sleep either." Sloan sat outside the door. "Don't lie and tell me you weren't awake."

"I was up," Joy conceded.

"Why didn't you play tonight?"

Since their meeting on the beach, Joy had avoided Sloan as much as possible without arousing suspicions. "I didn't feel up to it."

"Don't kid yourself. You weren't up to facing me."

"All right," she stormed. "I didn't want to see you. But it didn't do me much good, did it?"

"I can be as stubborn as you. Come out here and sit awhile."

Joy doubted that. "It's late." She searched for an excuse. "That's never stopped you before. I bet you didn't know I could see you out here with your flimsy silk nightgown pressed against you in the wind."

Joy decided the best thing to do was refuse to be drawn into his game. "I'm hungry," she said on a falsely cheerful note. "I think I'll fix myself a sandwich. Do you want one?"

"You know what I want," he whispered as he carried her hand to his lips.

"No!" She pulled her fingers free as if his touch were red hot. She didn't know what he wanted. Didn't want to guess, because whatever it was, her heart was willing. "I'm going to the kitchen."

"Then I'm coming too."

Her heart seemed to plunge into her stomach. Was there no escape? "It's your house," she returned with remarkable calm.

His laugh was short and mirthless. "At least we can agree on something."

Joy sliced a banana into thin pieces and laid them across a thick layer of peanut butter on bread. "Want half?"

Sloan's look was skeptical. "Peanut butter and banana?"

"It's good. Honest." She handed him half and poured them each a glass of milk.

Sloan joined her at the table. "I've been thinking all night of ways to thank you. But I never did have a way with words."

"Thank me?" She regarded him quizzically.

"I know what it cost for you to tell me about your

accident. Even now, just talking about mine produces a cold sweat."

The bite of sandwich nearly stuck in her throat. She swallowed around it and reached for the milk. As she stood, the chair scraped against the floor. "I think I'll go see to L.J. before going back to my room."

"Running, Joy?" he taunted softly.

She was glad her back was to him so that he couldn't see the flame of color that heated her face. "You're being ridiculous."

"I'll see you in the morning."

"Good night, Sloan."

The pause was only momentary before he whispered his own farewell. "Night, Joy."

Clara was busy in the kitchen when Joy returned from her run early the next morning. "Yum, that smells good. What is it?" Joy peeked under the lid of something cooking on the stove.

"Food. Now scat."

With a laugh, Joy took an apple off the table centerpiece and took a bite out of it. After a long run, she felt exhilarated.

"Here." Clara stopped her. "Take Mr. Whittaker his tray, will you?"

"Already?" Sloan wasn't normally up at this time of day.

"He's up. He called me soon after you left."

Clenching the apple with her teeth, Joy carried the tray down the long hallway. Her knock went unanswered. Resting the breakfast on one knee, she turned the knob and walked unheralded into Sloan's quarters.

Two steps into the room she stopped cold. Sloan and his father were busy going over some papers. Both father and son were so intent, neither was aware she was there.

Six

The apple fell out of her mouth, bounced, and rolled across the floor.

Myron Whittaker glanced up from the paperwork spread on the top of the large oak desk. "Good morning, Miss Nielsen. Could you set that tray outside? I'm hoping Clara sent an extra cup. I could use coffee this morning."

Sloan's expression was brooding. "Joy's my physical therapist, not a servant."

"I… I don't mind," she stuttered. "Really." She placed the breakfast tray on the verandah and came back through Sloan's room.

"Joy." Sloan stopped her. "Good morning."

His smile was devastating, her answering one weak but happy. "Good morning." A flowing warmth seeped into her limbs as she exited from the room.

"Does she normally dress like that?" Sloan's father's words followed her into the hallway. With a half laugh, she bit into the corner of her bottom lip. She was wearing baggy gray sweatpants and an old T-shirt.

Mindful of her appearance, she returned with the extra coffee cup and picked up the apple that had rolled halfway under Sloan's bed. "I'll be out of your way in a minute."

"No problem," Sloan assured her. She left in a rush, but not before she caught the look of concern in Myron Whittaker's eye as he glanced from Joy to his son.

Joy didn't need to be told what he was thinking. Sloan's father was worried. He didn't want Sloan to fall in love with her—and with good reason. Joy wasn't stupid. Myron's picture of Sloan's future wife was someone like Chantelle—as well it should be. Joy would never fit into the Whittakers' world; Sloan's wealth and lifestyle were as foreign to her as propositional calculus had been in her college days.

Later, the spray from the shower relaxed her muscles and soothed her body, but the look in Myron Whittaker's eyes continued to disturb her. He was right—she couldn't argue with him. Now she had to do her part to protect her heart and Sloan's.

Father and son worked until almost noon. Joy was sitting on a stool chatting with Clara when Myron walked into the kitchen. He looked relaxed, pleased, his eyes smiling.

"I owe you more than words can express," he said sincerely to Joy. "You've given me back my son. I'm going to see that you receive a generous bonus."

"Please, Mr. Whittaker, that's not necessary." The

harsh lines of strain about his eyes and mouth had re-laxed. That was all the appreciation Joy wanted to see.

"Nonsense." He dismissed her plea with a wave of his hand.

It was easy to see that arguing would do her no good. Myron Whittaker could be as stubborn as his son.

As soon as he left, Joy returned to Sloan's quarters to take back the breakfast tray and see if he was ready for their session in the pool.

"This was your idea, wasn't it?" he stormed as she walked into the room.

The anger in his voice stopped her. "Yes." She wouldn't deny it.

"Well, all I can say is thank God. You wouldn't be-lieve some of the things that have been going on. How my father could make some of these decisions is be-yond me."

A tiny smile broke out across her mouth. Joy battled to suppress it.

"What's so funny?" He didn't sound pleased.

"Nothing. Do you think you're going to have time to squeeze in the therapy today?"

Sloan set the papers he was working on aside. "I'll make the time."

Joy's mouth fell open.

"Don't look so shocked. You want to see me out of this thing, don't you?" He patted the rubber on the wheel of his chair.

"I'll get Paul and meet you in the pool."

"See you." He paused and glanced at his wristwatch. "Fifteen minutes?" He made it a question.

"Fine."

Joy was doing laps when Paul delivered him to the pool. Sloan sat on the edge watching her.

"Don't you ever get tired?" he called after a while.

Joy stopped and treaded water. "You should have said something. I didn't know you were there."

"You look like a sea nymph. That turquoise suit in the blue water leaves little to the imagination." His look was absent, his words thoughtful. "The scars were the reason you were always in the water ahead of me. It's also why you choose to wear pants."

Joy ignored his observations. She didn't want to talk about herself. "Are you going to come in the water or not?"

Sloan's smile was filled with warm amusement. "What will you give me if I do?"

"I think it's more of a question of what I'll do to you if you don't." The sound of his laughter rang in her ears as she swam toward him. She stood in the shallow end. "You're in a good mood today."

"Yes, I am," he agreed. "I can't tell you how good it feels to be needed again. Just looking over some of the things my father brought showed me how much things had slacked off since I've been away." He lowered himself into the water. "You knew that, didn't you?"

"Everyone needs to know they're wanted."

"Even you?" The words were whispered on a husky breath.

"Even me," she returned crisply. "Now let's get to work."

"Always business. Don't you ever let loose and have some fun?"

"Of course I do. In fact, I'm going out tonight." The statement came off the top of her head. But the idea was a good one. She needed to check her apartment in Oxnard, a small town a few miles up the coast highway, and it wouldn't hurt to call a friend and make a night of it.

Sloan's mouth twisted, drawing in his facial features. The look in his eye chilled her. "Anyone I know?"

"I'm sure you don't. It isn't like we run in the same circle, is it?"

"No, I guess we don't," he admitted, and stared at her.

Sloan was strangely quiet, almost brooding, for the remainder of their session. Even when she took him in his lunch, he did little more than give her a polite nod of acknowledgment.

That evening Joy's own feelings were mixed. She was sorry she'd said anything to Sloan about going out, and forced herself to dress in her best suit: black pants and a soft cream blouse with matching jacket. A strand of pearls graced her neck. While freshening her makeup, Joy tried to convince herself she was doing the right thing. The physical attraction between her and Sloan was growing more powerful every day. Of the two, she was the one who had to keep a level head, because she was the one who stood to lose the most. On the way out of the house, Joy stopped in the kitchen and told Clara where she could be reached in an emergency.

"I think it's time you took a day off, if you don't

mind my saying so," Clara murmured as she dried the pots and pans from dinner.

"I don't mind," Joy agreed and impulsively hugged the older woman.

"Must say you look beautiful."

"Thanks, Clara."

"Don't suppose Mr. Whittaker's taken a look at you yet?"

"I haven't seen him since dinner." Quickly Joy changed the subject. "You know where you can reach me." Joy realized the housekeeper was much too observant not to have noticed what was happening between Joy and Sloan.

"Got it right here." She patted her apron pocket. "Let your hair down, girl."

"Honestly, it's only three inches as it is," Joy said with a small laugh as she opened the swinging door that led out of the kitchen.

She was in the marble-floored entryway when Sloan spoke.

"Don't you ever wear dresses?"

Joy stopped and turned. He was in the living room, almost as if he'd been sitting there waiting for her. His hard expression was a shock. Sloan hadn't looked like that since the first days after her arrival.

"Sometimes," she answered softly. "Usually full-length ones so I can be assured no one is going to be shocked if they happen to catch a glimpse of my scars."

"That's considerate of you," he muttered.

"It's not consideration. It's protection for my ego.

These days women wear pants most anywhere, so it isn't any faux pas if I do."

His eyes held hers. "You look nice."

"Thank you."

"Have you decided where you're going yet?"

"Dan and I are going to dinner."

"Dan?"

"An old friend."

"How old?"

Joy inhaled a deep breath. "You're being ridiculous, you know that, don't you?"

"I suppose I am. Go on, go. Have a good time." He jerked the wheelchair around so his back was to her.

"Oh, boy, here it comes." Joy flew into the room and stood in front of him.

"Here what comes?" he barked.

"That 'poor little boy' act. You want me to feel guilty. You've even gone to great lengths so I'll experience this terrible guilt."

"Now you're the one being ridiculous," he declared, but his eyes refused to meet hers.

"Poor injured Sloan has to sit home while his physical therapist Joy paints the town." She raised her eyes heavenward in a mocking gesture. "I suppose you're planning to wait up for me, too?"

Sloan's nostrils flared as his eyes narrowed. "Get out of here."

"That's what I'm trying to do," she returned flippantly, and swung the strap of her purse over her shoulder in a defiant action.

She was halfway out the door when she heard him

draw in a quick breath and utter something violent. Joy decided she would prefer not to know what he'd said.

The small apartment in the heart of town looked exactly as she'd left it. Joy walked around, inspecting each room. She'd only been back once since moving into Sloan's. The rooms were compact and unappealing after the luxury she was accustomed to living in these past weeks. In some ways Joy doubted that her simple life would ever be the same again. Certainly her heart wouldn't. If she had a whit of common sense she'd pack her things and leave him now before their feelings for one another developed further.

A quick knock on the door was followed by a blond head. "I thought I'd find you here."

"Hi, Danielle." The one thing about tonight that Joy regretted was letting Sloan assume she was seeing a man. It seemed childish now, but vital at the moment.

They ate at a Chinese restaurant and drank several cups of tea while chatting over old times. When Danielle suggested a movie, Joy readily agreed. After a quick phone call to Clara, she sat through a nondescript movie. No matter how hard she forced herself to watch the screen, her thoughts continually drifted back to Sloan.

Danielle and Joy parted after the show, and Joy drove back to her apartment. Her watch said it was only ten. Much too early for her to head back to the beach house. If she was going to feel like a criminal because she took a night off, then he could sit and wait.

The television on, Joy slouched across a lumpy couch

and laid her head against the back cushion and closed her eyes. When she opened them again it was well past two o'clock. Oh, heavens, she hadn't meant to stay away this long. If Sloan had waited for her he'd be in a fine mood by now.

When she pulled into her parking spot in front of the house, she took in several calming breaths. Mentally, she prepared herself—for what she wasn't sure.

The porch light was on, and another in the long hallway that led to her room. She turned off the outside light and tiptoed into the entryway. "You look like a thief in the night." A deep voice flew out from the living room.

Startled, she let out a gasp. Her hand flew to her breast. "What are you doing there?" she demanded defensively.

"In case you've forgotten, I live here."

"I didn't mean that to sound the way it did," she apologized. "You frightened me."

He moved closer to her. "Did you have a good time?"

"Wonderful," she lied.

"How was Dan?"

"Good." She took in a deep breath. "Is this an interrogation?"

"No, just curiosity."

"I didn't mean to stay out so late." She could have kicked herself the minute the words slipped past her mouth.

"Time flies when you're having fun, or so they say."

"Yes, well, I think I'll get to bed."

"Did Dan kiss you good night?" The question came abruptly, issued with impatience.

"I don't think that's any of your business." Her hand tightened around the strap of her purse.

"You don't look like you've been kissed."

"Sloan, please." She released the words on a sigh.

"At least when I kiss you, there's no doubt. Your eyes grow warm and gentle, your face is flushed, and you have a look about you that begs for more."

Joy looked away, but not before she saw the way Sloan's fingers bit into the arm of his chair.

"Does Dan make you feel the way I do?" he continued, his voice raspy and deep. "Does your heart beat faster when he holds you? Or is it just the thrill of having a man, a real man, one you don't have to look down to?"

"Stop it," she cried, her voice strained and weak. "You don't know what you're saying." The temptation was to cry out that he was more man than she'd ever known, all the man she'd ever need. Were he never to take another step, she couldn't love him any more than she already did.

Joy inhaled a sharp breath, her eyes rounded at the startling realization. For days she'd been struggling with herself, refusing to accept the truth. Now, in her anger, she acknowledged her true feelings. It was too late; she was already in love with him.

"Joy?" Sloan paused and took her hand. "Are you all right? You look like you're sick."

"I'm fine," she mumbled, and pulled her hand free from his. "I just need to lie down." She felt like she was staggering as she rushed down the hall to her room. Of course, she wasn't, but it seemed her whole world had crumpled in on top of her and the weight was more than she could possibly manage.

"Joy, wait," Sloan called out after her, but she ignored him and firmly shut the bedroom door.

Even after she'd changed clothes and crawled between the fresh sheets, Joy couldn't sleep. Unreasonably, she was angry with Sloan. Irritated, because he knew as well as she did what was happening between them and had done nothing to stop it. Her feelings, emotions, and heart were only playthings to him, a small diversion until he was walking again. She could almost hate him. Almost.

She lay there for what seemed like hours, unable to sleep because every time she closed her eyes pictures of Sloan would flash into her mind. Not content with dominating every waking minute, he was determined to haunt her sleep as well. The room felt hot and stuffy. Throwing back the covers, Joy opened the sliding-glass door just a crack. A faint moaning sound stopped her. She had to strain to hear. Sloan.

Was he in pain? Thoughtless of her bare feet, she slipped outside. Sloan's glass door was also cracked. The sound of his moans was more distinguishable now, in addition to a faint thrashing noise. Joy peeked inside his room.

Sloan was asleep and in the throes of some horrible dream. His head tossed from side to side, his blankets a twisted mess around his legs.

"Sloan." She hurried to his bedside and placed a restraining hand on both shoulders. "Wake up. You're having a dream." Lightly she shook him. "Sloan, it's a dream."

He jerked himself upright, leaning the brunt of his weight on one elbow. For a second he looked at her blankly, then released a small cry of relief. "Joy, good heavens." His eyes were filled with some unspeakable torment. Forcefully he pulled her into his arms, his breathing hoarse and uneven. "Oh, Joy." His open hands caressed her back, shooting a tingling fire down her spine. "I thought I'd lost you," he continued. "You were in the school bus screaming for me to help you, and I couldn't get out of the chair."

"I'm fine, I'm right here," she assured him, her hands brushing the hair from his face. Her heart cried out to him.

"I couldn't bear to lose you now." He twisted his upper body, bring her onto the bed beside him. Positioned so that he was above her now, his anguished eyes stared into hers. "Don't stop me. I need you so much," he murmured before his mouth rocked over hers.

She gave in to him unselfishly, parting her lips with all the eagerness of her newly discovered love. Her hands roved his back, reveling in the muscular feel of skin under her fingers. He was warm, vital, and for this moment, this night, hers.

His mouth left hers and pressed against the gentle slope of her bare shoulder.

"You've been drinking," she whispered.

"Yes." He continued to kiss her neck, his tongue making moist forays against the sensitive skin. "It was the only thing that kept me sane tonight while wait-ing for you."

"Oh, Sloan. You didn't drink after taking any medi-cation, did you?"

"Don't 'Oh, Sloan' me. I know what I'm doing. For once stop being my therapist and be my lover?" His mouth blotted any objection she might have voiced.

Joy was reeling with the potency of his kisses. When his exploring hands cupped the soft undersides of her breasts.

"You shouldn't," she protested weakly.

"Do you want me to stop?" he whispered against her ear, his warm breath caressing her lobe.

"No," she admitted, her arms entwined around his neck, "don't stop."

Desire, raw and fierce, ran through her blood, spreading a path of fiery awareness that left no part of her untouched. Her senses were in turmoil. No lon-ger did she question right from wrong. No longer did it matter.

Sloan's kisses grew more deep, more passionate; their effect drugged her into submission and demanded a response. Trapped in the warm, rushing tide of her love, Joy responded freely, wholly. His lips began a downward path from the sensitive cord of her neck. Her long fingernails dug into the rippling muscles of his back as she arched, wanting to give more, needing to receive more.

"Joy," he moaned, and bruised her mouth with a scorching possession. "Do you realize how long it's been since I touched a woman like this?"

The whole world came to a sudden, abrupt halt. A woman. Any woman would have done. She was convenient, here, now. A passing fancy until he was ready for the Chantelles of this world.

Dragging her mouth from his, she pushed him away. "No more," she whispered, and struggled to sit upright.

Sloan went still. "Are you hurt? What is it? What did I say?"

The question was almost ludicrous. She was dying, and he wanted to know if he had caused her pain.

"Joy?" He raised himself up and brushed the hair from the side of her face. "What's wrong?" His tender concern was nearly her undoing.

"Let me go," she cried, her voice pitifully weak. She shut her eyes, and waited for him to let her go.

"Not until you tell me what's wrong." His voice was thick with frustration. "Are you crying?" A finger brushed the wetness across her cheek. "Joy, please. Tell me what I did."

"It has been a long time since you've touched a woman," she whispered achingly at last. "So long that you'd hold any willing woman."

"That's not true. I can't think of anyone else when you're in my arms. It's you I want," he muttered thickly. "Only you."

"That will change," she said confidently, "and soon."

He groaned her name.

"Please let me go," she pleaded, her voice quivering uncontrollably.

With a frustrated exclamation, Sloan rolled off her

and stared at the ceiling as she raced out of his room as if the devil himself were in pursuit.

For two weeks they treated one another like polite strangers. To avoid the curious stares of Clara and Paul, Joy took long daily walks along the beach. No longer did she play her flute on the verandah at night. L.J. was her companion and friend, often hopping along behind her on a walk.

On the first night of the third week, Joy delivered Sloan's dinner tray. He sat, his gaze centered on the ocean. Joy left it on the table outside.

"Can we talk?" he asked without looking at her.

Joy bit into the soft fleshy part of her inner cheek. "What do you want to talk about?"

"Us."

"No," she answered emphatically.

"All right, we won't talk about us. We'll simply talk."

Joy moved to the railing, watching the rumbling sea. The scent of the ocean filled the early evening. A gentle breeze brought in a salty spray. She turned and propped her elbow against the railing. "I don't know if we have anything to say to one another."

"That's a negative thought. I've never known you to be pessimistic."

"Oh, I can be," she admitted with a sad smile.

"Yes, I noticed."

"If you don't eat, your dinner will get cold." Her mouth felt suddenly dry, yet her hands were moist to the point of being clammy. She should have packed her bags and walked out the morning after she'd given in to his kisses. But she couldn't, not before it was time. When he was walking, at least on crutches, then she'd go.

His gaze fell on the tray she'd brought with her. "Leave it. I'm not hungry."

"Have you been busy?" she knew he met daily with his father now, and she had seen his light long into the night.

"Very."

"That's good."

He came closer to her side. "In some ways it's helped me…" He let the rest trail away.

"Helped you how?"

His smile was wry. "You said the subject was taboo."

"Oh," she said, and swallowed tightly.

Paul shouted from the far side of the yard and waved. Joy gave a guilty start. She'd told him she would join him for dinner at Mobey Jake's. They went there often now.

"I've got to go."

Sloan's mouth thinned with impatience. "I understand."

Quickly she moved into her own quarters and grabbed a light sweater.

"Joy." Sloan had followed her and slid open her glass door. "Will you play tonight? I've missed that." His smile was slightly off center, and her bones felt like liquid. "Almost as much as I've missed having you as my friend."

"I've missed it too," she murmured, refusing to look into his eyes.

"Hurry back, my Joy."

The words were issued so softly Joy was sure she'd misunderstood him.

Paul brought her a double order of fish-and-chips and joined her at the umbrella-covered table in the sun. The large order was far bigger than Joy could manage, but she automatically bought the double fish so there would be enough for L.J.

"You and the boss getting on better?" Paul questioned. Their camaraderie and mutual respect had grown over the weeks. They were a team, pressing toward one goal—Sloan. He would walk one day, and the credit would be due them all.

"I guess so." She wiped the corner of her mouth with the napkin and lifted one shoulder in a lopsided shrug.

"Sometimes I wonder how you two can work with one another, the ice is so thick."

"You have a good imagination," Joy denied uneasily.

Paul lifted one thick brow expressively. "If you say so."

Joy dunked a French fry in a small container of ketchup. "I do."

Later, she brought her flute onto the verandah. She hadn't played three notes when Sloan joined her. She lowered her instrument and offered him a smile.

"Are you taking requests?"

"Sure, what would you like to hear?"

"'Yesterday,'" he replied without hesitation.

Joy remembered the first time she'd played the song. Sloan had angrily proclaimed that yesterdays were gone forever, that they couldn't be brought back. Bitterness had coated his words. Now his voice was filled with hope.

The sweet melodic sounds of the Beatles' classic filled the night. When she was finished, there was a poignant pause.

"Why did you request that song?" she asked in a whisper, not wanting conversation to ruin the mood.

"Because I wanted to share with you some of my yesterdays."

"How do you mean?"

"Follow me," he answered cryptically, and turned sharply, leading the way through his quarters. Once he was in the hallway he paused in front of the door that was opposite her room. "Haven't you ever wondered what was in here?"

"No," she answered honestly. "I assumed it was probably your parents' room."

"Go on, open it."

Joy turned the knob and stepped inside. Because his chair wouldn't fit through the narrow doorway, Sloan remained in the hall.

The interior was dark, and she felt against the side of the wall for the light switch. Once she located it, she flipped it on. Immediately light sprayed across a room filled with awards, trophies, and sports equipment. Plaques lined one entire wall. On closer inspection, Joy saw that each one had been received by Sloan. There didn't seem to be anything he hadn't tried and mastered. Baseball, volleyball, skiing, bowling, and hockey.

Confused, she turned around, her smooth brow marred in thick creases. "All these are yours?" she asked incredibly. "It's unbelievable."

"I was quite the jock."

She picked up and inspected one of the smaller baseball trophies. "You were just a boy." She lifted her gaze to his.

"My father is credited with mounting most of these things. The albums on the desk—" he pointed to a large flat-topped desk on the far side of the room "—are filled with newspaper clippings from the time I could hold a tennis racket."

"My goodness, it's enough to take my breath away."

"I was good."

"I don't doubt it,"

"I'll never be as good again."

Joy didn't mince words. "No, you won't. Does that bother you terribly?"

The look in his eyes seemed to peel away every defense barrier she'd carefully constructed these past two weeks.

"It did, but you changed that."

"Me?" The one word echoed across the room.

"I accepted the wheelchair as my fate—until you came. It wasn't a conscious decision, but one I can see as clearly now as if I'd signed the contract in blood. I was a winner with remarkable talent and skill, if I was to believe everything that had been written about me. I had the world by the tail; I lived the good life. And then it all came tumbling down on top of me. After the accident I decided that if I had to be half a man the rest of my life, then I'd be no man at all."

Joy understood what he was saying. She came and knelt by his side.

"It wasn't the pain that bound me to the chair, but the fear." He took her hand and squeezed it tight. "I'm going to walk again, Joy Nielsen, because you had the foresight to understand what was happening to me on the inside. And just as you had your father, I have you." Very gently he lifted her hand to his mouth and kissed it.

Her heart plummeted to her stomach. Gratitude was what Sloan felt. Overwhelming gratitude, nothing more.

Seven

"You're sure about this?" Sloan regarded her skeptically.

Joy sat on the thick blue mat on the weight-room floor, her legs crossed Indian fashion. "Trust me."

"You said that when you asked me to roll around like a man whose clothes had caught on fire."

"Now I want you to crawl just like a baby."

"How much longer before I can work on the parallel bars?" He eyed the set she'd brought in.

"Not long, I promise. If you want, I'll test you for strength again today."

"No." He shook his head, and Joy could all but taste his disappointment.

"Don't push yourself so hard. You're doing remarkably well."

"But the progress is so slow."

"It isn't," she replied emphatically. "Look how long you sat in that chair—months. You can't expect to be out running again in a matter of a few weeks."

"Tell me what's next."

Joy must have repeated the procedure to him fifteen times, but she didn't hesitate when he asked again.

"Lying to crawling, crawling to kneeling, kneeling to standing."

"From there to the parallel bars, the walker, and lastly the cane," he finished for her.

"There's a light at the end of the tunnel."

"I'm just beginning to see it."

"Good." She smiled brightly. "I knew you would."

"Should I pretend I'm a dog and bark?" he asked as he moved into the crawling position.

"Go ahead." Joy laughed. "It'll give Clara a good laugh."

Sloan gave an Academy Award performance that left both Joy and Paul laughing.

"Mr. Jewett's here. I haven't seen Dale in nearly nine months."

The laughter drained out of Sloan's face and his eyes turned icy cold. "Send him away. I don't want to see him. Is that understood, Clara?"

"But Mr. Jewett's been your friend since you were a boy."

"It doesn't matter. I don't want to see anyone."

Joy tossed a glance to the obviously flustered Clara, then back to Sloan. Angrily Sloan reached out from the mat and grabbed the side of his wheelchair. With a violent shove he sent it crashing against the wall. The chair tilted onto its side and fell over.

"What's wrong?" she asked quietly, and knelt at his side. "Who is the guy?"

"A friend."

"You have a funny way of showing it."

"When I want your advice, I'll ask for it," he growled.

"That wasn't advice," Joy returned. "I was simply stating an opinion."

"Then keep those to yourself."

"Fine." She stood and wiped the grit from her hands. Walking across the room, she up-righted the wheelchair and brought it to his side. "I want you to make the transfer yourself today."

"I can't."

"Don't give me that, Whittaker."

"What is this? Put the person with disabilities in his place time?"

"Figuratively speaking, I think that's it."

"Kindly leave before I say something I'll regret later."

Joy's mouth formed into a humorless smile. "Gladly." Arms flying at her side, she stormed into the kitchen, plopped down on a chair, crossed her legs, and took three deep breaths.

"What's with that man lately? Mr. Jewett and Mr. Whittaker have been friends for a whole lot of years. Friends shouldn't treat one another like that. It's not right, it's just not right. But no one pays a mind to ol' Clara. No one," she emphasized.

"What's the matter with me lately?" Joy answered Clara with a question of her own. "I used to give as good as I took."

Clara apparently chose to ignore Joy. "I said to Mr. Jewett that Mr. Whittaker wasn't feeling like himself today. That's what I said because I know later Mr. Whittaker is going to want to see his friends again. No need to offend him. I did the right thing, didn't I?" Clara's look was eager.

"You did fine."

Clara clucked, and a look of relief relaxed the wrinkled face.

"Are you sure there isn't any reason Sloan wouldn't want to see his friend?"

"Mr. Whittaker sent all his friends away after the accident. He didn't want to see anyone. Mr. Jewett came around for a long time, but Mr. Whittaker wouldn't see him. Same as now. It's not right to treat friends like that."

"What's not right?" Sloan entered the kitchen and boldly glared at the cook.

"To send friends away," Joy answered for Clara.

Briefly renewed anger flashed from his eyes. "You two are beginning to sound like henpecking wives."

"Mr. Jewett's been your friend for as long as I can remember..."

With a burst of energy, Sloan wheeled himself out of the room, apparently not wishing to become involved in an argument.

Joy didn't see him again that afternoon. After his time with Paul, he met with his father and spent the remainder of the day in his room on his computer.

Joy sat on the beach with L.J. until dinner, wondering if she should press this thing with Sloan. She understood what he was doing all too well. She'd done it herself. Friends, especially ones who were whole and well, were a reminder of things that would never be again. Even Danielle, her best friend since high school, the one person who knew her so well, couldn't help or understand the adjustment Joy was making.

In some ways Danielle had hurt more than she helped. She came to visit, eager to share tidbits of news and gossip from school. Joy hadn't wanted to know or hear any of it. School, boys, teachers were so far removed from her life then that it only served to widen the gap between them.

Sloan met Joy that night on the verandah. She was sitting watching the sunset, a fiery ball of orange lowering into the ocean.

Sloan pulled up beside her. "Beautiful, isn't it?"

Smiling, Joy nodded. "I don't think I'll ever get tired of looking at it. The whole world seems so peaceful and serene. It's hard to remember the tragedies reported on the evening news when everything's so calm here."

"I often feel that way too."

She felt at ease with Sloan, relaxed, so unlike their first days of constant confrontation. Those times seemed in the distant past now. She turned to smile at him and noted the signs of stress about his mouth. His dark eyes looked tired.

"You're strung out from working all day," she whispered. "You should go to bed."

Teasing warmth kindled in his gaze as he smiled slightly. "Now that, my dear Joy, sounded suspiciously like an invitation."

The gibe was a gentle one, and Joy couldn't take offense. "No. When I issue an invite to my bed there won't be need for any speculation." Joy had hoped to sound breezy and sophisticated, but it came out all wrong. She could feel Sloan's puzzled gaze run over her.

"You're blushing, which leads me to believe you haven't had a lot of experience with men." His short laugh was soft, almost caressing.

Joy straightened. "I don't like the sudden turn of this conversation," she said stiffly. "Let's go back to what a beautiful sunset it is."

"Your cheeks are nearly as bright as the sky."

"Would you stop?" she demanded.

"No," he chided, and linked his hands behind his head, obviously enjoying himself. "Why?"

"Why what?"

"You're innocent…clearly you…"

"Honestly, Sloan, you're embarrassing me," she said, cutting him off. "Don't, please." She hung her head and pretended to be studying her fingernails. The sound of his moving drew her gaze. Sloan had turned his chair around and parked himself beside her so that only a few inches separated them. A finger under her chin turned her face to him.

"For most of my life I've stayed away from women like you." Joy swallowed uncomfortably. His eyes were tender, infinitely gentle.

"That was until I met you," he went on. "I'm pleased you are who and what you are. I wouldn't change a single thing about you." His hand slid behind her neck, urging her mouth to his.

Confused and unsure, Joy stiffened; she knew what

would happen if she let him kiss her. It would be lighting a match to gasoline. The feelings Sloan produced in her weren't a small spark, but a raging forest fire. She wanted him so much, but at the same time was all too aware of where it would lead.

He dropped his hand at her resistance. The puzzled look in his eyes deepened into pain. "Is it always no to every man?"

She looked away and nodded, because speaking was almost impossible.

"Is it the scars?"

"No."

"Then why?"

One shoulder was lifted in a halfhearted shrug, urgently hoping he'd change the conversation. "I'm not exactly a sex goddess."

"There's never been anyone I've wanted more."

Bounding to her feet, Joy stalked to the far side of the deck. "Stop. Please. I find this whole conversation inappropriate."

"If I promise not to mention it again, will you come back and sit with me?"

Joy didn't find the teasing light in his eyes encouraging. "Promise?"

"Scout's honor." Solemnly he raised his index and middle fingers.

Joy returned to the cushioned wrought-iron chair and relaxed.

"But then, I was never a Boy Scout," he inserted.

"Sloan!"

"I promise, I promise."

Joy sat and brought up her knees, resting her chin on top of one. "Tell me about Jewett." Joy could sense him drawing away from her. Not physically, but mentally.

"He's a buddy," Sloan returned in a tone that discouraged further discussion.

"A good friend?"

Irritably, he expelled his breath before answering. "At one time."

"Not now?"

"I know what you're doing, Joy," he breathed impatiently. "And I don't like it."

A gentle breeze ruffled the soft curls about her face, and Joy laughed lightly. "I love turning the tables on you."

"I don't want to talk about Dale or any of the others."

"Why not?"

"Because—" he hesitated "—because I'm not the same person I was before the accident."

"Dale knows that. He doesn't need a psychology degree to realize you've changed," she explained in a patient voice. "You couldn't help but change."

"The only friend I need is you."

"But I couldn't possibly hope to meet all your needs."

He cocked his head, and a teasing smile flirted at the side of his mouth. "You could try."

Joy ignored the glint in his eyes. "I did the same thing to my friends. Looking back, it's easy to see that my ego was involved, because I didn't want anyone to see me like that. Nor did I want to hear who was going with whom and what couple had broken up. My life had gone beyond all that, and it seemed trivial and petty.

They'd come with pitiful looks and talk as if I'd had brain damage."

"Exactly," Sloan agreed.

"But I didn't consider the fact that they needed me. I was their friend, and they loved me. It hurt them to see me the way I was, and desperately my friends wanted to do something, anything to help. For a long time I wouldn't let anyone near me. Then one day Dani—"

"Dani?" Sloan questioned.

"Danielle, for real," Joy supplied.

"Not the old friend Dan you had dinner with not so long ago?"

"One and the same," she supplied with a puzzled look.

Sloan went completely still, and she watched as the muscles worked along the side of his jaw. "You little devil. You did that on purpose."

Too late, Joy realized exactly what she had revealed.

"You purposely let me assume that you were going out with a man."

"Yes…well," Joy floundered.

"I sat here half the night going crazy thinking about you in the arms of this Dan. You should suffer for what you put me through." He wheeled around so suddenly, Joy was caught completely off guard.

Somehow she managed to escape his grip as she scurried out of the chair. Laughing, she ran down the deck, Sloan in hot pursuit. When she'd gone as far as possible, she turned, the wood railing pressing against her back. Joy stretched out a pleading hand. "Sloan." She couldn't keep the laughter out of her voice.

"Yes, my trapped little rat?"

"Would it do any good to apologize?"

"Not when I've got you where I want you." Slowly he advanced toward her, one inch at a time.

"Sloan," she pleaded a second time. Frantically she looked around for an escape.

"Mr. Whittaker, where are you?" Clara's high-pitched voice could be heard coming down the hall. There was a slight hesitation as the older woman stepped onto the verandah. "Oh, Mr. Whittaker, I was hoping I'd find you here."

"Yes, Clara, what is it?" Sloan's voice was thick with impatience.

"If you'll excuse me." Joy sauntered out of her corner and wickedly fluttered her long lashes. "It seems to have gotten a bit chilly out here all of a sudden. I think I'll take a drive into town."

"Are you going to meet Dan again?" Sloan taunted.

"Not tonight," she said with an exaggerated sigh. "But I think I'll give Mark a call."

His eyes narrowed for an instant before a smile broke out across his powerful face. For now she would escape, his eyes were telling her, but the time was fast approaching when he would extract his due.

"Are you ready?" Joy's voice was soft with encouragement.

Sloan nodded. Joy didn't know how he could be so calm. Her stomach felt like it had twisted to double knots. Even her mouth felt dry, her throat scratchy.

The parallel bars loomed before him. Sloan positioned the wheelchair so that he could reach up and pull himself upright.

Joy watched him with a ballooning sense of pride. Once he was upright, he beamed her an off-center smile.

"Well?" he probed. "How am I doing?"

Joy shook her head, because she was afraid the lump that filled her throat would make her words sound irregular and he would know how happy this new triumph made her. This was only the beginning.

"I don't think I realized how tall you are," she said at last.

Sloan continued to work his way across the bar, each movement cautious and measured. His face was furrowed with concentration.

"And I don't think I've ever realized what an elf you are."

"I am not," she denied.

His laugh was rich and deep. He stopped when he came to the end of the long bars and awkwardly turned around.

Joy watched him with her heart in her throat. She need not have worried; he was doing wonderfully well.

"Joy," he called to her, and she was immediately at his side.

"Yes?"

"Stand here." He indicated a place beside the bars. When she did as he asked, he manipulated himself around so that they stood facing one another. She came to just an inch or two under his chin. "An elf," he affirmed, "but a perfect one. Look how well we fit together." A hand grazed her cheek and cupped her neck.

"I've been waiting weeks to kiss you like this. Don't deny me now."

Joy could refuse him nothing. Had he asked for any part of her she would have given it to him gladly with all the love pent up inside.

When his lips touched hers, she released a small, weak cry of happiness. The kiss was sweet and gentle and left her craving for more. Somehow Sloan managed to keep his balance as he cradled her head against his chest and pressed his face into her hair.

"Thank you, Joy," he murmured, and again she was reminded that his emotions were confused, interwoven with a deep sense of gratitude.

"Has something happened to Sloan?" Margaret Whittaker rushed into the living room. Her face was pale and tight. Myron Whittaker followed close on his wife's heels.

"Not at all," Joy hurried to assure them. This whole production was Sloan's idea, and she was reluctantly playing her role. "Please sit down."

Myron eyed his wife and shrugged his shoulders. "You say Sloan's fine?"

"Yes." For a moment she was sure her smile gave her away. "Perhaps you'd like some coffee while you're waiting?"

"Please," Myron answered for them both, and stopped to run a hand across his forehead.

Joy excused herself and rounded the corner, pretending she was going into the kitchen.

"You should be shot for this," she told Sloan in a heated whisper. "They're both worried sick."

He was standing. The U-shaped walker accepted his weight as his hands gripped the metal bar. Joy continued to marvel at how tall he was. Tall and vital. But even the wheelchair had been unable to diminish the aura of powerful virility that was so much a part of him.

A happy smile skittered across his face.

"What's so funny?" she demanded.

"You. I still can't believe I let such a pip-squeak boss me around. I must have been weak in the head."

"Not weak," she countered brightly, "but exceptionally smart."

He bent his head and kissed her lightly on the cheek. "Don't tell me to break a leg."

She smiled, one that came deep from within her heart. "All right, I won't."

With a slow gait, every step deliberate and practiced, Sloan moved out of his hiding position in the hall. Joy stayed where she was, the sound of his steps, the drag of the walker against the floor, magnified in the enclosed area. She didn't need to be told the cries from Sloan's parents were ones of surprise and happiness. In her own way she was inexorably happy. The time was fast approaching when she must leave. Sloan wouldn't need her anymore.

"Clara, Clara." Myron Whittaker's voice boomed through the house.

Joy stepped aside as Clara bustled out of the kitchen.

"Bring out a bottle of my best champagne. There's cause to celebrate again."

"Joy," Sloan called to her.

Purposely she had stayed out of view. This was a time for family; she didn't want to intrude.

"Joy," he repeated, and she stepped around the entrance to the hallway and into the living room.

"Where did you go?" he questioned, his eyes watching her, his look vaguely troubled. "I thought you were right behind me."

Margaret was dabbing the corner of her eye with a scented handkerchief, and when she saw Joy she hurried across the room and hugged her tightly. "My dear Miss Nielsen, Myron and I owe you so much."

"Dad's bringing out the family's best." Sloan's eyes were bright with excitement.

"Do stay, dear," Margaret insisted. "After all, it's you we all must thank."

"Nonsense." Embarrassment heightened the natural color in her cheeks.

Sloan wrapped an arm around Joy's shoulders. "Mother, we owe this little pint-sized woman more than words can express."

A look of undisguised concern flickered briefly over Margaret Whittaker's eyes. Joy saw it but was certain Sloan was unaware of his mother's look.

Myron Whittaker returned with champagne and several glasses. A great production was made out of opening the bottle. Laughter filled the room as the bubbling brew foamed onto the marble floor.

Joy accepted the glass and stood stiffly apart from the cozy family scene by the fireplace hearth. Her smile was strained, but when Sloan's father offered a toast her response was genuine. She smiled warmly at Sloan, afraid her heart was in her eyes. Then purposefully she looked down into the sparkling liquid before taking a sip.

"This is fantastic," Sloan said, and reached for the half-empty bottle.

"French, of course," Myron Whittaker bragged. "Some of the world's finest."

"Honestly, dear, you sound like an advertisement."

Watching the small family interact naturally with one another produced an ache Joy knew she would endure for years hereafter. She would never fit into the Whittakers' social circle, with their wealth and position. It wasn't difficult to tell that Sloan's parents were concerned with their son's obvious attraction to her. And with good cause, Joy acknowledged.

"We must have a party." Margaret Whittaker's words broke into Joy's troubled musings. "Invite all your old friends."

Joy could almost visualize all the wheels turning in his mother's head.

"Here, of course," she continued. "It'll be easier for you that way. We'll invite the Jordans and the Baxters and the Reagans and the Considines."

"Mother." Sloan's sharp tone caused Margaret Whittaker to pause.

"Yes, dear?"

"There will be no party."

"Of course there will. You've been out of circulation for months. People are beginning to ask questions."

"Let them. There will be no party," he repeated forcefully.

"But, Sloan." His mother's eyes were soft and pleading. Joy didn't know how anyone could refuse the woman, and sincerely doubted that it happened often.

"I'm tired. Joy," Sloan called for her, and held out his arm. "Help me back to my room."

Joy set her nearly full champagne glass down on an end table and strode across the suddenly silent area.

"Don't say it," Sloan murmured as they reached his room and he lowered his weight in the wheelchair.

"Say what?" Joy asked, pretending not to know.

"For most of my life I've fallen into Mother's schemes, but not anymore. I have nothing in common with the Baxters, or any of those people."

Joy straightened, standing in the doorway, one hand braced against the wooden frame. "Don't look at me. That's your decision."

"Then why do I feel guilty?" He slammed his fist against the rubber wheel.

"Parents have the knack of doing that to us sometimes."

Sloan whipped a hand across his face. "I mean what I say, and Mother knows that. It'll be interesting to see what lengths she'll be willing to go to get her own way. I love my mother, but I'm not a fool."

It didn't take even twenty-four hours for Joy to learn exactly what Margaret Whittaker had in mind. Mid-morning, Clara handed Joy a phone message that asked Joy to meet Margaret Whittaker in the best restaurant in Oxnard for lunch. Joy dreaded the confrontation.

"You look nice," Sloan commented as she brought in his lunch tray. "Where are you headed?"

"I have an appointment in town."

"Oh?" He arched one thick brow curiously. When Joy didn't elaborate, he continued. "Anyone I know?"

"Honestly, who said I was meeting anyone? It could be with the dentist." Over the years Joy had gained a certain amount of poise. She didn't want to mislead Sloan; nor did she wish to cause ill will between mother and son.

"What time will you be back?" he questioned.

"You're beginning to sound like my guardian," she accused teasingly with an underlying tone of seriousness.

Sloan reached out and took her hand, squeezing it lovingly. Even his lightest touch was enough to cause chaos with her emotions. A tingling awareness spread up her arm. "That's the last way I want you to think of me." He smiled at her, his voice deep and calm while his eyes shone into hers.

Joy nodded and backed away. The need to escape was growing to the point of desperation. If she couldn't disguise her feelings for him, then everything would be lost and she would have to leave.

Margaret Whittaker was already seated when Joy arrived.

"My dear, how nice of you to come."

"How thoughtful of you to invite me," Joy murmured, hating small talk and knowing she would be forced to endure at least an hour of it until Sloan's mother came to the point of the meeting.

The waitress arrived, filled Joy's water glass, and handed her a menu. Joy ordered almost without looking. She doubted that she'd be able to choke down anything more than a salad. Already she could feel the sensitive muscles of her stomach tighten.

"Such lovely weather this time of year, don't you agree?" Sloan's mother murmured the question.

"Yes." Joy nodded. Her right hand surrounded the water glass, collecting the condensation. "May is my favorite month."

"You've done remarkably well with Sloan."

"Thank you."

"Believe me when I say I know how difficult he can be."

"He was in the beginning, but gradually he came to accept me as his physical therapist."

"How much longer will it be before Sloan's completely independent?"

"A few weeks, not much more than that." She swallowed a sip of ice water. It slid down her throat, easing the building tightness.

"One of the reasons I invited you here today is to ask about Sloan's social readjustment. I'm sure you've dealt with situations like this before."

Joy hadn't, but didn't say so. "I believe that, given time, Sloan will readjust automatically."

"I had hoped he would agree to letting me throw a party in his honor. He knows how much I love parties, and everyone has been so concerned. It seems like such a good way to help my son. Don't you agree?"

"I really couldn't say, Mrs. Whittaker." Uncomfortable, Joy lowered her gaze. So this was the reason Margaret Whittaker had invited her to lunch.

"Has he mentioned the party to you?"

"Not since yesterday."

"What did he say then?" the older woman probed.

"Mrs. Whittaker, please," Joy said, and breathed in softly. "I don't think it's my place to relay your son's feelings."

"But I had so hoped." She gave Joy a softly pleading glance, not unlike the one Joy had witnessed so recently.

The waitress arrived with their salads. Joy smiled her appreciation and reached for her fork. She didn't need to take a bite to know the meal would taste like overcooked mush.

"I think that if you talked to Sloan…" Margaret Whittaker continued, her gaze centered on the meal. "What I mean to say is that I've noticed the way my son looks at you."

Joy's heart leaped into her throat. "What do you mean?"

"It's only natural that Sloan would feel a certain amount of gratitude toward you. He respects and likes you. If you were to ask him about the party, I'm sure he would agree. Won't you, dear?" she quizzed softly. "For Sloan's sake?"

Eight

Joy laid the fork beside her untouched salad. "I sincerely doubt that my asking will have any effect on Sloan's decision."

"But you will try?" Margaret Whittaker entreated.

"Yes," Joy agreed, nodding reluctantly, when what she wanted was to keep Sloan to herself for the rest of her life.

As Joy returned to the beach house, she knew what she had to do. Sloan's mother had made the position clear. Joy's responsibilities went far beyond the physical therapy Sloan required. He was almost to the point of walking on his own now. Her last duty would be to bring him back into the mainstream of life.

Hands clenching the steering wheel, Joy drove to the shoulder of the highway and stopped completely. The scenery was spectacular. Huge waves pounded the rocky shoreline. Large gulls swooped low in a sky that was cloudless. Heaving a sigh, Joy lowered her face until her brow pressed against her coiled hands. What

Margaret Whittaker was really asking was that Joy relinquish her love. Of course, she had been subtle, but genuinely concerned that Sloan fit back into the lifestyle he had known before the accident. One that excluded Joy.

Sloan was in the hallway when Joy rounded the corner, eager to escape to her room unseen. She stopped abruptly when she saw him.

Large-knuckled hands gripped the walker. Slowly Joy raised her eyes to meet his.

"How was your appointment?"

"Fine."

A smiling knowledge lurked behind his dark eyes. "You don't look pleased about it. What's the matter, did the dentist find a cavity?"

"I wasn't at the dentist."

His mouth curved in a smile, the look deliberately casual. "I suppose my mother's been at it again."

Joy attempted to disguise her surprise. "How'd you know where I was?"

"I didn't. But I happen to know my mother. I didn't think she'd let this party thing drop so easily." He shifted his weight, and Joy recognized that he was getting tired.

"Go back to your room and I'll bring us coffee."

Sloan agreed, and Joy returned a few minutes later with two cups of hot coffee and freshly baked cookies from Clara.

When Sloan saw the tray he lifted one dark brow.

"You expect this is going to take a while?" The look he gave her was both amused and curious.

"It could," Joy responded noncommittally.

Her hand shook a little as she handed a cup to Sloan.

"You are nervous." The sharp gaze followed her movements.

"Not really," she said, attempting to smooth over her telltale tremble. With her cup resting on her knee, Joy sat across from Sloan, who was at his desk.

"All right, let's have it. What's Mother said to you?"

"Nothing so terrible."

"I can imagine."

"Don't," Joy said quickly in defense of the older woman. "You've spent a hellish nine months; I don't think you realize how hard this has been on your parents."

His mouth narrowed slightly. "I admit things haven't been easy for any of us."

"Now that you're walking again, your mother needs the assurance that things are going to be the way they once were."

Sloan rubbed his hands together, the movement marked with frustration. "I'm not the man I was nine months ago."

"You are and you aren't," Joy murmured, staring into the steaming black liquid.

Sloan's frown was curious.

"In some ways you can't change," Joy continued. "Certainly not who or what you are. But you're bound to see things differently. Life is suddenly precious, and what was once important means little to nothing." She sat awkwardly on the edge of the straight-backed chair. "I don't know if any of this makes sense."

"It makes perfect sense. That's exactly how I feel."

"The struggles, the pain, have made you…"

"Us," he interrupted, immediately linking them together.

"Us," she altered, and swallowed. The tightness in her throat was mounting until it felt as if someone's hands were around her neck in a stranglehold. "I know how it was with me. My whole world revolved around my family. I felt secure with them. I didn't want to face the world. People can be cruel, and I wasn't sure I could handle it if someone saw my scars." Her voice contained the rawness of remembered pain, but she continued steady and even. "Now that time has come for you too."

"Or so my mother says," Sloan murmured dryly.

"And I agree."

"Has it come down to taking sides?"

"I hoped it wouldn't," Joy whispered.

"Apparently Mother's conned you into believing this party idea of hers will bring me back into the social circle?" His tone was cynical.

"Your mother hasn't conned me into anything. She's concerned and wants what's best for you."

"And has appointed herself as my guardian to issue me back into a life I want to leave dead and buried."

Joy's responding smile was crooked despite her best effort.

"You find this situation comical?"

"No." She shook her head while her finger absently made a circular motion around the top of the cup. "You remind me so much of myself. The thing is, Sloan, as much as you'd like to remain a hermit in this beautiful retreat, there's a whole world waiting for you."

He emitted a harsh, bitter sound that Joy chose to ignore.

"My point is that I believe your mother may not be so far off base with this party idea. For weeks now, I've battled again the fortress you built against the outside world. The time has come to face these doubts straight on."

He was silent, intense, and to all appearances hadn't heard a word she'd said. "You're asking me to let my mother go ahead with the plans for this party."

"Yes." Her voice was faintly husky.

Sloan closed his eyes and uttered a low, frustrated groan. "By heaven she's done it again." He slammed his hand against the top of the desk, shooting pens and papers in every which direction.

Joy gasped, and her hand flew to her breast.

His mouth pinched tight, Sloan's head bobbed in cynical acknowledgment. "She knew the only person in the world I'd do this for was you."

"It's got to be for you, Sloan." If they didn't end the conversation soon, Joy was convinced she'd break into tears.

Margaret Whittaker couldn't possibly understand what she had asked of Joy. Not only must she relinquish her love, but she must give Sloan back to a life he claimed he didn't want.

"All right." Sloan ran a hand along the side of his

head, smoothing the dark hair. "I'll call Mother and tell her I'll agree to this stupid party idea of hers."

"Thank you." Joy stood before a sob escaped and humiliated her. "I'm sure you won't regret it."

"I already do." Sloan's muttered words followed her out of the room.

The party plans were set for the following weekend. Clara couldn't hope to manage everything, and extra help was brought in. Margaret Whittaker became a permanent fixture, bustling in and out, a flurry of activity following her wherever she went. The house, staff, everyone was thrown into an unbelievable tizzy.

As much as possible, Joy stayed out of the way. Tuesday she phoned Danielle to see if there was a possibility of their getting together that Saturday night, but Danielle had already made plans. Not wishing to involve herself, Joy decided to spend the night at her apartment and return the following Sunday morning.

Sloan joined her on the verandah the night before the planned gala event. He stopped his walker beside her and waited until she'd finished playing the musical score on the flute.

"Do you see what you've done?" he teased, referring to the party.

"Does your mother do everything like this?"

"Everything," Sloan confirmed with a chuckle. "But I admit this one tops the cake. I think Dad nearly had a stroke when Mother handed over the caterer's bill."

"I hope you don't mind if I slip out early tomorrow afternoon—" She wasn't allowed to finish.

"Slip out!" he repeated angrily.

"Yes, I thought I'd spend the night at my apartment. You don't need—" Again she was interrupted.

"Don't need!" he shouted unreasonably. "Listen here. It's because of you that I agreed to this whole fiasco. I have no intention of letting you get out of it."

"But I can't be here."

"What the blazes do you mean by that?"

Not for weeks had Joy seen Sloan so angry. "I... I don't belong there."

"The only reason I agreed to this craziness my mother schemed up was because you'd be with me."

"But, Sloan, these are your friends. I won't know anyone."

"You'll know me."

A feeling of desolation stole over her. "But I don't have anything to wear to something like this."

"Take tomorrow off and buy yourself a dress," he shot back.

"It doesn't matter what I say. You have an answer." Her chin jutted out defiantly.

"You're right. And you'd better decide soon. Otherwise this whole affair is about to be canceled."

Nervously Joy trailed her fingers along the railing. "But I don't want to go. I'll stick out like a sore thumb."

Sloan's sharp laughter filled the night. "And you think I won't? There's no way I'll endure tomorrow without you. Now, do you agree, or will I be forced to start a war within my own family?"

Her mouth thinned with anger and regret. "I don't like this, Sloan Whittaker. I don't like it one bit."

* * *

L.J. offered some comfort early the next morning when Joy walked along the sandy beach and plopped down on a log. With short strokes, Joy smoothed the gull's feathers down the back of his head.

"It isn't working like I'd planned," she complained. "Not at all."

L.J. cocked his head undisturbed. A few other seagulls flew overhead and landed down the beach. L.J.'s interest peaked as he squawked loudly. The returning sounds seemed to excite him, and he scurried toward his friends, his feet leaving wet indentations in the sand.

Joy's heart plummeted to her feet as she watched the bird she had come to love hurry away. Would she lose him? L.J. was tame now, at least for her. She couldn't help wonder if he'd fit back into the life he'd once known. She was almost glad when he turned around and hobbled back to her side. The gauze that held his wing against his body was what restrained him. Joy knew she shouldn't be glad, but she was.

The remainder of the morning and all afternoon was spent shopping. Joy gave up counting the number of dresses she tried on. By afternoon she was weak with worry. It didn't matter what she wore; nothing could change what she was: somewhat plain, short, and scarred.

The dress she finally chose was a deceptively simple design with elegant lines. The wide white belt contained a rose pin. By the time she made her decision, Joy had given up caring. The sales clerk told her it was lovely.

Joy was convinced the sales clerk was prompted by the thought of a big sale.

The hairdresser styled her short hair in bouncy curls that made her look like the comic strip character Betty Boop. Joy washed it out when she got home.

Sloan was nowhere in sight, and Joy stayed in her room, preferring not to interfere with everything that was going on around the house.

The knock on her bedroom door surprised her. She stood, running a light hand over the black skirt before answering.

Sloan, dressed in a dark suit and tie, stood supported by crutches outside her door. The sight of this virile, handsome man was enough to steal her breath. His smile was devilishly enticing and slashed deep grooves around his mouth. His dancing dark eyes were directed at her and slowly took in every inch of her appearance. Apparently, what he saw pleased him, as an immense look of satisfaction showed in his eyes.

"Will I do?" The words stuck in her throat and sounded almost scratchy.

His answering nod was absent. "I see you every day, but this is the first time I've ever seen you all dressed up."

"I feel like a fish out of water."

"And you look like a princess. My Joy, you are a beautiful woman." He said it as if it surprised him.

She felt the color seep up her neck. "And you, Sloan Whittaker, bear a striking resemblance to Prince Charming."

"So it's been said," he teased. "Shall we?" He proffered his elbow. Joy rested her hand lightly against the crook of his arm and inhaled a deep breath, readying herself for the ordeal.

"I'll be the envy of every man here," he whispered reassuringly, and paused in the hallway just out of view from the living room. "Relax. You're as stiff as starched underwear."

Under any other circumstances Joy would have laughed, but she felt like a coiled spring, her nerves in chaos.

"Joy." Her name was issued on a soft reassuring note. The gentle brush of his lips on her cheek sent a warm glow over her. "Now smile."

She painted one on her lips and prayed it would effectively disguise her nervousness.

People had already begun to arrive. Joy didn't know a soul, not even the help who sauntered in and around the guests with trays of drinks and hors d'oeuvres.

Just before they entered the room, Sloan paused and inhaled a deep, calming breath. Filled with her own misgivings over this evening, Joy had forgotten what an ordeal this must be for Sloan. She glanced at him, a protective spark burning in her eyes.

Sloan's mother was at their side the minute they entered the room. Dressed in a lovely silver creation, she looked years younger. Diamonds graced her neck and hung from her ears. The scent of gardenias followed her.

"Ladies and gentlemen," Margaret Whittaker announced solemnly, "the guest of honor, my son Sloan."

Sloan tossed his mother a look of severe displeasure, but graciously smiled at the small audience.

A flurry of introductions followed, for Joy's bene-
fit. After five minutes she gave up trying to remember
names and faces.

A path was cleared for Sloan as he purposefully
made his way into the room. He chose a far corner
chair and set the crutches at his side.

"Joy," he whispered tightly. "Get me something to
drink. I'm going to need it."

Joy felt exactly the opposite. More than at any time
she could remember, she needed her wits about her. But
getting something nonalcoholic in this crowd might be
impossible.

A waiter was readily available. Joy lifted a long-
stemmed wineglass from the silver tray. "Would it be
possible to have a Coke or something?"

"Right away, madam."

Joy relaxed. Maybe this wouldn't be as bad as she'd
assumed. Sloan took the wineglass out of her hand and
placed an arm around her waist.

"Sit here." He indicated the padded arm of the chair.
When she did as he requested, Sloan kept his hand
where it was. Joy knew she should object. The reason
for this gathering was to bring Sloan back into contact
with his friends—and that included women.

Joy spotted Chantelle a few minutes later. Blonde.
Beautiful. Perfect. Everything Joy would never be. Chantelle laid a thin cobwebbed lace shawl over Clara's
arm and smiled beguilingly into a tall man's eyes. Obviously her date. Joy relaxed.

"What was that for?" Sloan asked, his hand tightening possessively around her.

"What?"

"That sigh," he returned.

"Chantelle's here."

"Joy, whatever you do, don't leave me."

"Sloan?" She couldn't understand him.

"Don't 'Sloan' me. I want you here as protection."

"I'm your physical therapist, not your armed guard," she whispered back. Silently she gritted her teeth.

"Joy," he said again entreatingly. "If someone makes one condescending remark or patronizes me, I won't be responsible for my actions. I need you as a buffer."

"A pillow would have done as well. Why drag me into this? Haven't you any consideration for someone other than yourself?"

"Hello, Sloan." It was the man who had come in with Chantelle. He stood directly in front of them.

"Dale." The greeting was sadly lacking in warmth. "Forgive me for not standing up," Sloan mocked.

"That I can overlook. It's the constant brush-off you've been giving me these past months I'm having a hard time forgiving."

"I'd think after the first few times you would have gotten the message."

Dale directed his attention to Joy. "Since Sloan is delinquent in introducing us, I'll do it myself. I'm Dale Jewett, Sloan's friend, although that at the moment is questionable."

"How do you do," Joy responded primly. So this was the man Sloan had repeatedly sent away.

"I think there's something you should understand right now." Sloan's voice was coated in ice. "My tennis days are over, skiing no longer appeals to me, and my golf game is shot."

Dale laughed and loudly slapped his knee. "You mean that's what's been bugging you all these months? Do you think I care if you can do any of that?"

Joy slid off the seat. Sloan had released his hold, and didn't seem to notice that she'd moved. "If you'll excuse me a minute."

Sloan didn't answer. Joy stepped aside and watched as Dale pulled up the ottoman and sat down. Within seconds the two men were engrossed in conversation.

The waiter delivered her Coke, and Joy stood in the background. Someone she vaguely remembered being introduced to engaged her in a conversation, but Joy was only half listening, making monosyllabic responses when required. Apparently the woman was a distant cousin of the Whittakers and had heard all kinds of good things about Joy from another cousin.

Dale was joined by Chantelle, who proudly held out her left hand. A solitaire diamond sparkled from her ring finger. Joy felt like jumping up and down and applauding. She watched as the two men enthusiastically shook hands.

Sloan turned and started to say something, unaware she had left. His eyes briefly scanned the crowd until they found her. They narrowed slightly, indicating he wanted her.

"Excuse me, please," Joy told the friendly cousin. The Coke glass in her hand, she sauntered back to Sloan's side.

"You rang, master?" she teased.

His arm came around her waist. "The funny-girl is Joy."

"We've met," both Chantelle and Dale said at the same time, and laughed. The two were so obviously in love that Joy instantly shared in their happiness.

"From what I understand, you're the one responsible for this minor miracle."

"No, the credit goes to Sloan. The only praise I can accept is being tenacious enough to stick it out with him."

"This little lady pinched, poked, prodded, and punished me."

"All in the line of duty," Joy joked.

"Sometimes above-and-beyond duties' call," Sloan inserted dramatically.

Another couple joined them. Again Joy was introduced, his hand at her waist keeping her possessively at his side. When he handed her his empty glass, Joy stood to go refill it for him.

Dale had broken through the brick wall that Sloan had erected, and now the sounds of his laughter could be heard above the rest. The crowd around him had grown so large that Joy didn't bother to push her way through.

"Didn't I tell you what a good idea this party was?" Margaret Whittaker brushed past, cheerful and happy. "Myron and I couldn't be more pleased with everything you've done."

She held the fragile stem of Sloan's drink with both hands. "Thank you," she murmured humbly.

"We'd like to give you a generous bonus." Her husband had mentioned the same thing once before. Joy didn't want or need a bonus. It was enough that she had accomplished what she set out to do.

"Really, Mrs. Whittaker, that won't be necessary."

"Of course it's necessary. Now don't argue."

Joy was quickly learning that the Whittakers were accustomed to having things their own way. It wouldn't do her any good to argue.

Myron joined his wife, his hand cupping her shoulder. "Good evening, Miss Nielsen."

"Hello," she returned. "It's a lovely party."

"Are you enjoying yourself?"

"Very much." The lie was only a white one.

"Juliette's here." The words were directed to his wife.

Margaret was instantly alert. "Do you think inviting her was wise?" A curious note of concern entered her voice. "Juliette and Sloan were quite serious before the accident," the older woman explained.

"Oh." Joy struggled to sound as natural as possible.

"I'm so hoping they get back together again."

Joy tensed.

"They were perfect for one another."

"What happened?" Joy wanted a reason to hate the mysterious Juliette. Had the woman walked out on him after the accident?

"All Sloan's doing, I fear. He didn't want anyone around. I'm afraid he hurt her terribly."

"Don't worry, dear," Myron Whittaker commented. "I'm sure now that Sloan's walking they'll patch things up."

"What has been your experience in cases like this?" Margaret asked. Both parents looked to Joy.

She forced a reassuring smile. "I really couldn't say."

A middle-aged woman came up and whispered something in Myron's ear. He nodded.

"Miss Nielsen, would you mind checking with Clara in the kitchen. It seems we've run out of hors d'oeuvres."

"Of course not."

Her nerves felt raw as she sauntered into the kitchen. Clara was busy working with the caterers, placing large shrimp onto a silver platter.

"How's it going in here?" Joy asked.

Clara looked up, startled. "My goodness, what are you doing in here?"

"Mr. Whittaker sent me to see how the goodies are holding out."

"What he really wants to know is if the little pink fellows have made their debut yet." She held up a shrimp.

"I guess you could say that." She smiled.

"Tell him to hold his horses, for heaven's sake. There's only so much we can do all at one time."

"All right, I'll tell him. But if you don't mind, I'll use more delicate terms."

Clara's look was perplexed, her brow knit in deep creases. "Now scat before something spills on that pretty dress."

Sloan's wineglass was still in her hand as she returned to the party. The Whittakers were out of sight, and Joy suspected Myron had purposely sent her away in order to bring Juliette to Sloan's attention. It was probably best. Joy didn't want to meet someone that was perfect for him.

"There you are." Chantelle stepped to her side. "Sloan sent me to find you."

Joy took in a breath to make her voice sound calm. "I imagine he's ready for his drink. I got waylaid."

"His drink?" Chantelle returned hesitantly. "No, Dale got him a refill earlier. Sloan wants you."

What lovely words, Joy mused as she followed the blonde through the crowd.

Several people were standing in front of Sloan, some leaning against the furniture, drinks in hand, a friendly crowd that responded with laughing eagerness to his witticisms. The attention didn't bother him, but unnerved her.

Their eyes met and Joy stopped midstep. She didn't want to be thrust into the middle of this, and silently she relayed as much. Her hands balled into fists as she stood outside the circle of friends. She didn't belong here, and he knew it.

Someone whispered Juliette's name, and Joy's attention was diverted to another blonde who moved gracefully across the room toward Sloan.

A hush fell over the crowd.

"Hello, Sloan," the other woman's musical voice greeted him.

Joy couldn't listen, couldn't watch. Abruptly she turned away and for a timeless second was frozen into immobility as the sound of Sloan's warm welcome reached her.

Somehow she made it back to her room, which felt stifling and hot. The sliding-glass door made a grating noise as she opened it and stepped onto the verandah. Arms hugging her waist, Joy raised her face to the heavens. From the moment she arrived, Joy had known this would happen. There was no one to blame but herself. She was the foolish one to have given her heart to Sloan Whittaker.

Tonight had magnified their differences. From the instant she'd stepped into the party it'd been apparent she didn't belong. Sloan's world was light-years away from anything she'd ever known. He was accustomed to wealth, influential people, and a certain amount of power.

Her job was almost complete, and she couldn't be anything but happy with how things had worked out. Her heart, however, was weeping for the man who had cried out for her in his sleep. "I thought I'd find you here," Sloan spoke from behind.

"You should be with your guests," she mumbled, not turning.

"Why didn't you come back?"

She could hear the sound of his crutches as he moved closer to her side.

Tension crackled in the space separating them.

"I couldn't." Her weak voice was barely audible.

"That's not an answer."

"All right, I don't belong in there. Is that what you want me to say? Because it's true." Her lower lip quivered slightly.

"Don't give me that garbage." His words exploded into the still night. A hand on her shoulder turned her around.

Joy hung her head. "How's Juliette?"

"Fine. We didn't talk long. I was too eager to find you." A hand stroked the curve of her neck and down her shoulder. The other found its way to the back of her neck. A fiery warmth rushed down her spine. "How long is it going to take you to learn that the two of us belong together? We're a team."

The pressure of his hands brought her up onto her tiptoes.

"Don't," she pleaded, and her voice trembled. "Sloan, I can't bear it. Please don't."

His hand closed more firmly around her neck, bringing her against the solid wall of his chest. "Don't you know yet how much I love you?" His voice was incredibly gentle, caressing her upturned face.

Agony was tearing at her heart. "You can't love me."

"But I do." His mouth moved against her hair in a rough action. The heat of his body burned through the flimsy material of her dress. His heartbeat hammered erratically against her palm.

For a moment she managed to elude his searching kiss, but when his mouth found hers, all protest died. She wound her arms around his neck and gave herself completely to his probing kiss. Everything went spinning, a magical merry-go-round that ascended to dizzying heights. Feeling boneless, she molded her body to his. Sloan had once said that they fit perfectly together. For the first time, she was able to test how accurate his statement was.

"Come on, my Joy," he whispered against her nape.

"As much as I want to stay here and hold you the rest of our lives, we have to go back." He chuckled softly. "At this point, it would be best to avoid Mother's wrath."

Nine

Joy sat on a burned-out log along the beach. Her flute lay across her lap and L.J. hobbled about her feet. The early-morning air contained a crisp chill, but Joy was only vaguely aware of her surroundings.

"I should be the happiest woman in the world," she told the attentive seagull. "Sloan said he loved me last night." She raised the flute to her lips and played a few mournful notes. "Talk to me, L.J. Tell me why I feel so miserable."

The bird looked back at her blankly.

"Come on," Joy moaned regretfully. "This isn't doing any good. Let's go back."

She stood and continued to play as she walked along the sand-covered shore, L.J. trailing behind. Once she glanced back, and a smile lit up her face. She felt like a pied piper.

When the house came into view, she noted that Sloan was standing on the verandah, looking out. She paused and waved. He returned the gesture, but even from this distance she could see that something was bothering him.

He was still outside when she put L.J. back into the fenced yard and returned to her room. She carelessly laid the flute across the mattress and joined Sloan on the deck.

"What's wrong?"

He glared at her for a moment, his look thoughtful. "I didn't know you still had the bird."

"He's just like a pet now."

"The two of you made quite a pair walking on the beach like that." Somehow he didn't sound like it was a pleasant sight.

"Something's troubling you. What is it, Sloan?" She placed her hand on his forearm, and he covered it with his own.

"You say the bird is tame. For everyone?"

"No, only me. But I was the one who treated him and I'm the one who feeds him."

"Hasn't he ever given any indication he wants to be free?"

"No…" She stopped, remembering his reaction the other day when some gulls were near.

"I notice his wing is still bandaged. I'd think by now it would be healed."

Joy straightened her back and took a step in retreat. "What you're suggesting is that the time has come to set the bird free." She struggled to take the protest out of her words.

"I know how you feel about him."

"You couldn't possibly know. I found him; I was the

one who took care of him. He eats right out of my hand now. He's tame, I tell you. He doesn't want his freedom; he's content to stay here." Her voice became thinner with every word as she argued.

"You're right," Sloan reasoned. "The bird is yours; you're the one who worked with him. I'm just asking that you think about it."

Joy tried to smile, but the effort resulted in a mere trembling of her mouth. She squared her shoulders. "I think you're right. L.J. deserves a better life than this." Abruptly she turned around, intent on doing it while the strength of her conviction remained strong.

"Where are you going?"

"To set L.J. free."

"It doesn't have to be done now."

"Yes, it does." Unreasonably, she felt like shouting at him.

Her mouth was set in a firm line as she marched down to the back portion of the yard and opened the gate. She didn't need to say a word for the gull to come rushing out. Like a tiny robot, he followed her down to the beach.

Tears blurred her eyes as she knelt at his side and unwrapped the gauze bandage from his wing. Carefully she extended it, checking for any further damage. There wasn't anything that she could see.

"We've become good friends over the last few weeks, haven't we, Long John?"

He tested his new freedom, then quirked his small head at an inquiring angle when he experienced the first unruffling of his broad wingspan.

Joy bit into the corner of her bottom lip at the happy squawk he gave.

"The time has come for you to go back to your other friends." Her voice was incredibly weak.

The bird continued to stare back at her.

"Go on," she urged. "Fly away. Scat."

He didn't budge.

"Sloan's right," she spoke in a whisper. "He told me it was time to set you free." Joy choked on a sob. "But it wasn't you he was talking about. Sloan's ready too. Long John," she groaned. "This is hard enough without your making it any more painful." She rose and brushed the sand from her pants. "You're free. Go." She waved her arms, indicating that he should fly away.

Still he didn't move.

Joy began to run, and to her horror the bird followed behind as he'd done so many times in the past.

"No." She shouted and continued waving her hands in an effort to frighten him away.

He looked at her as if he were laughing.

She picked up a pebble and tossed it at him. It bounced a few inches away.

He let out an angry squawk.

"Go," she shouted with all her strength. Just when it didn't look as if anything she did would make any difference, another gull swooped onto the beach.

"Your friends are here," she told him in a gentle voice that probably confused him all the more. "Go to them. It's where you belong."

He glanced from her to the sky. Testing his wing a

second time, he rose and hovered in the air above her. He seemed reluctant to go.

Standing completely still, Joy placed a hand over her mouth and raised the other in a final salute to the bird she had come to love. Burning tears streamed down her cheeks.

Her heart breaking, she stayed on the shore until he was out of sight. She turned, and the beach house loomed before her.

Almost from the beginning she had found similarities between Sloan and L.J. They were two of a kind. In the beginning each had been arrogant and proud. She had been the one to tame them, and she must be the one to set them free. The decision was long overdue. Sloan didn't need her anymore. Within a matter of days he'd be able to go from the walker to the cane. Why had she waited? It only made the parting more painful.

Her lower lip trembling, Joy returned to the house. Mercifully Clara wasn't in the kitchen, and Joy hurried down the hall to her room. The suitcases were under the bed, and she knelt down to pull them out.

The first thing she packed was her flute in the small black carrying case that resembled a doctor's bag. Without rhyme or order she began tossing her things inside the open bags.

When the largest one was filled, she dragged it off the bed and out of the house. Somehow she managed to get it into the back of her car. Sloan was in the hallway outside her bedroom when she returned. Without a word, she scooted past him.

"What are you doing?"

"Packing."

He laughed. "You're kidding."

"No," she said forcefully, "I'm not."

"You can't mean it." He sounded shocked.

"Isn't it obvious?" she returned flatly. "Look in my room. My bags are out; my clothes are on the bed. To put it plain and simple, I'm leaving."

"But why? I don't understand."

Holding her expression tight, Joy released an impatient sigh. "What's there to understand? My job is finished. You're up and around. That's what I came here for. Now it's time to move on." She strived to sound as unemotional as possible.

She saw his hands tighten around the metal bar that supported him. "It's that damn bird, isn't it?"

"Of course not."

"I knew the minute you left that something was wrong. Let's talk about it, at least. Don't just walk out."

"Mr. Whittaker." Clara ambled down the hall. "I haven't seen Joy this morning."

"She's here," he replied, obviously irritated by the interruption.

"But she didn't bring you breakfast."

"She claims she's leaving," Sloan announced.

"No." Clara emphatically shook her head to deny the truth. "Joy wouldn't leave without saying something. That's not like her."

Joy came through the doorway carrying as much as possible under both arms. Only one suitcase remained. "I was coming back to say goodbye to you and Paul."

"But not me?" His look cut her to the quick.

She didn't answer.

"Joy." Frustration coated his voice as he stepped aside to allow her to pass. "Why are you doing this?"

"Because I have to, don't you see?"

"No, I don't," he returned angrily.

Joy hurried out of the house and threw her things into the car. She paused long enough to take in several deep, calming breaths.

Clara was standing in the front doorway, her face tight with concern. "What's happened?"

"Nothing." Joy attempted to brush away the housekeeper's doubts. "The time has come for me to leave, that's all. You knew from the beginning I would eventually go."

"But not like this, so sudden and all."

"Sometimes it's better that way. Clara, you've been a dear. I'll never forget you." Briefly she hugged the warm, generous woman. "Where's Paul?"

"He's gone into town," Clara replied, her look preoccupied.

"Then give him my best. I can't wait."

"Why can't you?" Clara demanded in uncharacteristic sharpness.

Joy didn't answer; instead she stepped back into the house and headed straight to her room. Sloan was inside waiting for her. He slammed the door shut after she entered.

Hands clenched, Joy whirled on him. "Why'd you do that?"

"I'll lock you in here until hell freezes over if you don't tell me what's going on."

"What's there to explain? The time has come for me to take on another case, that's all."

"But I need you."

"Nonsense. Everything I do, Paul can do," she explained tersely.

"That's not it, and you know it."

Her chin jutted out in challenge. "I know nothing of the sort." Her hand closed around the suitcase as she lifted it off the bed.

"Doesn't last night mean anything to you?"

Joy's greatest fear was that he would bring up his love. Silently she prayed God would give her strength. "Of course it does. But those feelings of gratitude are common—" She wasn't allowed to finish.

"It isn't gratitude." He was all but shouting now. "What does it take to reach you?"

With the suitcase in her hand, she rolled it across the floor.

"Don't walk out on me, Joy…we both know that in time you'll regret it."

A sad smile briefly touched her mouth; she would come to regret this day? Slowly she turned to face him. "Goodbye, Sloan. May God grant you a rich and full life." At the moment her own felt empty and desolate. Tears clouded her eyes as she turned around, her back to him, one hand on the door.

"Don't leave me. Not like this." A wealth of emotion filled Sloan's plea.

The temptation to turn around and run into his arms was so strong that Joy felt as if she were fighting an invisible force that was pulling her apart.

"Goodbye," she repeated, her voice trembling and weak.

Something exploded behind her. Joy swung around just in time to see Sloan hurl a vase against the opposite wall. It shattered into a hundred pieces.

"Go ahead, then, go," he shouted, knocking the bedside lamp aside. "You're right. I don't need you. Get out of my life and stay out." Defiance glared from his dark eyes.

All color drained out of her face as she stood frozen and immobile.

"What are you waiting for? Do I have to kick you out the door?" He took the walker and slammed it against the dresser. "Like you said I don't need you."

Joy understood all too well. Swallowing, she walked out of the room. Her legs felt as if they could buckle under her, but somehow she managed.

Clara stood in the entryway, wringing her hands. "Sure gonna miss you around here. It won't seem the same with you gone."

"Thank you, Clara." Tears ran freely down her face. "Take care of him for me." Her voice was breaking, and she paused to take in a breath, then tilted her head toward Sloan's room so Clara would know what she meant.

"I will, but it's you he needs."

"He'll be fine."

"But will you?"

The confirming nod was weak. "I think so."

Without looking back, Joy walked out of the house, climbed in her car, started the engine, and pulled away.

"I won't do any more private cases," Joy emphasized

as she spoke into the telephone receiver. She knew that
Dr. Phelps was upset with her, but Joy had learned her
lesson. Never again.

"You're sure? The money is good," Dr. Phelps persisted.

"The money is always good."

"You did a fabulous job with Whittaker."

"Thank you." Joy bit her lip to keep from asking how
he was. Three weeks had seemed more like three years.

"I understand you're working at the Sports Clinic
now."

"Yes, I started a couple of weeks ago."

"How do you like it?"

Joy couldn't very well admit it was boring, unchal-
lenging, and that every day away from Sloan she was
dying a little more. "It's regular hours, no hassles and…"

"Crummy pay," Dr. Phelps finished for her.

"And that," she agreed with a weak laugh.

"I can't talk you into this case?"

"No, I'm afraid not."

"Should I try again?"

"You can try, but I doubt if I'll change my mind." She
knew Dr. Phelps was disappointed in her. "I'm sorry,"
she murmured, and replaced the receiver.

Her hand rested on top of the phone. No less than
twenty times after she'd left Sloan, she'd been tempted
to call and see how things were going. The only thing
that had stopped her was the fear that Sloan would answer. Some nights she had lain awake and allowed her
mind to play back the memories. They'd shared some
happy times, good times. Her favorite had been when

they'd sat on the beach, Sloan at her side, his hands fingering her hair.

So many times they'd sat on the verandah late at night and discussed a myriad of subjects. Amazingly, their tastes and opinions were often similar.

Joy hadn't expected to miss his companionship so much, nor his friendship. Sloan had been her friend, a very good friend.

A long sigh escaped her as she tucked her feet under her in the big overstuffed chair. Joy rested her head against the back cushion and closed her eyes. Three weeks, and she'd yet to sleep an entire night through. She felt exhausted and frustrated with herself.

The decision had been the right one. Both times. L.J. was free to join his own kind and live the life he was meant to. Just as Sloan was now. She would no more fit in Sloan's world than she would in L.J.'s. For a time they would miss her. It would be a natural reaction. But later those feelings would change. Soon, if not already, Sloan would realize she'd been right. What he felt was gratitude, not love. Her only desire was that in the future he would think kindly of her.

Days took on a regular pattern. She rose early and continued with her running, sometimes going as far as five miles.

Her work offered few challenges. Patients were shuffled in and out of the treatment room every thirty minutes, sometimes longer, depending on the nature of the damage. The clinic specialized in treating sports injuries. Usually little more than ice packs, electric muscle stimulation, and a workout schedule with weights. But there was little personal satisfaction.

Usually Joy didn't eat until late in the evening. Her appetite was nearly nonexistent. Clara's good cooking had spoiled her, and when it came to fixing herself something to eat it was easier to open a can or toss something in the microwave.

Friday night, after a long week, Joy left the front door of the apartment open while she sat drinking from a glass of iced tea, her leg draped over the side of her chair. Her attention flittered over the glossy pages of a woman's magazine.

When the doorbell buzzed, Joy assumed it was Danielle, who sometimes stopped in unexpectedly. Unlooping her legs, she set the tea aside and sauntered to the door.

The welcome died on her lips. Was she hallucinating? Dreaming? Sloan, standing erect without the aid of crutches or walker, stood before her.

Dressed in tan slacks and a blue knit shirt, he looked compelling and handsome. The vigorous masculine features broke into a ready smile.

"Hello, my Joy." The lazy, warm voice assured her that her mind wasn't playing cruel tricks.

"Sloan." His name slipped from her lips as the magazine fell to the floor. She stooped to retrieve it, conscious of her rolled-up cotton pants and bare feet.

"Aren't you going to invite me in?"

"Of course," she muttered, her voice trembling as her fingers fumbled with the lock on the screen door. "You're using the cane." The observation wasn't one of her most brilliant. But she knew how hard he must have worked in the three weeks since she'd last seen him to be using the cane.

"Yes, but only for a few days." The limp was barely noticeable as he walked into the room.

"You're doing great." It was so good to see him that she had to restrain herself from throwing her arms around him. Her heart was singing a rhapsody.

"Thanks."

Her hands were clenched self-consciously in front of her. "Would you like something to drink? I made some fresh iced tea earlier. From scratch, the way Clara does."

"That sounds fine."

Joy felt like skipping into the kitchen. Her mind whirled at the virile sight of him. He looked magnificent. Oh heavens, why hadn't she washed her hair tonight? She was a mess.

"Make yourself comfortable," she said, and motioned toward the chair she'd vacated. "I'll only be a minute."

Joy had opened the refrigerator door and taken out the pitcher of tea before she noticed that Sloan had followed her.

"Aren't you going to admit it's good to see me?" His gaze shimmered over her.

"It is," she said, and beamed him a bright smile. "It really is. You look great."

"So do you."

The tea made a swishing sound at the bottom of the glass as she poured it over the ice cubes. Her hand shook as she added a lemon slice to the side of the tall glass. When she held it out for him, Sloan's hand cupped hers.

"I've missed you, my Joy."

"And I've missed you." She forced a light gaiety into her voice.

Sloan set the tea on the counter without releasing her hand. His eyes held her prisoner as he tugged gently on her arm, bringing her closer to his side.

"I want you to come back."

"Oh, Sloan," she murmured miserably, and dropped her gaze. "You don't need me; I can't come back."

"I love you, Joy. I've loved you from the time you held up your head and walked out of the pool, letting me see your scars. Proud, regal, and so beautiful I nearly drowned just watching you."

"Don't, Sloan, please." She injected a plea into his name.

"I can't change the way I feel. I love you."

Backed against the kitchen counter, she was grateful for the support it gave her. "Listen to me, please."

"No," he said, and sighed heavily. "I listened to you the last time. Now it's my turn."

"All right." Her hesitation was pronounced. She didn't want this, but there was little choice. Nothing he could say would change her mind.

"I know what you're thinking."

"I'm sure you don't—"

"It isn't gratitude," he interrupted her, his voice heavy with building frustration. "We're a team; we have been almost from the day you arrived. We were even injured in the same kind of accident. I could have fallen off a cliff skiing or broken my back a hundred different ways. But I didn't. We like the same things, share the same ideals. I am thankful for what you did, I can't deny that, but it's so much more."

"I'm a therapist." She placed her palm across her breast in an identifying action. "I've worked in tons of cases like yours. Patients always fall in love with their therapists. It's common knowledge that it happens all the time."

"In other words, I'm one of the scores who have fallen for you."

She avoided the question. "What you feel isn't a true emotion, but one prompted by appreciation for what I've done."

Sloan took in a deep, angry breath. "In this case I think you outdid yourself," he returned flatly.

"Your parents' bonus check was very generous." Her heart was crying with the agony she was causing them both.

His handsome face twisted with something she couldn't read.

"You're wrong," he argued. "I know what I feel. I'm not a young boy suffering from my first case of puppy love." His voice was low and rough with frustration, almost angry.

"The thing is, we've been through a lot together. We've worked hard; I've seen you at your best and your worst. You've shared a part of yourself with me that probably few others have ever seen. It's only natural that you would come to think you love me. Believe me when I say sincerely that I've never been more honored."

"Don't say that. I want to share my life with you. I want you to be the mother of my children and stand by my side in the years ahead. When I wake up at night, I want to feel your softness at my side. Tell me you want this too."

"Sloan." Tears blurred her eyes as she lifted her gaze. She loved him desperately and at the same time hated him for what he was forcing her to do. Perhaps now he wanted these things. But later that would change. His gratefulness would diminish and he'd realize what a terrible mistake he'd made.

"Say it, Joy. Tell me you want me." His hands, warm and possessive, cupped her shoulders.

"You're being unfair." Her throat felt raw, and it throbbed.

"I'm being more than fair. All I ask is a simple straightforward answer. I love you; I want to marry you. Yes or no?"

She stood, unable to formulate the word, not when every part of her was crying out for her to go to him. A huge lump had a stranglehold on her voice.

"Joy?" he prompted. "Just say yes." His voice was a caressing whisper. His fingers pressed lightly into her shoulder as if that would encourage her.

Tightly she closed her eyes, unable to bear looking at him. A tear squeezed through her lashes and ran down her cheek.

With infinite tenderness, Sloan kissed the moisture away.

"No." Somehow the word managed to slip out.

Joy felt his shock.

"I see." He dropped his hands from her shoulders.

She blinked through a curtain of tears. "I'm sorry; so sorry." She felt raw and vulnerable.

"Not to worry." The grim voice was cutting. "I appreciate the honesty." He turned abruptly and moved out of the kitchen.

Dazed, hurt, dying, Joy watched him leave as the tears slid down her face. He didn't hesitate.

Ten

Mutely Joy walked to the screen door to catch one last glimpse of Sloan as he strolled out of her life. His limp was more pronounced now, his shoulders hunched. Joy bit viciously into her bottom lip, and the taste of blood filled her mouth. Never had anything been more difficult; never had anything been more right.

Someday the hurt would go away and she would be stronger for it. At least that was what Joy told herself repeatedly in the long, dark days that followed. She had no energy. Listlessly she lay around the house. Food held no appeal, and she began skipping meals. Her weight began to drop. She wouldn't allow herself the luxury of tears. The decision had been made; she had done the right thing. It would be useless to cry over it now.

Five days after Sloan's visit there was no doubt that summer had arrived in Southern California. Heat and humidity filled the tiny apartment, and Joy turned on a fan in hopes the small appliance would stir the heavy heat.

The thin cotton blouse stuck to her skin, and she unfastened the second button. Perspiration rolled down the hollow between her breasts.

Impatiently she walked into the kitchen and took a soft drink out of the refrigerator. Empty calories for an empty life, she mused as she ripped the pull tab from the aluminum can.

Her cell rang, and she felt like plugging her ears. There wasn't anyone she wanted to talk to. Not her mother. Not her brother. Not even Danielle. No one. The whole attitude was so unlike her that Joy knew it was important to shed this dark apathy as quickly as possible.

"Hello." Her voice held little welcome.

"Hi, Joy. This is Paul. How you doing?"

"Paul," she spoke into the mouthpiece, surprise raising her tone. "I'm fine. How are you?"

"Great. Listen, I know this is sudden and all, but how about dinner? We could meet at Mobey Jake's."

"I… I don't know." She hesitated. Why torture herself? Paul was sure to mention Sloan.

"Have you eaten?" he asked.

"No. It's too hot to eat."

"Come on," Paul encouraged. "It's the least you can do, since I didn't get so much as a goodbye when you left. That still rankles." He was playful and teasing.

Joy laughed, and the sound surprised her. It'd been weeks since she'd found anything amusing. "All right," she agreed, "but give me an hour."

"Do you want me to pick you up, or can you meet me?"

"I'll meet you."

* * *

Mobey Jake's held fond memories. The flashing neon whale, round tables with faded umbrellas, and some of the best fried fish on the California coast. The first barrier she had hurdled in her relationship with Sloan had been the night she had brought him an order of fish from Mobey Jake's. Even L.J. had liked this fish the best. And who could blame him?

Joy was sitting at a table that overlooked the seashore far below when Paul arrived. He came from the direction of the beach home, which answered Joy's first uncertainty. Paul was still with Sloan. She had to wonder if Sloan sent him to talk to her. As soon as the question formed, she knew the answer. Sloan did his own talking.

Paul parked the older-model convertible and waved. Joy returned the gesture. He looked fit, tan, and muscular.

Tucking the car keys in his jean pocket, he smiled as he strolled toward her. "You look good." The hesitation was slight enough for her to notice.

"I don't, either."

"Lost weight?"

"A few pounds." Her fingers curled around the tall foam cup. "I'm ready to order." She changed the subject abruptly, not wanting to be the topic of their conversation.

She waited while Paul stood in line at the window and placed the order for their meal. He returned a few minutes later with their standard. Joy looked at the large double order of fish, knowing there wasn't an L.J. to eat the leftovers. The memory of her little friend tightened her stomach.

"I don't suppose you've seen L.J.?" She looked up at Paul.

"That darn bird of yours? No, I haven't."

"I wonder what ever became of him."

Paul shrugged his shoulders and slipped a large piece of fish into his mouth. Avoiding her gaze, he looked out over the scenery. "Don't you wonder about anyone else?"

Deliberately obtuse, Joy returned, "Of course, I do. How's Clara?"

"Ready to quit."

"Clara? I don't believe it. She's been with the Whittakers for years."

"Neither one of us can take much more of what's been going on lately."

Joy nearly choked on a French fry. "Oh?"

"Aren't you interested?"

"I don't know." Joy managed to sound offhand and unconcerned, when she was terrified Paul would even mention Sloan's name.

"I understand where you're coming from," he began, "and whatever's between you and Sloan is none of my business, but something's got to be done."

"What do you mean?"

Paul took a swig of beer and with deliberate casualness placed it back on the table. "I shouldn't trouble you with this. After all, you were the smart one to get out when you did."

"Paul!" For the first time, Joy wanted to shake the younger man. "Obviously there's something you want me to know. Now either get it over with or shut up."

"It's Whittaker." Paul sounded uncertain now.

"Well, for heaven's sake, who else would be causing you any problems?" Joy was quickly losing her patience.

Paul avoided her gaze, fingering the fish. "He's in a bad way."

"How do you mean? Did he fall and hurt himself? Why didn't anyone let me know? Paul, does he need me?" All her concerns rushed out in one giant breath.

"He needs you all right, but not because of any fall."

"What do you mean?"

"I wish I knew. Listen, I don't know what happened last week, but Whittaker hasn't been the same since he came back from seeing you."

Joy hadn't been the same either. "How's that?"

"For nearly three weeks he practically killed himself— and me," Paul added sheepishly, "so that he could walk with the cane. His goal was to come to you. He never said as much, mind you, but it was understood. I don't know what you said, or what *he* said, for that matter, but Sloan's been locked up in his room ever since."

"I don't believe it."

"It's true. Ask Clara. He shouts and throws things at anyone who comes near him. If you think he was an angry beast when you first came, you should see him now. I think he's drinking, too."

"Oh, no." Joy's shoulders sagged. "Oh, Paul, no."

Joy hardly slept that night. Everything Paul told her seemed to press against her as she tossed and turned fitfully.

Before the sun came up the next morning, she was

dressed in the same outfit she wore while working with Sloan. The ride down the highway was accomplished in short order, and she pulled into the long driveway that led to the beach house. Pausing, she looked apprehensively at the closed drapes and prayed that she was doing the right thing.

Clara answered her timid knock and gave a cry of welcome when she saw it was Joy.

"I'm so glad you've come." She hugged Joy briefly and hurried on to explain. "I just didn't know what to do for Mr. Whittaker anymore. He doesn't want to see no one. He hardly eats and keeps himself locked up in that room. Not even his father, but he'll see you, Joy. It's you Mr. Whittaker needs."

Joy's returning hug lacked confidence. "If he thinks I went through months of work so he can lock himself away and sulk, then I'll tell him differently."

"That-t-a girl." Clara patted her across her back. "I'll be in the kitchen cooking breakfast. Mr. Whittaker will eat now that you're here."

"You do that."

"I'll fix my best blueberry waffles. I'll cook some up for you too."

Food was the last thing that occupied her thoughts, but Joy gave the old woman an encouraging nod.

Hands knotted at her side, Joy squared her shoulders and marched down the hall to Sloan's room. Boldly she knocked long and hard against his door.

"I said leave me alone."

Pushing in the door, Joy was immediately assaulted with the stale and unpleasant odor of beer. Wrinkling her nose, she proceeded into the room. Dirty clothes littered the floor, the bed was unmade, and the sheets hung off the edges.

In the dim interior, Joy didn't see Sloan at first. When he spoke, her attention was drawn across the room to the far corner. He sat in the wheelchair, the cane lying on the floor at his side. Two or more days' growth of beard darkened his face. His normally neatly styled hair was tangled and unruly. Paul hadn't been exaggerating when he said Sloan was in a bad way.

"What do you want?" The anger was unable to disguise his shock.

Joy didn't answer him; instead she walked across the room and pulled open the drapes. Brilliant sunlight chased away the shadows and filled the room with its golden rays.

"Get out of here, Joy."

"No." Hands on hips, she whirled around. "What's the matter with you?"

He didn't bother to answer. Instead he stood, limped across the room, and closed the drapes. "Wasn't it you who said if I wanted to keep the drapes closed I'd have to do it myself? I just have. Now get out."

"Oh no you don't," she flared, and jerked the drapes open a second time. Not an inch separated them.

Sloan squinted with the light. "Who the hell let you in here anyway? They'll pay with their job when I find out."

"What's that doing sitting in here?" She pointed to the wheelchair. "When I left, it was because you would never need that thing again." Now she was angry, just as angry as Sloan.

"Is that what it takes to bring you back in my life? A wheelchair?"

"No," she cried. "But I didn't spend long, hard weeks working with you so that you could sit in the dark."

"I thought I told you to get out of here. This is my life, and I'll live it as I please," he shouted back harshly.

"Not when I've invested my time in it you won't."

"I need a beer." A hand against the side of his head, he looked around the room, carelessly throwing clothes and anything that impeded the search.

"Alcohol is the last thing you need."

"Go home, little girl. I don't want you."

"Sloan, for heaven's sake, look at what you're doing to yourself. This is ridiculous."

"No more crazy than your coming here. I don't need your devotion or your pity."

"Pity?" She nearly choked on the word. "I can't believe you'd even suggest anything like that."

"You've made your feelings crystal clear," he told her roughly. "If it isn't sympathy, what is it?"

Joy pressed her lips together.

"Why are you here?" he demanded a second time.

"I... I don't know why," she lied, and stalked across the room, arms hugging her waist. He shouted at her again, and she grimaced, not even hearing the words. "All right," she cried, "you want to know why? I'll tell you. I didn't go through the agony of giving you back to the Chantelles of the world so you could waste your life."

"Have you gone crazy?"

"Yes, I'm nuts, and another week like the last one and I'll be carted off to a mental hospital." She knew she was being irrational, but she had lost the power to reason. She didn't know what she'd planned to say when she walked into his room. But nothing was going right, and everything looked so hopeless.

"Joy." An incredulous note entered his voice. "Do you love me?"

Joy opened her mouth to deny herself again, but the words wouldn't come.

"Do you?"

"Yes," she snapped.

"You idiot. You crazy idiot," he muttered, and pulled her into his arms, his hold strong and sure. He expelled a rush of air and relaxed against her.

Somehow Joy had never heard anything more beautiful.

"Why did you send me away?" His breath stirred the hair at the crown of her head.

She slid her arms around his neck, reveling in the feel of his body close to hers. "I couldn't let you waste yourself on me because you're grateful."

His arms tightened around her. "Grateful." He spat the word out. "I've come to almost hate that word. What does it take to convince you that what I feel is love?"

"Thirty years?" she breathed, and laid her head against the muscular chest.

"That's not near long enough," he told her huskily, his hand weaving in her short curls, pressing her to him.

"But, Sloan, how can you love me? I'm not pretty or rich or—"

"Stop," he interrupted her, almost angry again. "I love you, and I won't have you saying those things about yourself. When you first came, for all intents and purposes I had a disability. Then I was walking again, and you left. Everything should have been perfect, but I was worst off without you."

"But I don't fit in—"

"The only thing that's going to stop you from arguing with me is kissing you."

She laughed and nuzzled his neck. "That might work," she said shakily, and raised her head to meet his descending mouth. Her lips parted under his, and the blood rushed through her veins. No longer did she question if Sloan's feelings were interwoven with a deep sense of appreciation. He loved her; she knew that now as intuitively as she had recognized her own feelings.

Possessively his hands slid over the womanly curves of her rib cage to cup the swelling fullness of her breasts. He shuddered and buried his face in her neck. "You'll marry me." It wasn't a question, but a statement of fact.

"Yes," she breathed in happily. "Yes."

"Children?"

"As many as you want."

"My, my, you're agreeable."

"All right, no more than ten."

He rubbed his chin along the top of her head. "You won't go away if I take a shower and change clothes, will you?"

Her arms curved around the broad expanse of his

chest. "Are you kidding? You've given me enough reason to hang around for a lifetime."

Chuckling, he kissed the top of her nose. "Are you always going to be this stubborn?"

"You'll find out," she teased.

"I can hardly wait."

An hour later, their arms looped around each other's waist, they slowly sauntered down the flawless beach. Their bare feet made deep indentations in the sand, their footsteps punctuated by Sloan's cane.

A brisk breeze whipped a curl across Joy's face. Sloan tucked it around her ear and kissed her hard and deep.

"I love you," she told him shakily, her voice still affected by his kiss.

"I wondered how long it would take you to say it."

"I admitted it to myself a long time ago."

Above, a flock of seagulls circled and let out a loud squawk. Joy paused and shielded her eyes with her hand.

"Sloan," she whispered in disbelief. "It's L.J."

"Honey, there are a thousand birds out here that look exactly like him."

"He's up there. That's him," she cried, pointing him out for Sloan. Happiness trapped the oxygen in her lungs. "It's got to be him."

"Joy." Sloan arched both brows.

Her attention was directed to the flock of birds that flew down the beach. Only one stayed behind, landing a few feet away.

"It is him," she whispered.

"You didn't tell me I would be forced to fight off

flocks of admirers," Sloan teased with a smile of intense satisfaction.

L.J. quirked his head as if to say he didn't have time to chat, spread his wings, and flew back to his friends.

"He just stopped by to say hello," Joy murmured happily.

"And I," Sloan whispered, pulling her into his arms, "have come to stay a lifetime."

* * * * *

ADAM'S IMAGE

One

He stood across the room, nursing his drink. Not for the first time that evening, Susan Mackenzie found her attention drawn to the tall, rather lanky man. Her first impression was that he was strikingly unattractive. His face was too narrow, the chin square and abrupt; the dark brown eyes were friendly, but small. And his hair, although short and well trimmed, did little to disguise ears that tended to stick out. But there was a kindness about him, a gentleness she hadn't seen in a man for a long while.

Susan was situated in a corner by herself. Cocktail parties were not her forte. She tended to be more comfortable communicating with an individual instead of a whole room full of strangers. But she had seen to the obligatory chitchat and was free to sit and observe.

Several editors from rival publishing houses were present and Susan enjoyed looking them over, learning what she could about the people from the way they interacted with others. The games they played—

the games everyone played—could be amusing when viewed from a spectator's position.

That was what interested Susan about the stranger across the room. He too was an-onlooker. Twice she had watched couples approach him. His smile had been warm and genuine, and although Susan couldn't hear his voice over the conversational hum, the sound of his laugh had drifted across the extensive living room, deep, rich and full. Just listening to him had made her want to smile. He gave whomever he was speaking to his full attention. A man who listened, another rarity.

She stood, taking her wineglass with her as she approached him. He saw her coming and straightened slightly. Susan wondered if he'd noticed her and shared some of the same thoughts.

"Susan Mackenzie." She held out her hand.

"Adam Gallagher." He took her petite hand in his huge one and shook it firmly.

"I wanted…"

"I was going…"

They both spoke simultaneously and stopped to laugh.

"You first," Adam said, and gestured with his old-fashioned glass, his dark eyes smiling.

"I don't believe we've met, and thought I should take the opportunity to introduce myself." There were probably dozens of people she hadn't met tonight, but he was the only one who interested her enough to seek out.

"I was thinking the same thing."

"Are you a friend of Ralph's?" Ralph was the man giving the party. The cocktails were part of the celebration for Ralph, who was opening his own literary agency after several years of working for L & L Literary Services.

"We attended college together." He smiled, displaying a flash of pearl white teeth. "Are you in publishing?"

Susan nodded. "Associate editor." She could feel his surprise although he didn't comment. People were often amazed that someone as young as she would be an editor. It wasn't uncommon; most romance editors were in their mid to late twenties. Nearly everyone at Silhouette's office was. Susan was twenty-four. "And you?"

"No." He shook his head. "I'm a doctor."

Now it was her turn to be surprised, although why she should she didn't know. The profession fit perfectly with the man, his kindness, the gentle quality about him. He was a healer.

"Do you have a complaint?" he asked with a rueful gleam.

"A complaint?" The questioning look produced small dimples in her naturally rosy cheeks.

"You know, headaches, a bad back, indigestion?"

A breathless laugh came from her as he held her gaze. "Now that you mention it," she said, "my feet are killing me."

"New shoes?"

A strand of long brown hair fell loosely down the side of her cheek as she nodded. Susan looped it around her ear.

"Would you like to sit down?" he suggested.

What she wanted was to go home, but not if it meant missing the opportunity to talk to this intriguing male.

There were quite a few things she planned on finding out about Adam. She liked him, had liked him almost from the first moment she'd begun observing him. That in itself was unusual. "I suppose I should."

Adam left momentarily and returned with two chairs. "Here, that should take some of the pressure off your feet."

They sat and talked for an hour. Adam told her how he'd met Ralph and how they'd maintained their friendship over the years, Susan's own dealings with Ralph Jordan had been limited. Most of his clients wrote mainstream fiction, although he represented one of Silhouette's best authors. That was why she was there tonight.

Adam wasn't shy, and somehow she found that surprising. He wasn't like her; he didn't possess the same reasons for blending into the background that she did. Her reticence came from a deep-seated shyness that she had struggled to overcome most of her life.

The more they talked, the more attractive Adam became. Less than an hour after she introduced herself, Susan no longer saw the too square chin, or the large ears; she saw the man. And the man was the most compelling, interesting one she had met in two years of living in New York.

Adam paused and glanced at his watch. Something flickered over his face. "My goodness, I've been talking up a blue streak." A scowl briefly touched his brow. "I don't usually do that." He stood. "Would you like a refill?" His gaze centered on the empty goblet she held in her hand.

"No, I'm fine. Thanks."

He examined his own empty glass. "What I'd really like is a cup of coffee. How about you?"

"I doubt that we'll find that around here." Had she unconsciously hoped he'd suggest they go someplace else?

"Sure we will, come on." His hand cupped her elbow as he directed her toward the back of the house. His touch was gentle, assuring, pleasant. While they'd been talking she had studied his hands. They were exceptional. Large, with long tapered fingers and square-cut nails. If she had noticed them before they spoke, she might well have guessed he was a doctor.

"Hey, Adam, who's the pretty girl?" A husky male voice impeded their progress.

Susan felt Adam tense. He dropped his hand from her elbow and let it fall to his side. Although he gave no outward sign, Susan could sense that Adam didn't like the man behind the voice.

"Susan, this is Tony Dutton." The introduction was made grudgingly.

Nodding politely, she purposely didn't offer Tony her hand. He was one of the men she had studied earlier, tittering from one beautiful woman to another dispensing his male charm like a bee collecting nectar from a variety of flowers. Sleek, handsome, a womanizer.

It hadn't taken her more than a minute to recognize his type.

"Tony."

"Hello, Susan." He drawled her name as he did an appreciative sweep of her appearance. His gaze paused on her full breasts and then her soft mouth. "Just where have you been all night?"

"With Adam." She hoped to convey her lack of interest in the clipped reply.

"If you'll excuse us," Adam inserted, his hand again gripping the underside of her elbow.

Tony looked taken aback for a moment, but he quickly recovered and gave Adam a bold wink. "Sure thing, good buddy, sure thing."

Again Adam gave no outward sign, but Susan knew he was repulsed. He directed her through the small groups that were milling around chatting. He stopped at the entrance to the kitchen and held open the swinging mahogany door.

"Betsy will make us a cup of coffee."

A large-busted woman of about fifty was preparing a tray of hors d'oeuvres. She turned at the sound of someone intruding on her territory, the blue eyes stormy. But the minute she recognized Adam, the frown turned to a wide grin.

"Dr. Gallagher," she exclaimed in delight. The high-pitched voice was filled with devotion. "I wondered if you'd come back to see ol' Betsy."

"I couldn't very well leave without saying hello to my favorite girl, could I?" he joked, giving the older woman a bear hug.

"Oh, be away with you." Betsy laughed, and a dancing gleam sprang from the tired face. "I suppose you're after a piece of my apple pie again."

"Not this time," Adam said, and moved slowly to Susan's side. He reached out and took her hand; the touch, although impersonal, produced a warmth within her. She was beginning to feel some of the things her writers spun stories about.

"Susan and I would like a cup of that marvelous coffee you brew."

Hand on her hip, Betsy glared at him mockingly. "Excellent brewed coffee, indeed," she quipped. "Been serving the same brand around this house for ten years. Nothing fancy, either," she mumbled under her breath as she brought down two mugs from the cupboard. "Comes straight from a can."

With a boyish grin creasing the grooves at the sides of his mouth, Adam pulled out a kitchen chair for Susan.

"I'll take care of that, Betsy."

"Sit down," the gray-haired woman ordered. "I won't have anyone fiddling in my kitchen but me."

Adam's gaze met Susan's, and the quirk of his thick brows showed his amusement.

No more than a minute passed and they were served mugs of steaming coffee and thick slices of apple pie with hot cinnamon sauce. Susan wasn't hungry, but she wouldn't have offended the older woman. The pie was delicious.

Adam carried their plates to the sink when they'd finished, and kissed Betsy on the cheek. Susan watched as the woman flushed with pleasure. Lifting the glass coffee pot, he brought it to the table and refilled their cups.

Susan leaned back in the chair and held the mug with both hands.

"Here." Adam sat beside her and lifted her feet onto his knees. "If you take these off, you'll be able to relax.

Nothing can ruin an evening more than shoes that are too tight." Carefully, he unbuckled the strap and slipped the sandal off her foot, letting it drop to the floor. Gently his fingers massaged the toes, the circular motion extending to the arch of her foot. The gentle rotating action was repeated on the other foot.

The ache all but disappeared as a tingling sensation ran up the back of her legs. Susan felt her throat tightening as she struggled not to purr. The sensations he was producing in her were incredible. The feather-light touch was strangely, inexplicably intimate. She lowered her lashes because to look at him would reveal the havoc his touch was playing on her senses.

"Are you asleep?" The question was whispered.

"If I am, I don't want to wake up," she answered in a subdued, husky voice.

"Me either." The words were issued so quietly that Susan wasn't sure he'd spoken.

She opened her eyes to watch his gaze move slowly over her.

"You're very beautiful." He'd stopped massaging her feet. "Those eyes are fantastic. I don't think I've see anything so brown in my life."

From any other man it would have sounded like a line designed for its devastating effect. But not from Adam.

"Your hair is the same warm shade as your eyes. I imagine I'm not the first man who's wanted to run his fingers through it."

Their gazes met and held, and for an unbelievable moment Susan felt as if she'd never need to take another breath. Again she was forced to restrain herself. It took every dictate of her will to keep from standing and pulling the combs from her hair to allow the long chocolate brown curtain to fall free. Her heart was pounding so loud she was sure he must hear it. His gaze lowered to rest on her generous mouth. He didn't need to voice his thoughts; they were there for her to read.

A dish clanged against the counter in the background, breaking the spell. Adam shifted uneasily and looked away. "Want some more coffee?"

Susan shook her head because speaking would have been impossible.

"I'll buckle these for you." Leaning over, he gripped the straps of one black leather sandal and slipped it onto her foot.

"You make me feel like Cinderella." Susan had attempted to make a joke, but her voice sounded incredibly weak.

"I'm no Prince Charming." The cynical tone of his voice surprised her.

A frown of confusion knit her brow. "Is something wrong?"

He paused, compressing his mouth into a thin line. "No. I'm sorry."

"Adam." Her hand reached out, and her fingertips gently stroked the angular line of his jaw. "Would you kiss me?"

He caught his breath audibly, his eyes burning into hers. "Now? Here?"

A smile tugged at her mouth as he nodded in answer to both questions.

His eyes turned a deeper shade of brown as he stood, looking around him.

Susan's gaze followed his. Betsy was busy at the kitchen sink, her back to them. At the moment Susan wouldn't have cared if they'd been in the middle of the living room with its tens of guests; all she knew was that she didn't want to wait another minute to discover what it would be like to taste his mouth once it was placed over hers.

"Outside." An arm around her waist led her out the back door. A dim light illuminated the cement patio. At least, Susan thought it was a light; maybe it was the moon.

There wasn't much time to survey their surroundings before Adam slipped his arms around her and brought her against the muscular hardness of his chest. His hold tightened and his mouth moved closer.

Susan linked her arms around his neck and stood on tiptoe, anticipating the union of their mouths. Adam didn't rush the process. His eyes seemed to burn into hers. The tip of her tongue moistened suddenly dry lips, and with a muted groan, Adam lowered his mouth to hers.

The kiss was soft and gentle, as if she were as delicate and precious as fine porcelain. Parting her lips in welcome, Susan yielded. A rush of intense pleasure washed over her and left her trembling. The kiss deepened as his hands roamed over her back, arching her closer and closer as if he wanted to fuse them together for eternity.

When Adam dragged his mouth from hers and buried it against the side of her neck, Susan felt cheated. This shouldn't end; it was too beautiful, too right. She was on the brink of discovering in a few short minutes more of what it meant to be a woman than she had in all her twenty-four years.

She was conscious of the pressure of his body pressing against her and of Adam's uneven breaths. Had he felt it too? Surely he must have…certainly he knew. She gave a small protesting moan as he pulled away.

His hands moved to her upper arms as he took in deep, ragged breaths.

"You are very kissable," he murmured, his eyes half-closed. "But then, I imagine more than one man has told you that."

Several had, but Susan didn't want to think about anyone or anything except Adam. How could she possibly hope to explain that she felt more wonderful with him than she had with any man…ever. Was it conceivable that she could be falling in love with someone she had met that night and had kissed only once? Even to herself it sounded ludicrous.

Placing two fingers over Adam's lips, she hoped to silence him. "Your mouth is equally desirable." Leaning forward slightly, she softly pressed her lips over his. His hands tightened as if to restrain her, but the tenseness quickly flowed from him. Instead of pushing her away as she was sure he intended, he gathered her to him, holding her in his embrace. One palm rested over his heart and Susan sighed as she felt the erratic hammering beat. The flame that was blazing within her had touched him too. She couldn't remember a time she felt more happy, more content.

"Susan." Her name had become a gentle caress as he held her, his chin resting on the crown of her head.

She breathed in deeply, drinking in the scent of musk and cinnamon.

"We should be getting back," he said, and she could feel his mouth move against her hair. The reluctance in his voice made her want to sing.

"We've probably been missed by now."

"Probably," Adam said with a sigh.

But neither moved, unwilling to break their embrace. Just knowing that he was sharing these same inexplicable feelings excited her almost as much as being in his arms.

"Are you cold?" Adam questioned as if suddenly conscious that the early-October night might be uncomfortable on her bare shoulders. His hands ran up and down the silky length of her arms in an effort to chase away any chill.

Susan couldn't prevent the small laugh. "Cold? Are you joking?"

"I guess that was a silly question." Adam spoke softly.

Silence stretched between them. The party would be breaking up soon, and although he continued to physically hold her, Susan could sense him mentally withdrawing. The horrible sensation that they would part tonight and she would never see him again tightened the muscles of her abdomen. The thought, even after this short a time, was intolerable. Yet Adam said nothing, made no suggestion they meet.

"Can I see you again?" she asked with an eagerness she didn't often reveal. "Tomorrow?" she asked with a half smile.

"I'm on duty at the hospital in the afternoon." He drew away, dark eyes narrowed on her face.

"Morning's fine. I'm an early riser." Normally she was anything but. It wasn't often that she could think clearly without a minimum of two cups of strong coffee.

"I've got a soccer game."

"You play soccer?" He'd be a natural. Tall, lean, quick. For a moment the image of Adam running down a field, manipulating the ball with agile feet flashed through her mind.

"I coach a team for the Boys' Club." He drew in a deep breath. "Not tomorrow, maybe sometime next week. I'll give you a call." The softness had left his face.

Stunned for a moment, Susan stared at him disbelievingly. His mood had changed so quickly. "You're giving me the brush-off, aren't you?" She had come on strong, a lot stronger than she did with others. Some men didn't like that. Adam was obviously one of them.

"I'm not." Just the way he said it told her he was lying.

Susan took a step in retreat, studying him in the soft moonlight. She clenched her hands nervously. A chill that had nothing to do with the weather raised tiny bumps over her forearms. For the first time she saw displeasure in Adam's features. His jaw was clenched and tight; a muscle twitched by the corner of his eye.

"Don't worry, I get the message. Don't call me; I'll call you." She laughed tightly. Pride dictated that she hold her head high; her chin was tilted at a slight angle. "I've got better things to do than wait around for a phone call."

"I'm sure you do." The words sounded grim, final. "I enjoyed meeting you, Susan. I wish you well."

"Oh, me too," she replied flippantly. "It's been grand, just grand." With a sweeping gesture Loretta Young would have envied, Susan turned. "Now if you'll excuse me."

"Of course."

The back door closed and Susan thought it must have weighed three thousand pounds. It felt so heavy and hard. But then, so did her heart. Pausing just inside the kitchen, she glanced out the window. Adam remained exactly as she'd left him, a solitary figure standing in the moonlight. His shoulders had hunched, and she watched as he wiped a weary hand over his face. Indecision and some kind of inner turmoil seemed to be troubling him.

"Mighty fine man." A voice sliced into Susan's thoughts, and she swiveled her attention around.

"Pardon?"

Betsy was wiping her hands on a linen dish towel. "I said Dr. Gallagher is a fine man."

"I'm sure he is." Susan meant that sincerely.

"Not much to look at though." The older woman chuckled, but her eyes were serious as they seemed to appraise Susan. "That means a lot to some people. My Ben was a good-looker. Biggest mistake of my life was marrying that man. Caused me nothing but heartache all his life."

"Looks aren't everything," Susan agreed, walking across the kitchen. "Thanks for the coffee and pie, Betsy."

The woman's gaze followed her. "Good night, miss."

"Good night." The words nearly stuck in her throat.

"Did you have a good time last night?" A sleepy, disheveled Rosemary Thomas sauntered into the cozy living room and looked questioningly at Susan early the next morning. Rosemary was employed in Silhouette's contract department, and the two shared a tiny one-bedroom apartment off east Eighty-Eighth Street.

"As good as can be expected." Susan sat sideways on the sofa, burrowing her feet beneath the opposite cushion as she sipped from a steaming mug of coffee. The dark liquid burned her lips, and she blew into the cup before taking another drink. The coffee was bitter. "Meet anyone?" Rosemary persisted while pouring herself a cup. Long auburn hair tumbled over her flannel nightgown.

The dark eyes widened. "What makes you say that?" Rosemary shrugged one delicate shoulder. "I don't know, you look different. Brooding, like you ate too much pâté or met Mr. Wonderful."

"I didn't eat the pâté, and I've given up on the dream of ever finding Mr. Wonderful."

"Do my ears deceive me?" Rosemary placed a hand dramatically over her heart. "How can a romance editor forsake Mr. Wonderful?"

"Mr. Wonderful's an illusion," Susan announced, turning her head to avoid looking at her friend. "I'm looking for Mr. Nice Guy."

Rosemary sat in the worn chair covered in the same material as the sofa. She lifted her knees and pulled the long nightgown down over her legs.

"What did you do with your hair?" Susan asked, noticing for the first time the way the auburn curls seemed to spring in every direction. "You look like you stuck your finger in a light socket."

Rosemary giggled good-naturedly. "I gave myself a perm last night. I think I may have left the solution on a bit longer than necessary."

A smile threatened to crack the tight line of Susan's mouth. "You may have."

"Doing anything this weekend?" Rosemary asked, taking her first sip of coffee. She paused to grimace. "What'd you make this with? Shoe polish?"

"No to both," Susan answered evenly.

"I think I'll head out after breakfast. It's Mom's birthday Wednesday, and she'll be disappointed if l don't spend some time with her. You're welcome to come if you want."

With a quick shake of her head, Susan declined the invitation to visit her friend's family in New Jersey. Her hair flowed unrestrained down her back and seemed to dance with the movement. "I've got some proposals I want to go over this weekend." Bringing work home from the office was essential in order to keep current with the demanding load. Working with as many as fifty authors made it impossible to find the time to read all the material she wanted and give it her undivided attention. Therein lay the root of the problem. Constant interruptions were all part of being an editor.

The remainder of the weekend passed in a dull shade of gray. With Rosemary gone, Susan spent the rest of Saturday and all day Sunday going over material from the slush pile. Some of the best authors Silhouette published had started out by submitting unsolicited material. One of the most fulfilling aspects of her job was the chance to spot and develop new writing talent. Wednesday afternoon, Susan did something that shocked her. She phoned the Boys' Club and discovered the youth soccer games were played at nine and ten-thirty on Saturday mornings in Central Park.

If she felt like a fool then, she felt more of an idiot the next Saturday as she zipped up a baby blue warmup jacket and headed for the park.

"Why am I doing this?" she repeatedly asked herself as she walked the distance. Brilliant fall colors cloaked the avenue as multicolored trees lined the entrance. The day was glorious. One of the few remaining Indian summer days that would grace New York, Susan thought. At least it wasn't pouring rain. If she planned on running into Adam, she had to make it look as if she were on a casual stroll enjoying the weather.

The soccer fields were on one end of the Great Lawn, exactly where the man at the Boys' Club had said they would be. A quick glance at her watch, and Susan noted it was ten to nine. She hadn't been up before nine on a Saturday morning in six months; Rosemary would be shocked to wake and find her gone.

The playing fields were chalk lined. She didn't know that much about soccer, except what she'd read the night before in the encyclopedia. It seemed to be a natural sport for young children and didn't require much finesse or skill. Only the ability to run and kick. As she advanced toward the fields, Susan picked out Adam easily. He stood head and shoulders above and in several cases was a couple of feet taller than the nine- or ten-year-old boys on the team.

Just watching him, even from this distance, did something to her heart. What was it about this man that had haunted her all week? She couldn't sleep without dreaming of Adam. And if the nights were bad, the days were worse. There hadn't been a single day that she didn't force herself to rein in her thoughts or force Adam's image from her mind. What had happened that night at Ralph Jordan's for him to suddenly pull back, withdraw from her? In the beginning she was sure it was because she'd come on so strong. Some men preferred shy, retiring females. But there had been nothing that evening to indicate that those were his views. After all, she had been the one to make the first move and introduce herself. That had seemed to please him. She had even asked him to kiss her. Color invaded her face at the memory, creeping up from her neck. Even then he had shown no displeasure. Everything had seemed to indicate that he was as caught up in this attraction as she.

This whole thing was probably an occupational hazard for her, something that came as the result of reading thousands of romances. Leaning back against a huge oak tree with one foot propped against the bark, Susan expelled her breath slowly. That's not what it was and she knew it. She had been attracted to Adam Gallagher physically, mentally and spiritually almost from the moment she'd first seen him.

The players were on the field, and at the sound of the official's whistle one player ran forward and the ball was kicked. Knobby-kneed boys raced from one end to the other with boundless energy. Even from her position, camouflaged by the trees, Susan discovered she couldn't remain unaffected. Several times she kicked her own foot as if the movement would aid the players. When Adam's team scored the first goal, Susan all but leaped in the air with excitement.

On more than one occasion Adam cupped his mouth to shout instructions to his team. She might have been out of earshot, but it was easy to see these boys adored him.

Sometimes—Susan didn't know why—the action was stopped and a boy would step onto one of the sidelines and throw the soccer ball onto the field. Immediately a fierce scramble would result and the game would resume.

The official's whistle blew, and for a moment Susan thought the game had ended. Instead the players ran off the field and Adam's boys huddled around him. Adam knelt on one knee in front of the group.

Half time, she mused. The second half of the game proved to be as exciting as the first. Adam's team won the game, and Susan couldn't restrain her sense of pride. Her intention had been to saunter past him casually and act shocked that they happened to run into one another.

Now she realized she couldn't do it. Turning, she stuck her hands in her pockets and headed toward the sidewalk, her feet kicking up the leaves as she walked.

Ten-fifteen and the park was alive. She took a deep breath of the autumn air.

"Susan." Someone was shouting her name.

She turned to see Adam running toward her with long strides. He was slightly breathless when he caught up with her.

If she'd hoped for a friendly greeting, she was in for a disappointment. His eyes were dark and brooding. Forbidding.

"What are you doing here?"

Two

"Oh, hi. Adam, isn't it?" Susan hoped to give an impression of indifference.

But the knowing look his eyes flashed at her told her she hadn't fooled him. Yet she persisted in the charade. "I just happened to be enjoying a walk and stumbled onto the soccer game. You have a good team. Nice day, isn't it?"

"Beautiful." Adam smiled ruefully.

"Well, I won't keep you. I've got some errands to do," she said with forced cheerfulness. "It was good seeing you again. Give Ralph my best." She offered him a weak smile and turned. He's actually going to let me leave, her mind screamed. He's going to let me walk away without saying a word! She kicked at the leaves with the toe of her shoe, angry with him and the world.

She didn't need to turn around to realize he was standing there watching her. His eyes seemed to be boring holes into her shoulder blades.

Without even knowing she would do anything so

crazy, Susan collapsed to the ground. Totally relaxed, she slumped onto a huge mound of leaves the parks department had collected.

"Susan."

Never had she heard so much emotion in the simple sound of her name.

The clamor of running footsteps followed. At precisely the right moment, she turned and threw a huge handful of maple leaves into his face.

Adam looked stunned, his hands fighting off the attack of foliage. Before he could recover, she stood, picked up another armload and tossed those at him.

Susan was laughing harder than she could remember doing in a long time.

Adam stared back at her in bewilderment. "What did you do that for?"

"Because I couldn't stand for us to talk to one another like polite strangers," she yelled. "What's the matter, don't you like to fight?" Bending down, she scooped up more leaves, preparing to do battle.

She never got the chance. One gentle push against her hip toppled her onto the soft pile. Immediately she was deluged with leaves as Adam dumped several armloads over her head.

In an effort to escape, she rolled onto her side, kicking up the leaves as she turned. Laughter hindered her movement, and a second later Adam had joined her on the ground, his hands pinning her to the earth.

Her breasts heaving with the effort to breathe evenly, she gazed into the powerful face that had haunted her all week. Amusement glittered from his dark eyes, and the corners of his mouth were quivering. Their looks met, and the world about them seemed to fade into oblivion. The leaves, the sun, the trees were gone, as were the sounds that filled the heart of Central Park in New York City. The hold on her hand relaxed, and Adam brushed the hair from the side of her face. His touch was gentle, sweet. The laughter had left his face as his attention centered on her softly parted lips.

Susan inhaled deeply, anticipating the union of their mouths. He didn't want to kiss her; she could see it in the determined set of his jaw. But at the same time, he couldn't stop himself. The knowledge thrilled her, and instinctively her arms curved around his back as he lowered his head.

The kiss renewed every sensation she had experienced the night they met. Somehow deep inside she'd been hoping it had been the wine or the romantic surroundings. The memory of being held in his arms and standing in the moonlight filled her thoughts. But she was kidding herself. This was real, so real and wonderful. Magic.

She hadn't realized she'd whispered the word until Adam raised his head, his look quizzical. "Magic?" he repeated.

She smiled and nodded, her hand fitted over his cheek; the growth of day-old beard gently prickled the skin of her palm.

Adam released her and sat up. He linked his hands around bent knees and stared into the distance.

Susan joined him, sitting in the same position. "Why?" she murmured softly. There wasn't any need to explain the question. The one word asked so much. Why had he made it plain he didn't want to see her again after the party? Why had he looked so unwelcoming when she'd come to the park? And why was he so reluctant to kiss her?

"I knew someone like you once," he began, and there was a deep sadness in his voice. Still he didn't turn to look at her. "Gail was as beautiful as you are."

"Pretty girls are a dime a dozen." She shrugged her shoulders and looped a long strand of hair around her ear. The movement captured Adam's attention. "She had the most incredibly thick auburn hair."

Susan hated her already. "Mine's brown." Expelling her breath forcefully, she rested her chin on top of one knee.

Adam didn't seem to notice her; he was entangled in his own thoughts. So he'd been hurt, she thought, probably jilted; maybe his red-haired beauty was dead. None of it had anything to do with her. Unless…unless he had been pretending he was holding Gail, kissing Gail.

"Are you still in love with her?" she questioned bluntly, desperately needing to know.

Adam looked taken aback for a moment. "I don't think so. No." He shook his head, adding emphasis to the response.

"Well, that's encouraging." She didn't mean to sound ill-mannered, but love's course hadn't been all that smooth for her either. She didn't know that it was for anyone.

She bounded to her feet, suddenly angry. The one thing she thoroughly detested was being confused with someone else, especially when that someone else happened to be his one true love. "It was nice seeing you again, Adam. As always, it was an adventure."

He stood too, brushing the leaves from his pants. He started to say something but she interrupted him.

"The name's Susan, in case you forget. That's S-U-S-A-N. It doesn't even come close to Gail. And the hair's brown, dark brown." She weaved her fingers through its length. "And for that matter, I'm not all that beautiful. My nose is a little odd. But you hold on to the illusion of Ms. Perfect. I'd hate to be the one to force you to come to terms with reality." Pivoting sharply, she strode with purpose-filled steps out of the park. He didn't try to stop her. Somehow she knew he wouldn't.

Susan lifted her eyeglasses and pinched the corners of her eyes with her thumb and index finger. This job was definitely taking its toll on her eyes. She coughed.

Her health too. The little romp in the damp leaves last Saturday had resulted in a horrible cold. That's what she got for behaving like an idiot. A sneeze was coming, and Susan grabbed a tissue just before the gigantic burst of air shook her body.

Another violent sneeze caught Rosemary's attention that night. "You know what you need, don't you?"

If Susan heard about the wonders of vitamin C one more time she thought she'd scream. Her roommate had been on a health-food kick for weeks. For her own part, Susan felt she ate a balanced diet, half good food and half junk food. "I can't imagine what, Dr. Pauling."

Rosemary had the good grace to look slightly

abashed. "Well, yes, vitamin C would help, but what would really help is some good old-fashioned exercise."

"That's how I got into this mess in the first place, if you recall."

Rosemary shook her head. The perm had been tamed considerably and was styled attractively, feathered away from the petite oval face.

"I'm serious," her friend said forcefully. "What you need is to get those endorphins pumping through your body."

Susan sighed and shook her head scornfully. "Endorphins? Have you been reading too many Intimate Moments again?"

"I can't believe anyone can graduate from Cornell and not know what endorphins are."

Susan sneezed again. Her throat ached and her eyes were beginning to water. She couldn't miss any work; her desk was stacked high enough as it was. She looked at Rosemary, who was bright and cheerful while she felt wretched. "All right, tell me all about it." She might as well capitulate. From the look in her eye, Rosemary would tell her anyway. Why fight it?

"Endorphins are a secretion your body produces that gives you a natural high, both physical and mental. I was reading about it in one of the books I picked up from the health-food store. The book said that exercising will actually make you feel good. That's why I've started to walk to work."

For over a month Rosemary had trekked the two and a half miles to The Avenue of the Americas every week-day morning. Susan had scoffed and been far more interested in sleeping the extra forty-five minutes. Maybe Rosemary's ideas weren't so loony after all.

Her friend was as fit as an Olympic runner, and Susan felt steps away from missing a week's work.

She sat on the sofa and leaned her head against the back cushion. "I feel awful," she admitted verbally for the first time.

"Scratchy sore throat? Eyes burning? Ears plugged?" Rosemary questioned softly.

Weakly, Susan nodded and placed two hands over her breasts. "I think my chest is tightening up too."

"I can help," Rosemary said with a cheerful note. "In fact, I can absolutely guarantee every cold symptom will be gone by tomorrow morning."

Susan lifted her head and tilted her chin at a disbelieving angle. "Guarantee?"

"Absolutely," Rosemary confirmed. "But you have to trust me."

Trust Rosemary? What did she have in mind? "What do you mean?"

Rosemary plopped down in the chair opposite Susan. "There's a way. I promise it'll work, but it won't be pleasant and you'll have to do everything I say."

"Everything?"

"Everything. Are you game?"

A fit of uncontrollable sneezes convinced her she was. "Oh, all right, let's get it over with." She coughed. "And the sooner the better."

A half hour later Susan couldn't believe what was happening to her. Rosemary had insisted Susan change into her pajamas and housecoat. Then she'd hung a huge head of garlic around her neck and applied the most horrible-smelling gook over her chest.

"It's made with mustard," Rosemary explained. "Wonderful stuff, it'll draw the poison right out of your system."

Susan murmured something sarcastic under her breath, but chose not to voice her serious doubts in front of her friend. "This better work, Rosemary. That's all I can say."

"Trust me," she declared, leading Susan into the bathroom.

"There's more?" she protested loudly, and the garlic bounced against the mustard plaster, cracking it.

"Trust me."

"For heaven's sake, is that all you can say?"

"Sit," she ordered, and helped lower Susan onto the edge of the bathtub. She left, only to return a moment later with a steaming bucket of water. Immediately the small room was filled with the scent of lemons and spice. At least it helped kill the garlic odor.

"Lean forward," Rosemary instructed next. "It's important for you to breathe in as much of this as possible."

Releasing a troubled breath, Susan did as she asked, taking in deep breaths of the rising steam.

"That's not going to work." Rosemary's voice held an impatient edge. "Here, this should fix it." She draped a thick towel over Susan's head.

"How long do I have to sit like this?" The words sounded muffled even to her own ears, and she lifted the towel to be sure her friend had heard.

Scratching her head, Rosemary quirked her mouth to

one side. "I don't know. Let me check the book again. Keep your head down until I get back."

"Wonderful, just wonderful," Susan muttered, feeling wretched. "This had better work, Rosemary. And if you dare say a word to anyone…"

"I wouldn't, don't worry." Mockingly, she crossed her heart. "Now keep your head down."

Obediently, Susan replaced the towel and sat in a dejected heap on the edge of the bathtub, breathing in the citrus-scented steam.

Somewhere in the distance she heard a buzzer. It sounded as if it had come from the stove in the kitchen. Susan groaned inwardly, wondering what other wild concoctions Rosemary assumed she could get away with. As it was, she'd about had it.

"Susan, it's for you."

Her fingers gripping the edge of the towel, she lifted her head and peered out. "What's for me?"

"The door."

"The door?" she repeated, dumbfounded, and as she did her heart leaped wildly to her throat. Adam Gallagher moved into her line of vision, standing directly behind Rosemary.

"Hello, Susan. It's Adam, spelled A-D-A-M."

Immediately Susan lowered her head, hiding under the towel. "Rosemary," she shouted, "do something."

"I didn't know he was following me," Rosemary defended her actions. "I thought he'd sit down."

Apparently her friend found it necessary to exonerate herself.

"I should have," Adam said, a smile evident in his

voice. "But I confess to being curious about a certain smell that seemed to be coming from this room."

"Would you two mind leaving?" Susan screamed, and seethed silently. Nothing in the world could induce her to remove the towel. She would prefer to sit and evaporate in the steam than have Adam see her like this.

At the sound of the door closing, Susan ripped the garlic from her throat and let the towel fall to the floor. Dear heaven, she'd never be able to look Adam in the eye again. How would she ever live this down? Both hands covered her face as she sat in misery.

A couple of minutes later there was a light tap on the door. Without waiting for a response, Rosemary stuck in her head.

The thin line of each delicately shaped brow was arched in question. "You're not mad, are you?"

Susan gestured weakly with one hand. "Why should I be? Just because I was made to look like a complete idiot? Just look at me, Rosemary." She held up two limp strands of wet hair, and her voice wobbled. "How could you do this to me?"

"I'm sorry, Susan. Really sorry."

Dismissing the apology with a wave of her hand, Susan turned toward the bathtub. "I'm going to do what I should have done in the first place. Take a hot bath, down two aspirin and go to bed. And if there's a merciful God in heaven, I'll die peacefully in my sleep and never have to face the world again."

As much as Susan hated to admit it, she felt much better the next morning. Rosemary had already left for work, but there was a note waiting for Susan beside the coffee pot on the kitchen counter. It read: "Hope you feel better. Adam wanted me to ask if you'd meet him tonight, six o'clock at Tastings for a drink. I would have said something last night, but I didn't think you were in the frame of mind to talk to me. I don't blame you. Hope to see you later. Rosie."

Her frame of mind last night had been strictly forbidding. After a long soak in a hot bath, Susan had gone directly to bed. Rosemary had watched her anxiously as Susan walked from the bathroom to the bedroom. But the tight set of Susan's mouth had apparently convinced Rosemary to leave well enough alone.

Susan picked up the piece of paper, crumpled it and tossed it into the garbage can. Every encounter she'd had with Dr. Adam Gallagher had been disastrous. Why make a fool of herself again? She wouldn't go.

By the time she broke for lunch that afternoon, Susan had decided she was behaving childishly. Of course she'd meet Adam. Wasn't that why she'd gone to Central Park Saturday morning?

Sure, she countered mentally, but that was before she knew about his long-lost love and how much she reminded him of Gail. Her mind spat out the name distastefully.

At five-thirty, Susan cleared her desk, or as much of it as she could. There seemed to be a sense of never really being finished. There were always more manuscripts, more correspondence, more stories. If she didn't love the work and New York, her job could have depressed her. Instead she was challenged.

No, she wouldn't meet him. What was the use? She wouldn't be a stand-in for any woman.

Making polite conversation in the elevator with her co-workers, Susan wasn't sure what she was saying or even to whom she was speaking. Her thoughts were muddled. Her heart was telling her she should meet Adam. But the more practical part of her personality was issuing repeated warnings that pursuing a relationship with him would eventually lead to pain and heartache.

Without ever admitting to herself that she would or wouldn't accept the invitation, Susan strolled toward Tastings, a popular restaurant six blocks up the street from the Simon and Schuster Building. She preferred to think that she was leaving her options open. At any time she could turn around and head for the apartment. Early October and the day was glorious. The air was crisp, and she stuffed her hands into her long beige raincoat. Her heels clicked against the cement walk as she strode purposefully along her way.

Adam was arriving just as she got there. Maybe if Susan hadn't seen him, hadn't felt the physical stirrings just looking at him created in her, maybe then she wouldn't have kept the appointment. But she did see him. He was there, walking toward her with a wide grin that was directed at her alone. And like a magnet drawn to steel, she returned his warm greeting with a smile of her own.

"Hello, Susan."

"Adam." She couldn't look away. He really was plain looking. He was tall but muscular, and his wide shoulders narrowed to lean hips and long, long legs. Plain, but compelling in a way she couldn't describe.

"I see you're feeling better," he said with a smile. "Your roommate mentioned you were under the weather."

Susan flushed, silently praying that he wouldn't say anything about last night. "Yes, much better. Thank you."

A low chuckle rumbled from his throat. "The wonders of modern medicine never cease to amaze me. I was rather shocked to discover such advancements since I left medical school."

"Adam Gallagher." Susan stopped mid-step. "If you so much as mention one word about last night, I'll leave."

A large hand cupped her elbow as a mesmerizing smile crinkled the lines at the corner of his eyes. "No more, I promise."

Tastings was a long and narrow room with emerald green tablecloths on the square tables. One wall contained a huge wood bar with upholstered stools. Behind the bar was a glass case containing the hundreds of bottles of expensive wines Tastings was known for. It was a popular place to meet for drinks. Although it was early evening, the room was nearly filled. Adam found an empty table and helped her out of her coat. He folded it along with his own over the back of a chair. A waitress took their order and returned a couple of minutes later with Susan's California Cabernet Sauvignon and Adam's French Beaujolais Nouveau.

Adam cupped the long-stemmed glass, and again

Susan was impressed with his hands. A smile briefly touched her mouth as she thought there was a magical quality about his fingers. She had known doctors before, had even dated one briefly a couple of years ago. But no one had affected her the way Adam did.

His shoulders were hunched forward slightly, and Susan asked, "Tired?"

He ran a hand over his eyes and nodded. "But it's not the company I keep." His gaze rose to meet hers. "The stork got me out of bed this morning about four. A beautiful baby girl, but the mother had a difficult labor and I wanted to be with her. Her husband left her, and she was alone and needed someone. By the time I finished there, it was time to go to the office."

It's not his hands, Susan mused, but his heart. His capacity to love and care was larger than any man's she had known. He was the kind of person who would carry the whole world on his shoulders if it would help someone.

"We can make it another time if you'd rather," Susan offered.

"No." He reached across the table and squeezed her fingers. "In fact, I don't know about you, but I'm starved. I'm not dressed for anything fancy, but I know where we could find a decent meal."

Susan nodded, pleased at the invitation. "Yes, I'd like that."

He took her to a small restaurant not far from Times Square that served charcoal-broiled hamburgers and fresh-baked bread. The owner shook hands with Adam and personally escorted them to a booth. From the way the man spoke, it was obvious that he'd been a patient.

Adam introduced Susan, and Ambrose Lockridge shook her hand so hard Susan was sure she'd lose feeling in her fingers.

Ambrose wouldn't allow them to order from the menu, insisting he would personally cook the specialty of the house in their honor.

"You'll have to forgive him." Adam looked faintly chagrined. "Ambrose tends to be overenthusiastic."

"I don't mind," Susan insisted, her face gleaming with an inner happiness. Some men would have felt the need to impress her with an extravagant restaurant, but not Adam. In his own way, he was making a statement about himself. He preferred the simple life.

Their seats were situated against the outside wall by a window that ran the length of the building. Susan watched, fascinated, as dusk settled over the most exciting city in the world.

Ambrose delivered hamburgers that looked as tall as the Empire State Building. Melted cheese, sliced pickles, thick slices of tomato, lettuce and a sauce oozed from the sides of the buns. The meat patty alone must have weighed half a pound. One person couldn't possibly manage to eat the entire hamburger.

Susan did her best, downing almost half. Again she discovered how much she liked Adam. He talked for a long time, telling her about his office and the decision to go into family practice, which in itself was a specialty. He told her a little about the woman whose baby he had delivered that morning.

Not until they finished their meal and several cups of rich coffee did he mention Saturday morning. "I feel I owe you an explanation."

Taking a sip from her coffee cup, Susan avoided looking at him. She didn't want to hear about Gail; she wanted to build her own relationship with him. Leave the past buried.

"You don't owe me anything, Adam," she said, hoping to conceal the frustration in her voice. "I got the picture from what you said Saturday."

"I'm sure you thought exactly the wrong thing," he contradicted gently. "I wasn't comparing you to Gail, although there are striking similarities."

"I doubt that very much." Susan took another sip of coffee. The hot liquid felt good against the slight thickening building in her throat.

"I like you, Susan."

He was saying so much more. Susan wished she knew exactly what. Could the attraction he felt for her be half as potent as what she was feeling? She set the cup back on top of the table. "I like you too."

Again his gaze settled on her facial features. "You're a beautiful woman, and I'm not exactly a knight in shining armor."

"I'm not Lady Diana, either," she countered. If it would have made any difference, Susan would have gladly erased the smooth, silky skin, the brilliant brown eyes and gentle curves of her womanhood. With any other man her attractiveness would have been an asset. But not with Adam.

"You're prettier than royalty. Prettier than Gail."

Susan felt as if her heart would burst. She turned her troubled brown eyes toward him. "Did this…other woman hurt you so bad that you can't trust again?" Susan chose not to say her name.

"Gail," he supplied again, as his index finger did a lazy circle around the rim of the cup. "I loved her very much. But I was young and stupid."

Adam may love Gail, Susan thought, but she had never felt such intense dislike for someone in her life. "Here," he said, and took the paper napkin from her hand. "If you don't stop, you'll have that thing shredded to a thousand pieces."

Susan wasn't aware that she had been doing anything to the napkin. "What happened?" she asked. Adam wanted to tell her; maybe it would help him finally obliterate Gail from his memory. Susan, however, wasn't so sure she could sit and listen while he spoke of another woman he had loved so intensely.

Adam's look was thoughtful. "We met when I was in med school."

That long ago! Susan thought with a sense of frustration. Adam had to be thirty-four, maybe thirty-five. He had loved Gail all these years? Involuntarily, she stiffened.

"There's really not much to say except that we fell in love. I fell in love," he corrected. "Gail fell for dollar signs she was sure, were in my future. I should have known a beautiful, popular girl like Gail couldn't really love someone like me."

Susan had to swallow back words so as not to interrupt him. It had been on the tip of her tongue to say

she was half in love with him and they'd only been together three times. Her declaration would have embarrassed them both.

"At the end of my first year we got engaged. A couple of months later my father became seriously ill and I
decided to discontinue my studies and help out at home
until Dad was better. Gail was adamantly opposed to
my leaving school. We had a bitter argument. I couldn't
understand how she could be so uncaring, so heartless
toward my father. I must have been naive, because she
chose to spell it out to me."

Indubitably there was a lot Adam was leaving unsaid.
"Anyway," Adam continued with brooding thoughtful-
ness, "I did go home, and my father died a couple of
weeks later. I was glad I was there. By the time I returned to school, Gail was engaged to another medical student."

"And you still care about her?" The question was
hurled at him in disbelief.

"No." His voice was a soft, caressing whisper. "But
a man doesn't easily forget his first love."

They'd been lovers. The thought was so unbearable
that Susan downed the remainder of her coffee in one
giant swallow. What was the matter with her; was she
going crazy? She had never been the overly jealous
type. At least not until now.

"How can Gail and I possibly be alike?" she questioned grimly.

"In addition to being beautiful, you both have the
tendency to go after what you want. Neither of you is
easily dissuaded."

Pinching her lips tightly closed, Susan released an inward groan. She knew it! They had gotten off to a bad start because she'd been the one to cross the room and introduce herself. She'd asked him to kiss her, and when it looked as if he wasn't going to suggest they meet again, she'd said something. Not only that, but she had another mark against her because she'd gone to Central Park hoping to see him on Saturday. If Adam only knew how extraordinary such behavior was for her. Never, she promised herself, never again would she instigate anything with him.

"I'm not like her, Adam. But that's something you'll have to discover yourself." She straightened and reached for her purse.

For a moment he didn't reply. "I was afraid you thought I was pretending you were Gail when I kissed you. I wasn't." His voice was husky and soft.

Susan doubted he raised his voice to anyone. He was a gentle man. Scooting out from the chair, she stood and reached for her raincoat. "I should be going. Thanks for the drink and dinner," she murmured.

Adam stood and paused to place some money on the table before taking his coat and following her outside. She heard him call something to Ambrose.

The sky was a magnificent purple and pink. Silhouetted against the skyline were huge buildings of concrete and steel. But she hardly noticed.

A hand on her shoulder halted her progress as she moved to the street to wave down a taxi. "Just a minute." Adam expelled his breath forcefully. "I've offended you, haven't I? That wasn't my intention."

Susan already knew that. Adam would never knowingly hurt anyone. "I'm sure it wasn't," she replied
stiffly, keeping her face averted so she could capture
a cab's attention.

"When you're in my arms, Susan, I can think of
little else."

Well, she certainly hoped so! With one foot off the
curb, she looked down the street. Where were the taxis
when she needed one?

"It doesn't matter to me if I'm at a party with tens
of guests, any one of which could step onto the patio. It
doesn't matter that it's the middle of Central Park on a
bright fall morning." The pressure of his hands turned
her around. His eyes were smiling into hers with a mis-
chievous light. Slowly he lowered his mouth to claim
hers in a gentle but surprisingly ardent kiss.

Susan melted into his arms as he wrapped her in his
embrace and half-lifted her from the sidewalk. A soft,
involuntary moan came when he lifted his head, but he
quickly lowered it again, parting her lips with a plundering kiss that sent the world in a tailspin. Obviously
one kiss wasn't enough for him, either.

Susan buried her face in his light jacket and sighed
unevenly. Adam's mouth was pressed against the top of
her head. "What should it matter if I kiss you in mid-
town Manhattan?" It wasn't really a question.

A taxi pulled to the curb. "You looking for a ride?"
he asked in a surly tone.

"Yes," Adam answered for her.

With a determined effort, she dropped her arms.
Adam held open the car door.

"Good night, Susan."

She smiled softly and pressed her fingers to her lips and waved a good-bye. Still caught in the rapture, speaking would have been difficult.

"Where to, lady?"

Susan had to stop a minute before relaying her address.

Not until she was almost home did Susan realize Adam had done it again. No mention had been made of seeing her again. And after what he'd said tonight, she couldn't invent opportunities to see him. For all she knew, Dr. Adam Gallagher was out of her life.

Three

Susan offered Jack Persico an apologetic smile. The bored, frustrated look he shot back didn't encourage her. The evening had been a waste. What was the matter with her? Couldn't she have fun anymore? Why should her life hinge on whether she heard from Adam Gallagher again? She hadn't, and that was the crux of the problem. For over two weeks she'd lived and breathed anticipation. As each hour, each day passed, she grew more uncertain.

"I had a nice time. Thanks, Jack," she murmured flatly, unable to force any enthusiasm into her voice.

"Little liar," he said, and laughed lightly. "What's wrong? Problems at the office?"

Shaking her head, she turned and inserted her key into the lock of her apartment door. "I hope you aren't offended if I don't invite you in, but I really am tired."

"I understand," he told her gently, and in a strange way Susan was sure he did. He gave her a knowing smile and kissed her lightly. One finger trailed a path across her cheek. "I'll give you a call later."

Her throat muscles constricted painfully. "Thanks, Jack." She let herself into the silent apartment. Rosemary had gone out after all, she mused. Leaning heavily against the door, she felt the hopelessness of the situation wash over her. Friday night and she'd turned down two invitations, hoping to hear from Adam. When she didn't, she accepted Jack's casual offer for a movie. A half hour afterward and she couldn't remember the title, let alone the plot. The entire evening had been spent worrying if she was missing a phone call. Maybe Adam had stopped by? Jack and several others were anxious for her company. Why was it the one man that mattered couldn't have cared less? Releasing a slow, uneven breath, she hung up her coat.

Just as she closed the closet door, Rosemary came out of the bathroom, her face covered with a green conglomeration that resembled avocados and mayonnaise.

"Oh, you're back. How was the movie?"

"Great. Any phone calls?"

"One, he didn't leave his name."

Susan's heartbeat nearly tripped over itself. Adam! "Was there a message?"

"No, he said he'd call back later."

Glancing at her wristwatch, Susan asked, "When did he call?"

"About an hour ago," Rosemary mumbled, barely moving her lips as the facial plaster began to slip. "But I don't think it was your doctor friend. This guy sounded sexy."

"Adam's sexy," she shot back heatedly. Her dark eyes flared with defiance.

Rosemary looked stunned for a minute. "I know, what I meant was that this guy's voice was different from Adam's."

"Oh," she whispered, deflated. "What's that on your face?" Maybe if she changed the subject she could gloss over the small outburst.

"Avocados." The timer buzzed, and Rosemary returned to the bathroom.

Susan could hear the faucet running as she glanced over the TV Guide looking for a late, late show to distract her. Nothing but old monster films. Sighing, she tossed the guide on the end table and absently reached for a magazine. Two weeks! Why hadn't Adam called? He couldn't help but know how crazy she was about him. How could he not know? She'd practically thrown herself at him. If she'd given a dozen men half the encouragement she had him, they'd be married by now. Married. The word had slipped into her mind so easily. Almost from the beginning she'd recognized that Adam was what she'd been searching for in a husband. That gentle, caring quality about him made him so attractive to her.

The clock radio went off early the next morning and Rosemary groaned in protest. "Susan," she mumbled. "It's Saturday. Turn the radio off."

Stretching out a hand, Susan fumbled with the switch that killed the music. One eye fluttered open to note the time—seven fifty-five. She hadn't been kidding herself; the alarm had been purposely set. Perhaps that had been Adam phoning last night. Then it'd be entirely proper for her to contact him in return. And since she'd been thinking about how good an early morning walk in Central Park would be for her health, there was no better time than Saturday morning. If she just happened to run into Adam coaching his soccer team, then that would be the perfect time to ask.

Slipping out of bed, she grabbed jeans and a sweater and silently walked into the bathroom. With luck she could be out the door before Rosemary knew she was gone. Since she was unable to fool herself, she wasn't likely to outsmart Rosemary. In addition, she didn't feel like answering questions this early in the morning. As far as this health-food kick went, most of which Susan thought of as silly, she did agree with Rosemary on the importance of eight hours sleep. Something she rarely got, especially when they sat up to 3:00 A.M. playing Monopoly. And people thought editors lived glamorous lives.

Forty-five minutes later, fortified with several cups of strong coffee, Susan let herself out the apartment door. A chill ran up her arms as the crisp October air hit her face. One look at the threatening dark sky and she cringed. Only for Adam; there wasn't another reason on earth she'd be out this early on a Saturday morning. Her breath formed a foggy curtain as brisk strides carried her into the park. After the initial chill, she had quickly become accustomed to the cold. Even walking had been pleasant. Maybe Rosemary wasn't so loony after all, and a little exercise was just the thing she needed. No, quickly she dismissed the thought. No need to be hasty.

After a few minutes of following the meandering cement walkway into the park's interior, she saw Adam. Pausing, hands clenched tightly in her pockets, she stopped and watched him for several moments. Her gaze was drawn to the craggy features, the proud look. It was unfair that after two miserable weeks she should be this affected by him. One glance and she felt relief flood through her.

Standing on the sidelines of the soccer field, Adam was talking to his team. Everyone clapped their hands once and ran onto the field. Even Adam. Dressed in jeans and a gray sweatshirt, he stood in front of the boys, who were in an orderly line. Even from the distance she could hear his shouts as he called and counted the exercises. First they did jumping jacks. Adam's arms flew into the air in perfect rhythm with his boys. Blood pounded in her veins at the virile sight he made. Pride touched her heart at the way the boys respected him. Much the same as she did.

Hoping to look as casual as possible, she strolled to the field and stood on the sideline. Her toe played with the chalk line that bordered the field. When she glanced up, her eyes met Adam's. She knew hers were round and a little apprehensive, but her doubts quickly faded at the welcome in his.

He shouted something to one of the boys, who ran forward and took his place. Agilely he trotted from the field to her side.

"Hi."

"Morning." She glanced away, fearing he'd read the eagerness she felt.

"I was hoping you'd come."

He was hoping she'd come! Her mind tossed back the words bitterly. For two miserable weeks she'd heard nothing from him. She'd turned down dates, sat by her phone, toyed with a hundred crazy excuses to see him, and he said he was hoping she'd come! Of their own volition, her eyes shot him an angry glare.

Surprise flickered briefly over his face. "Is something wrong?"

"Nothing," she lied. "I got a phone call last night. Rosemary said she thought it might have been you."

"No," he said casually, "it wasn't me."

No need to fool herself; she'd known it hadn't been. Inhaling deeply, she hoped to calm herself and fight off the attack of indignation. "It seemed like such a nice morning for a walk. I didn't mean to intrude."

"You're not," he assured her quickly, and exhaled a slow breath. "Are you always this beautiful in the morning?"

Beautiful! She'd barely worn any makeup, just a light application of lip gloss. Her hair was brushed away from her face and held in place with two barrettes. A hurried glance in the mirror on her way out the door had assured her that he wouldn't think she was planning to meet anyone.

Struggling for a witty reply, she murmured, "You should see me before I've downed two cups of coffee."

"I'd like that very much."

The words were issued so softly that Susan wasn't

sure he'd said anything. But the way her heart somersaulted into her throat assured her she hadn't imagined it. When she turned to search his face, she found that his gaze was directed onto the field.

"We're going to need lots of encouragement today. We're playing the first-place team."

"Terrific," she said, and beamed him a smile. "I'll have you know I was a high-school cheerleader."

"It doesn't surprise me," he returned. "I suppose your school team went to the state championship."

"No." A puzzled frown marred her brow. "Why?"

"If I'd been on that team, I'd have played my heart out for you."

"You're on my team now, coach. So let's win this game."

Chuckling, Adam ran back onto the field.

As before, Susan was quickly caught up in the action of the game as the young boys ran back and forth kicking the black and white ball. Several calls made by the officials confused her, but rather than break Adam's concentration by quizzing him, she said nothing. But anytime Adam's boys had the ball, she gave her full support by shouting. As soon as she heard one of the boys' names, she called encouragements to him. The game was clearly a defensive one, and neither team had scored by half time.

The boys hurried and got a drink from the water faucet before gathering around Adam. Down on one knee, Adam drew a couple of pictures in the dirt with a stick, illustrating a play. Each youth was held in rapt attention. Adam asked a couple of questions, to which the boys nodded. A few minutes later the team was back on the field.

Like an anxious parent, Adam moved up and down the sidelines. Susan was convinced he'd forgotten she was there until one boy weaved the ball through the defenders and kicked it past the goalie, scoring for the first time. Before she knew what was happening, Adam's arms shot around her waist and she was lifted from the ground and swung around. Happiness gleamed from his eyes, and it was all Susan could do not to throw her arms around his neck and kiss him.

His team didn't score again, much to Susan's disappointment. Soccer could easily become her favorite sport if Adam took her in his arms every time his team made a point.

The final score was one to nothing, and the boys left the field triumphantly waving their hands high above their heads and shouting their glee. Again Adam gathered them around him. His eyes spoke of his pride as he congratulated each one. Every boy placed a hand in the center of the circle with Adam and shouted a cheer. They raced excitedly across the field to shake hands with the opposing team members. Adam stayed a couple of minutes longer to speak with the other coach, then turned and ran back.

The team had already gathered their coats and snapped up cookies and cups of hot chocolate one of the mothers was handing out.

"Congratulations, coach," Susan said with a warm smile when Adam joined her.

"I told you what would happen with you cheering,"

he said with a happy laugh. A hand on her shoulder brought her close to his side. "Have you had anything to eat? I'm starved."

"Me too."

"What would you like? The sky's the limit."

"Anything I like?" she asked, her voice low and seductive. "For openers," she said, and she swung her body around so that she stood directly in front of him. Placing a hand on both sides of his waist, she tipped her head back to look him in the eye. "For openers," she repeated, "I'd like to know why you haven't called me. Following an acceptable excuse, I want you to find a reasonably secluded corner and kiss me before I do something rash. And lastly, I'd like the assurance another two weeks aren't going to pass before I'm forced into making an excuse to see you." Taking in a deep breath, she continued. "And that's just the beginning."

Something unreadable flickered in his eyes, and his mouth thinned into an uncompromising hard line. Susan groaned inwardly, knowing that she had displeased him. She'd done it again. When would she stop making a fool of herself? Fiery color stained her cheeks. Adam preferred to handle their relationship in his own way, without her prodding.

Dropping her gaze and her hands, she stepped aside. "On second thought, a hot dog with mustard would do."

"But not for me," he murmured thickly. Fingers pressing the back of her waist, he directed her to a small stand of trees. Before she could say anything, he turned her into his arms. With his hands looped easily around her trim waist, his eyes, serious and dark, met hers. As if in slow motion, he lowered his mouth to hers. An eternity passed before his lips found hers in a kiss that told her everything she needed to know. He claimed her with a mastery that was unquestionable, as if he were a starved man invited to a banquet. His hands moved against her back, arching her closer, half-lifting her from the lawn.

As she linked her arms around his neck, her breath became ragged and irregular. One kiss and her senses were inflamed. "Two weeks," she moaned in frustration. "Why did you make me wait that long?"

"I don't know," he whispered against her hair. His fingers cupped her face and raised her head as his mouth crashed down a second time. The fierceness, the intensity stole her breath, and her knees threatened to buckle.

"Now for that hot dog," he whispered, and brushed his chin and jaw across the creamy smoothness of her cheek. His warm breath stirred the hair at her temple. "Hot dog?" she repeated, still caught in the rapture. "Food," he reminded her. "You said you were hungry."

"Oh, that." She tried to laugh, but the sound came out high and wavering.

He kissed her neck once fleetingly. The nibble shot delicious shivers down her back. "There's a place not far from here we can walk to if you don't mind."

"I don't," she assured him. Not when he had his arm around her; not when his eyes were laughing into hers; not when she felt as if she were walking on air.

As they strolled out of the park they met a vendor with a red cart selling giant pretzels. "Want one?" Adam asked. "They come with mustard," he added, as if she needed an inducement.

"Sure."

He handed the burly man some money and was presented with two doughy pretzels with mustard. Susan bit into hers and was surprised that they were still warm.

"Hey, these are good."

"You mean you've never had one of these?"

"To be honest, I've lived in New York two years and you wouldn't believe the things I haven't done."

"Climbed the stairs up the Statue of Liberty?"

"Nope."

"Toured the United Nations?"

"Nope."

"My goodness." Adam looked surprised. A hand cupped her elbow as they crossed the street.

"Visited the Museum of Natural History."

"That I've done, twice. I liked it so well the first time that I went back again." They continued strolling down Fifth Avenue with no clear destination. "There's one thing I've wanted to do. I mean, we don't have these things in Oregon."

"What?" He threw her a curious gaze. "Subways."

"You mean to say you've lived in New York two years and you have never taken the subway?"

"Don't look so shocked. You're talking to a girl born and raised in Tillamook, Oregon. I thought I'd hit the big time at Ithaca."

"You attended Cornell?"

"Why are you so surprised? I'm not an air head."

"I know that." He took her hand and squeezed it

tight. "Come on, I've got a gun permit. You'll be perfectly safe."

An entrance to the underground station was three blocks east. Adam paid for their tokens while Susan stared at the green walls littered with graffiti. Most everything was spray painted, and the messages scribbled across the walls were enough to curl her hair. "What's this, the library?"

Adam chuckled. "In a way you could say that."

"Well for heaven's sake, if they're going to write on the walls, the least they can do is learn how to spell. Some of their efforts are pretty creative."

Capturing her hand, Adam carried her fingers to his mouth, his eyes smiling into hers. "Do you find yourself doing this often?"

"Doing what?"

"Editing the world."

"All the time," she admitted. "I can hardly read anymore without changing a word here or there, or questioning punctuation."

The tender look he gave her created a whole series of new sensations within her.

"By the way, where are you taking me?" she asked as a way of disguising the overwhelming effect his touch had on her emotions.

"Wait and see."

A roaring sound filled the tunnel as the huge metal monster soared into view. Susan took an unconscious step closer to Adam. The roar dissipated into a swishing hiss and came to a stop. Steel doors glided open and several people filed out. Susan and Adam waited until there was a clear path before hurrying inside. The compartment was crowded with people from various walks of life. Businessmen, shoppers and a few rough-looking souls who would have made Susan uncomfortable if Adam hadn't been standing protectively at her side. Because there wasn't any seating available, they stood. Susan kept her balance by clasping a steel pole. Adam's arm was wrapped around her waist to cushion her from any abrupt moves. At the first stop, the force of the train made her falter, and she would have stumbled backward if not for Adam.

"You okay?"

"Fine." Her voice was slightly choked; but not from the sudden movement. Adam had never held her this close for so long, and she couldn't help but marvel at the power he had over her senses. Everything about the day held a glorious promise, and she felt as if she'd been sipping champagne at noon instead of nibbling pretzels with a boys' soccer coach.

"We get off here," he told her as the train came to a halt a second time. Weaving their way between the other passengers, who weren't inclined to clear a path, they stepped off the train without difficulty. Adam's hand held on to her with a firm grip.

"What did you think?" he asked once they reached the street.

Tilting her head to one side, Susan shrugged. "I'm not sure. I do know I'm going to appreciate those surly cabdrivers a little more the next time I need to get someplace."

They'd walked several blocks before she ventured to

ask the question a second time. "Are you going to tell me where we're going or not?"

"You'll see."

Adam directed her into a multistory building on the next block, and he gave her an amused glance as he led her into the elevator and pushed the button indicating the tenth floor.

She ventured a guess. "Your apartment?"

Dark eyes feigned shock. "We hardly know one another."

"Adam," she groaned softly, "I hate surprises."

"I'll have to remember that at Christmas time."

The suggestion that she would continue to be part of his life pleased her more than she cared to reveal.

Stepping off the elevator, he took her hand again, not giving her the opportunity to study her surroundings. Together they walked down a long, narrow hallway. It didn't take her long to guess.

"Your office?"

"The girl's a marvel," he issued softly. His mouth curved into a tantalizing smile. "There's someone I want you to meet. But before I go to the hospital I've got to change clothes, and here is closer than my apartment. You don't mind waiting?" Thick brows arched with the question.

"Of course not, but, Adam…" She hesitated, glancing down at her jeans and leather loafers. "I'm not really dressed to be meeting people."

"No one's going to look past that gorgeous face to notice."

"Adam," she sighed in protest.

"You look fine, trust me."

"The last time someone asked me to trust them I ended up with garlic dangling from my neck."

Placing a hand on each shoulder, he brought her close. "I don't make many promises, but that's one I have no qualms about." He kissed her lightly, effectively silencing any further protest.

He brought her into his private office, then left to change in an examination room. Her gaze swept the walls, and she paused to read the framed degrees and certificates. Of more interest was a bulletin board in the reception room. She'd noticed it on her way in and was eager to examine it. Moving from his office to the front reception area, she saw pictures of newborn babies he'd delivered and several thank-you notes from children. A proud smile softly curved up the edges of her mouth as she waited.

"I told you that wouldn't take long," he said from behind her. Susan turned to discover he was dressed in a thick Irish cable-knit sweater and dark slacks.

Smiling, she held her arm out to him. "Now I look like something the cat dragged in. I wish you'd said something before. I hate to meet anyone looking like this."

An arm around her shoulders firmly guided her out of the office. He paused to lock the door, placing a plain brown bag under his arm as he did so. Susan assumed the bag contained his clothes.

"To be honest, I don't think Joey will notice."

"Joey?"

"A leukemia patient of mine. He's going home today,

after a long stay at the hospital. Poor fellow's been through quite a bit, and I wanted to stop in and see him before he's released. Interested?"

From the look in his eye Susan realized this wasn't an ordinary patient, but someone Adam cared about deeply. "You bet." No doubt Joey worshipped his doctor. As everyone else seemed to, if the bulletin board was any indication.

"If I ever get sick, can I make an appointment?" The question was asked in a teasing tone, but there was an underlying note of seriousness that Adam didn't fail to recognize.

The hesitation was enough to make Susan edgy. "Of course," he said at last.

"I don't think you need to worry. I'm fit as a fiddle."

A hand slid over her hip and buttocks. "You can say that again," he said, his gaze dark and meaningful.

The hospital was only three short blocks from his office. Several people waved greetings as he walked up the front steps. Adam was cornered almost the minute he walked through the wide double doors onto the polished tile floor.

After brief introductions, the nurse, a white-haired older woman, engaged him in a series of questions. Adam flashed Susan an apologetic smile. She returned the gesture, assuring him she didn't mind. Ten minutes later he directed her to the pediatrics ward and into the nine-year-old's room.

"Hi, Joey."

"Dr. Gallagher," the youth responded with an enthusiastic smile, sitting up in bed.

He was dressed in Star Wars pajamas, and a watchman's cap adorned his bald head. Blue eyes sparkled with mischief as he directed his gaze toward Susan.

"This is my friend, Susan Mackenzie," Adam introduced, curving an arm around her shoulders.

"Hi, Susan." A huge smile revealed a wide space between two front teeth. Joey looked at Adam. "She's real pretty."

Something Susan couldn't define flickered across Adam's face.

"Congratulations, Joey. Dr. Gallagher tells me you're going to be released today."

"Honest?" Excitement vibrated through the boy as he turned his attention to Adam. "Do I really get to go home?"

"Seems that way," Adam admitted with a wry chuckle. "As much as the nurses would like to keep you, I thought it was time your mother had the chance to shower you with some of that attention."

"Yippee," he shouted. He threw his cap in the air, then made a wild dive to catch it before it fell onto the floor, which nearly sent him off the bed.

"Remember what we talked about before you had the chemotherapy?" Adam's eyes suddenly turned serious.

Some of the excitement faded from Joey's eyes. "I remember," he mumbled, glancing away. "I know I wasn't as good as I should have been, but I tried real hard."

"I know you did." Adam tossed a teasing glance to Susan. "Nurse Perkins and I talked it over, and I contacted a friend of mine. He wanted me to give you this."

Opening the bag, Adam took out a baseball and handed it to Joey.

For a moment the boy stared at it with openmouthed disbelief. "Dave Winfield signed this?"

"I think he might have put your name on it there someplace."

"Wow." The one word was barely above a whisper as he reverently turned the ball over and over in his hand. "But then the rest of the Yankees felt deprived after I told them about you, so they wanted me to give you this." Placing his hand inside the sack, Adam produced a leather mitt covered with autographs.

"Everyone on the whole team?" Joey raised questioning awe-filled eyes to Adam.

"It seems they don't hear about boys as brave as you all that often."

Tears shimmered in the boy's blue eyes as Joey threw his arms around Adam's neck. "You've got to be the best doctor in the whole world."

Sometime later Susan sat across from Adam at a small Italian restaurant not far from the hospital.

"How'd you manage that?"

"What?" he asked, looking over the top of the menu. "The autographed baseball and mitt."

A wry grin drove grooves into the sides of his mouth. "Don't ask. I owe so many people favors for that one, I may be giving free exams until the year 2000."

"You don't know Dave Winfield?"

"Heavens no," he admitted with a chuckle.

"You really love that little boy, don't you?" The

question was unnecessary, the answer obvious, but she wanted to watch Adam when he admitted it, praying she'd see the same look in his face when he looked at her one day.

"I do. There aren't many people I admire more than Joey Williams."

"Is he going to make it?"

"Yes." The lone word was issued forcefully, as if the strength of Adam's will would be enough to heal him. "What would you like to order?"

They'd barely had time to look at the menu, and Susan realized he didn't want her to question him about the boy. Doing a quick survey of the dishes listed, Susan quirked her mouth thoughtfully. If she were Rosemary, she'd order the salad. "The lasagna," she said with a determination that caused Adam to look at her curiously.

He ordered two of the same when the waitress came to their table.

Everything was delicious, just as Adam had claimed it would be. When their dishes were cleared away and the girl refreshed their cups of coffee, Susan glanced at her watch and sighed with disappointment.

"What's wrong?" Adam asked, both hands cupped around his coffee cup.

"I've got to get home. I didn't even tell Rosemary I was going to be gone. We're supposed to attend a party this afternoon. Do you know Charlie Johnson?"

Adam shook his head. Susan didn't suppose he would. "He's a friend."

"In publishing?" The casual interest was a pose.

Susan was intensely aware that Adam was more than curious.

"Yes," she said, and breathed heavily. This was the time when she'd sit in eager anticipation to see if Adam would follow true to pattern. Would he make the suggestion that they meet again? He hadn't in the past, and she'd been left wondering.

Replacing her cup in the saucer, she glanced at Adam. He seemed to be lost in his own thoughts. "Adam?" she whispered, then bit into her lip to keep from asking. Hadn't she promised herself she wouldn't?

He looked up expectantly. "Yes?"

She shrugged her shoulders lightly. "Nothing," she said, and glanced down. A long strand of dark hair fell forward, and she looped it around her ear.

"Susan." Her name was spoken softly. Eagerly she looked up. "Yes?"

"There's another game next Saturday. Would you like to come?"

"Adam Gallagher," she cried happily. "I could kiss you."

Four

Panting, her breath coming in ragged gasps, Rosemary Thomas let herself into the apartment. Susan looked up expectantly from her position on the sofa.

"My goodness, you really are taking this physical fitness stuff seriously."

Beads of perspiration poured down Rosemary's face as she gave a weak nod and staggered into the bathroom, returning a minute later with a hand towel to wipe her face. Collapsing onto the carpet, she attempted to speak, but the sounds she emitted were barely recognizable.

Concerned now, Susan set the cookbook aside and leaped to her bare feet. "Rosie, are you all right?"

An emphatic bob of the brown head assured Susan she was. "Wonderful," she gasped.

Hurrying into the kitchen, Susan opened the refrigerator and took out a diet soda. "Here." She removed the pull tab and handed the soft drink to her friend.

"Are you crazy?" Rosemary choked, and looked at

her with wide-eyed disgust. "I'm not going to poison my body with that junk."

Susan looked from her friend to the soda and lightly shrugged. "Okay, then I will." Resuming her cross-legged position on the couch, she tipped her head back and took a large swig out of the aluminum can.

"Susan," Rosemary groaned. "I worry about you. I swear you'll be half-dead by age thirty. Look at you. Already your arteries are becoming clogged with cholesterol, and bags are beginning to form under your eyes."

"That's from so much reading," she returned, not in the least troubled.

Undaunted, Rosemary continued. "And physically, you're a wreck."

"That's not what Charlie Johnson said last week," she replied easily, then took another drink from the can.

Rosemary chose to ignore the comment. "Really, Susan, I'm worried."

"Don't be. I'm happy, and that's all that counts."

Groaning, Rosemary lay back on the carpet and took in huge gulps of air until her breathing returned to normal. "Aren't you going out tonight?" Glancing at her wristwatch, she looked back at Susan, her eyes questioning. "You've always got a date Friday night."

"No," she murmured without looking up from her book. There had been a couple of invitations, but she wanted to get to bed early for the sheer practicality of getting enough sleep for the game with Adam in the morning. "What about you and Carl?" she asked, keeping her place in the book with her finger as she glanced over to Rosemary.

"We're attending a lecture relating fiber in the diet to sound mental health."

Susan bit her lip to keep from saying something sarcastic but couldn't keep from rolling her eyes dramatically. More than once she suspected that Rosemary had become a health-food fanatic because it was the only common ground she shared with Carl, who was part owner of a gentlemen's gym. The two had dated steadily for over a month. Susan liked her roommate's friend, but somehow the picture of Rosemary and Carl as a couple didn't gel. Maybe if Rosemary hadn't been so eager to have Susan join her in the craziness, she could have looked at them in a different light.

"Scoff all you like. But Carl and I find that sort of discussion enthralling."

"I didn't say a word," Susan replied defensively. "You didn't have to." Making a show of standing, Rosemary wrapped the towel around her neck and headed for the bathroom.

A few minutes later Susan heard the shower running. Her smile threatened to break into a full laugh. Fiber and mental health. Honestly!

After having read each cookie recipe, Susan decided to stick with her original choice, chocolate chip. Lining up the ingredients on top of the small Formica counter, she blended the sugar and butter. She had just cracked the eggs against the side of the bowl when Rosemary sauntered in.

"What are you making?"

"Cookies." Susan looked up and smiled. "Hey, you look nice."

Rosemary beamed her pleasure at the compliment. "It's all part of the cardiovascular program Carl's designed for me."

"Gee, and I thought it was the new dress," Susan teased.

"You're not putting processed white sugar in those cookies, are you?" She asked the question as if Susan were about to add strychnine to the batter.

"Yup." She already knew what was coming.

"White sugar is the curse of America. Mark my words, Miss Know-It-All, mark my words."

Again Susan had to bite her tongue, but she managed to let it pass without comment.

A half hour later, Rosemary and Carl were on their way and Susan was left alone in the apartment. That she was the one sitting at home was definitely a switch. Usually it was her own social calendar that was tightly booked. She'd turned down several invitations since meeting Adam. It wasn't that she didn't want to go out, but that she'd rather go with him.

The entire week had passed without a word. Not that she'd expected Adam to call. Expected, no; desperately hoped, yes. What was it about this one man that made him so fascinating? More and more he dominated her thoughts. It had become impossible not to compare him with every other man she'd known and dated. In every instance Adam came out better. True, he wasn't as good-looking as the others, but his appeal was by far stronger.

The alarm rang early the next morning, and Susan threw back the covers and immediately climbed out of bed. Feeling in an unusually chipper mood, she hummed softly as she dressed. A quick glance out the bedroom window revealed heavy clouds and a good possibility of rain. Instead of taking her leather jacket, she pulled on a beige belted raincoat and matching cloche. A pink hatbox contained the saucer-sized chocolate chip cookies she'd promised Adam she'd bring for the team.

"I must be dreaming," Rosemary said between two yawns, sitting up in bed and rubbing her eyes.

"Sorry, I didn't mean to wake you."

"You didn't. It was such a shock to hear you humming that it drove me straight out of bed. I mean, Susan Mackenzie, the original morning grouch! The girl who said if God had meant for man to see the sun rise, He would have made it happen later in the day. The same girl who needs two cups of coffee before she's civil."

"One and the same," she said with a wide smile, and tucked a thermos of coffee under her arm.

"It must be love," Rosemary said under her breath, and Susan was sure her friend hadn't meant for her to hear. In twenty-four years she couldn't remember having been happier, and it was all because she was on her way to Adam.

By the time she entered the park, a light sprinkle had begun to fall, dotting the ground. Brisk steps carried her to the soccer fields. But when she arrived, there wasn't anyone else around. Had the game been canceled? Surely Adam would have let her know, wouldn't he? Looking around, she noted a tall male figure walking toward her and felt a flood of relief. Until this moment she hadn't been aware how important it was that she see him this morning.

When he lifted his hand and waved, she returned the gesture and started walking toward him.

"Morning," she greeted cheerfully once he was within hearing distance. "What happened? Has the game been called?" Tiny waves of pleasure pulsed through her at the raw, virile sight he presented. He wore a tweed jacket and dark slacks, and Susan couldn't remember a time he looked more enticingly masculine.

"The other team forfeited the game."

"Oh." She tried to disguise her disappointment.

"I didn't know about it until yesterday afternoon," Adam said in a low-pitched voice.

"You should have said something. I brought the cookies."

"The cookies, damn. I'm sorry, I'd forgotten about them."

"No problem," she assured him. "Want one? There's coffee too."

"You think of everything." He took the hatbox and thermos out of her hand and led the way to a sheltered picnic area not far from the field. "I would have phoned last night," he said, placing the items on the picnic table, "but I thought you probably had a date." When he glanced up, his expression was bland and guarded.

"I did," she said, her meaningful gaze meeting his. "In the kitchen making cookies. And since I went to all this trouble, the least you can do is eat every last one of them."

"Then I will." A smile brightened his face, and a

happy light gleamed from the dark depths of his eyes. "Hey, these are good. You didn't tell me you could cook."

"I have talents you've only begun to discover, Adam Gallagher." She didn't really mind that he hadn't phoned, knowing that she probably wouldn't have seen him if he had.

"That I don't doubt." His voice was husky and filled with a sweet intensity that made her glance up.

Turning her around and into his arms, he placed a hand along the side of her neck and tilted her head back with the subtle pressure of one finger.

Susan's breath became shallow. Anticipating his kiss, she parted her mouth willingly and slipped her arms around his neck as she yielded to the mastery of his power over her senses. The kiss lingered and lingered as if they were both unwilling for the intimacy to end. When he buried his face against the slim column of her neck, Susan moaned, not wanting him to stop. She trembled, afraid he would pull away from her again, mentally more than physically. She couldn't bear it. Lifting herself onto tiptoe, she arched against him, her hands clinging to his neck. One kiss and the whole crazy world took a tailspin.

Adam raised his head, and his thumb lightly traced her throbbing mouth.

"I need some of that coffee," he said finally. "Why?" Susan asked in confusion, knowing it would feel cold outside of his arms.

"Because we're in the middle of Central Park on a

Saturday morning and are about to be joined by half of New York City."

"Oh, of course," she said, and dropped her hands just in time to see several runners dressed in various outfits enthusiastically jog past. "What was that?"

"Runners." Adam's voice was full of contained amusement.

"They jog in packs now?" As far as Susan knew, Rosemary ran alone. "And just where do these herds graze?"

"Do I detect a sarcastic note?" Adam asked. His mouth quivered, and Susan knew he was fighting a smile. "Don't be so hard on us."

"Us?"

"Sure, I'm a runner. I thought you knew."

"No," she said, and breathed softly. "No, I didn't. When do you run?"

"Weekdays right here in the park. I usually follow the same route as everyone else. Two and a half miles is all I have time for, but I love it."

Susan could recall a time she'd thought he was a soccer player, but what a natural runner he must be. His long strides would display a panther-like grace. Already her mind was buzzing. Perhaps Rosemary wasn't so crazy after all. Maybe it was time she thought about joining the physical fitness craze.

"You look a million miles away."

"Oh, sorry." She snapped herself out of her private thoughts. Lowering herself beside Adam on the bench, she opened the thermos and poured out the steaming coffee. "We'll have to drink from the same cup and share all those disgusting germs."

His gaze was warm and teasing. "I think my immunity system can take that."

He reached for a cookie and handed it to Susan before taking another for himself.

"Hey, I was only teasing. You don't have to eat them all. Save some for next week."

"Next week?" He looked at her blankly.

"Yes, coach, remember your team. The game's soccer."

Adam took a sip of the coffee and placed the red plastic cup within easy reach for her. "I guess I forgot to tell you today's game was the last one of the season."

Disappointment washed over her. How quickly Saturdays had come to be special, knowing she would meet Adam. Now that was over. "Yes, I guess you did." The realization was a threatening one. "Do you coach anything else?"

He flashed her a brief smile. "Only soccer. I don't have time for anything else."

Was he saying he didn't have time for her either? "You can keep the cookies then."

"I have no intention of giving them up," he said. His gaze slid to Susan, and she realized he was referring to more than the cookies.

It may have been a raining, depressing and yucky morning, but Susan couldn't recall a more glorious day. "Are you going to treat me to a decent breakfast?"

"I imagine that could be arranged."

"First thing we're going to do is take you to the

health-food store and introduce you to Fred. He'll set you up on a vitamin program." Rosemary's deep brown eyes gleamed with enthusiasm.

"I want to start running. Not once did I mention taking vitamins."

Placing one hand on her hip in challenge, Rosemary sighed meaningfully. "You've got to learn to trust me, Susan. Without the proper vitamin fortification, you could be desperately sick within a week."

"How much is this going to cost me?" Susan demanded, mentally calculating the fifty dollars she had already spent for a multi-shaded turquoise running suit.

"Does your health have a price?"

"This month, yes," she returned forcefully.

"Okay, okay. We'll start with the bare essentials." Rosemary was at the height of her glory. Susan had trouble restraining a laugh. Her friend seemed to believe it had been her influence that had changed Susan's thinking. And Susan was her first convert.

An hour later she looked over the balance in her checkbook and knew she'd barely have enough to live on for the rest of the month. Rosemary's bare essentials consisted of five bottles of high-potency vitamins. She did have to admit that Rosemary's friend, Fred, had been helpful and friendly. In her eagerness, Rosemary had assembled twenty different minerals and vitamins she considered indispensable. Fred had narrowed the field, helping Susan stay within a reasonable price range.

Their next stop had been the grocery store. By the time they arrived at the check-out stand, Susan was staring at the items with a sense of disbelief. Tofu, yogurt, sunflower seeds, cottage cheese, fresh fruit and vegetables. No potato chips, no diet soda, nothing that so much as hinted of processed white sugar or flour.

"Hot dogs!" Susan exclaimed. "I forgot the hot dogs."

"Never," Rosemary cried righteously. "They're pure poison."

Defeated, Susan shook her head numbly. "Yes, but they taste so good."

"Wait until you've had tofu spread thick across a stone-ground wheat cracker," Rosemary countered. "That's what good is all about."

A multitude of doubts surfaced, but Susan left them unvoiced.

The first alarm rang early Monday morning. Snuggling contentedly under her blankets, Susan rolled over, assured of another hour of sleep. Rosemary spent the early morning doing her exercises and left early to walk to work.

"Susan," the soft voice broke into her dream. "Humm," she purred, pulling the sheet closer to her ear.

"Time to get up."

"No, it's not," she mumbled.

"If you're going to become physically fit, then the best way to start is with walking."

The thought passed fleetingly through her mind that sleep was of more value than exercise. But the warm vision of being with Adam every morning, even if it meant running, was enough inducement for her to struggle to a sitting position.

"Here." Dressed in shorts and a T-shirt, Rosemary cheerfully handed her a steaming mug.

Susan forced one eye open, not awake enough to thank her friend. Bless Rosemary's heart, she mused, forcing a poor facsimile of a smile across her face.

Susan took one sip and spit the horrible-tasting liquid back into the cup. "Good Lord, what is this stuff?" she cried distastefully. A shudder ran through her at the unfamiliar taste.

"Seeped parsley leaves," Rosemary returned proudly. "It's just the thing to get the ol' juices flowing in the morning."

"Parsley?" Susan handed the cup back to her friend. "I've got to have coffee."

"It's all in your head," Rosemary said with a certainty that sounded irrefutable.

Susan staggered into the kitchen, poured water into the pot, scooped grounds from the container and turned on the stove.

"You can't," Rosemary insisted. "The caffeine in one cup will undo everything we're trying to…"

One fiery glare was enough to sufficiently convince Rosemary that maybe this was one point on which it would be best to compromise.

Twenty minutes later, Susan stared at her friend incredulously. Rosemary had completed one hundred and fifty sit-ups, Susan fifteen. An equal number of jumping jacks had been done by Rosemary with an ease that shocked Susan, who had managed twenty-five.

"How do you feel?" Rosemary shouted, hands on her hips as she lifted her knees while running in place.

"Like I should quit while I'm ahead."

"That's probably not a bad idea. Don't make the mistake of doing too much at once."

"There's little fear of that," Susan said with a laugh, and realized that although she wasn't about to give up her morning cup of coffee, she didn't mind the exercise. "Didn't I tell you this is great!" Rosemary shouted, still running, her knees coming up higher and higher. "Yes, you did," Susan admitted. "How long before I'll be ready to jog?"

"Depends on how far you want to go?"

She shrugged, hoping her friend would believe the figure came off the top of her head. "I don't know, two miles, two and a half at the most."

"That'll take weeks."

"Weeks?" Susan cried. She couldn't wait that long. True to character, Adam hadn't set a time to see her again. It had only been two days since she'd met him in the park, and already she was worried. "I've got to be able to hit the streets faster than that."

"Why?" Rosemary stopped, taking in huge breaths and slowly sauntering around the room before placing her hands on her knees and bending forward.

"Well...because." Her mind struggled for a plausible excuse. "I just want too, that's all."

"I don't suppose this has anything to do with Adam, does it?"

A denial rose automatically to her lips, but she refused to let it escape. "What makes you ask?"

Wiping her face with a hand towel, Rosemary gave her an odd look. "We've been living together for almost two years. I know you. I've seen men come and go. But I've never seen you act like this over any one of them."

"I've never felt this strong about anyone else." Her gaze leveled with her friend's. "I learned last week that Adam's a runner."

A look of understanding flashed over Rosemary's face with a clarity that was unmistakable. "Ah, now I get the picture."

"Good, how long will it be before I'm capable of holding my own on a two-and-a-half-mile course?"

Rosemary's eyes widened and she shrugged helplessly. "Weeks."

"I can't wait that long," she said with a groan. "There isn't any way you'd be able to get in top physical condition any sooner?"

"Who said top condition? I'd be willing to settle for breathing normal while doing sit-ups."

Rosemary's laugh echoed from the bathroom as she strolled inside and turned on the shower.

A week later, Susan was almost desperate: It'd been ten days since she'd last seen Adam, and she hadn't heard a word from him. In the past when she'd been uncertain over their relationship, she'd had trouble sleeping. That was no longer the case. Rosemary had devised a workout program that left Susan exhausted. Every night she crawled into bed and fell into an easy slumber.

Within six days Susan was matching Rosemary in sit-ups and jumping jacks. Although she wasn't thrilled about the two-and-a-half-mile walk to the Simon and Schuster Building in Rockefeller Center, she faithfully made the trek each morning. For, as hard as she had berated her roommate's enthusiasm for physical fitness, Susan found she enjoyed it—not the early-morning hours, or even the exertion, but the overall good feeling afterward. Rosemary claimed it was the endorphins. Susan didn't know what it was.

Wednesday morning she woke at five-thirty, long before the alarm sounded. Lying on her back and staring at the ceiling, she released a slow, quivering breath. Wouldn't Adam ever phone? Hadn't he guessed how much he meant to her? Nothing seemed to be going right. Tuesday afternoon she'd had an argument with an agent that had weighed on her mind all night. Now, in the darkness that preceded the first light, Susan realized it wasn't that she wanted to see Adam; she needed to see him. Needed him.

Without questioning the wisdom of her actions, she laid back the covers and quietly slipped out of bed. Making the least amount of noise possible, she took the running outfit hanging in the closet and tiptoed into the bathroom. With any luck she'd be out the door before Rosemary knew she was gone.

Although the morning was crisp and the sky dark, several runners were already in the park. Susan knew enough not to take a coat. She'd be warm as soon as she started jogging. But until she saw Adam and joined with him, she'd have to suffer the cold. Limbering up on her way to the soccer fields, she jiggled her arms at her sides and made a pretense of the same with her legs. Jogging shouldn't be so difficult; after all, she'd been walking the same distance every morning with Rosemary. Running couldn't be that different. Now all she needed was a little luck. She had no idea what time Adam ran, but she'd noted that his office hours weren't until midmorning and assumed he did hospital rounds before then. So if he ran every morning, it had to be around six. All she had to do was wait around by the picnic area until he came into view and she could casually join him.

Fifteen minutes later, Susan stood shivering and miserable, convinced that Adam wasn't coming. With her arms cradling her midsection, she didn't know how she would ever manage to give the impression she'd "accidentally" run into him.

"Susan." Her name was shouted from the distance and she had to squint to see the source. Adam! It took all her restraint not to run and throw herself into his arms.

"Hi," she called, and waved, forcing herself to smile cheerfully. Her mouth felt cold and brittle. If she didn't start moving soon she'd freeze to death. Trotting toward him, she hoped he was impressed with the color-coordinated jogging outfit.

"I didn't know you ran?" He slowed his pace to match hers.

"Yes," she mumbled, already feeling breathless. Rosemary had told her the first few minutes were always the worst. "Since I hadn't heard from you, I thought maybe I'd join you once around the reservoir and see how you've been."

"Great, and you?"

"Wonderful," she lied. Just once, couldn't he tell her he'd been thinking of her? That he'd missed her last Saturday? Her lungs were beginning to hurt, and she struggled to maintain the pace. Talking and breathing were almost impossible.

"How many miles do you run a week?" Adam said, breaking the silence.

"Ten." Somehow she managed to get out the one word. She didn't have the breath to explain that she usually walked the distance.

"Have you ever averaged your minutes per mile?"

"No." Centering her vision on the pavement in front of her, she concentrated on placing one foot in front of the other, nothing more. She wasn't going to embarrass herself. She'd finish the course if it killed her. Her lungs felt as if they were on fire, the pain extending up her throat as she took in ragged breaths. Every muscle in her legs was screaming in protest. At just the moment Susan was convinced she was either going to faint, vomit or die, Adam came to a stop.

Hands on his hips, he tipped his head back and took several deep breaths. "Wow, that felt good."

Susan didn't respond. Instead she collapsed onto the wet ground, her entire body feeling like a limp rubber band.

Adam joined her on the dew-covered grass. Susan didn't mind the moisture; it felt cool and comforting against her burning flesh.

"You okay?" Concern drove creases into his wide brow as his face appeared above hers.

She didn't even have the breath to assure him.

Nodding her head and waving her hand was the most she could offer.

"I imagine my pace is a bit faster than yours. I like to

maintain seven-minute miles. I imagine we were doing eight, maybe a nine-minute mile."

"Oh," was all she could manage.

A hand brushed a long strand of hair from her temple and lingered. "It's good to see you." The intensity in his look created a tidal wave of emotions within her. Every painful step of the run was worth that one tender look.

She struggled to sit up. If he wouldn't say it, she would. "I missed you."

"I was going to call," he murmured, and looked away.

"Why didn't you?" she whispered, hoping to hide the hurt and disappointment in her voice.

"You're an extremely attractive woman." There was a ragged edge to his voice that hadn't been there when jogging.

"That's an excuse?" Had she misread his look that day when he'd told her he had no intention of letting her go?

"Susan," he said, then paused and dragged in a deep breath. "I'm not a plain-looking man. People are going to take a look at us and see beauty and the beast. I don't think…"

"Stop it, stop it right now." A reserve of energy she hadn't known existed loaned her voice the strength to shout at him. "Don't you ever say that to me again." Raising herself up so that she was on her knees, she jabbed a finger into the muscular wall of his chest.

"You are the most attractive, wonderful, fun person I know, and if I ever hear you talk like that about yourself or me again, I'll… I'll…" She didn't know what she'd do. "I'll scream," she added finally.

"You're managing to do a fair job of that now." He glanced around them self-consciously, his look showing he was grateful that there weren't many others nearby. "I know what I'll do," she cried desperately. "I'll scar myself and then maybe you won't look at me like I'm Miss Perfect...or Gail. That was her name, wasn't it? Then maybe you'll treat me like a normal woman—like everyone else treats me." She recognized how irrational she sounded, but she was hurt and resentful and had said the first thing that came into her head.

A muscle jerked angrily in his jaw, and Susan knew she had gone too far. He didn't like her to mention Gail. What was so sacred about his long-lost love? If he still cared for his college sweetheart, Susan thought she'd die.

"Have you ever stopped to think that maybe I didn't want to see you?" he demanded in a low growl. The line of his jaw was hard, the look in his eyes almost savage.

The words hurt more than if he'd slammed his fist into her stomach. For a stunned second she didn't breathe. Tears filled her eyes and she lowered her gaze, not wanting him to know the power he had to hurt her. Crying was the final humiliation; if he saw that it would be too much.

"No, I guess I hadn't." She whispered the words in a husky, pain-filled murmur. Wearily she stood, her back to him. "I'm sorry, I won't bother you again." By the time she made it to the outskirts of the park, her vision had become a watery blur and she hardly knew where she was walking.

Pausing outside her apartment door, she wiped the tears from her face, then let herself in.

"Susan," Rosemary cried. "Where have you been? I was worried." She stopped abruptly. "Susan...you're crying." She sounded shocked.

"Go to work without me today, will you?" Susan asked, keeping her face averted. "Tell Karen I'm sick. Maybe I'll be in later...if I feel better."

"Sure." The one word was whispered soothingly. "Are you going to be all right?"

"No." She tried to laugh. "But you go on, I'll live."

"You're sure?"

She wasn't, but she gave a weak nod.

Rosemary left a few minutes later and Susan sank onto the couch, bringing up her knees and cradling them with her arms. Her chin was tucked against her breast as the recriminations washed over her. Why couldn't she leave well enough alone? Why couldn't she have waited until Adam contacted her? He would have eventually.

Someone banged on her door. The sound reverberated around the silent room and her head shot up. Adam? No, she decided. If he'd just finished telling her he didn't want to see her, then he wasn't likely to follow. Besides, he had his hospital rounds to do.

"Yes." She unlocked the door and quickly opened it. Her gaze collided with Adam's as his presence loomed before her.

Five

"Susan, I'm sorry." He didn't bother with a greeting. "I didn't mean what I said." After a brief hesitation he reached out and touched her shoulder.

Susan didn't need any more encouragement. Wordlessly, she walked into his arms and buried her face in his chest. His deep breathing stirred the hair at the crown of her head, and she closed her eyes to the healing balm his embrace offered.

"Why?" The sound of her voice was muffled by the strength of his hold. Susan didn't need to explain further. She had made a fool of herself from the beginning with Adam. Never before had she waited around for a man to ask her out. No one else in the world could have induced her to push herself beyond her physical capabilities just for the opportunity to see him.

Two large hands cupped her face as his gaze probed hers. Susan noted a curious pain that tinged his eyes.

"You're so beautiful."

For the first time in her life, being attractive was a

detriment. With anyone else it would have been a plus. An involuntary protest slipped from her lips. "Adam, please," she said, and groaned. "I'm not."

"Enough for anyone to question what someone like you is doing with me."

"That's nonsense." She wasn't angry. Strangely, she felt devoid of emotion, as if the tears had depleted her. Raising her own hand, she cupped his face and turned her head so that she could press a kiss into his palm.

A sound came from deep in his throat as his mouth descended to hers, plundering her ready lips with a kiss that was fierce and hungry. Gradually the hard pressure lessened to a gentle possession as his mouth moved lazily over hers. The longings, the yearnings he created within her left Susan trembling. Again she was a willing victim to the sweet, rapturous intensity of this man.

"When I'm with you," he began, his voice slightly uneven, "I think I'm the luckiest man in the world. I treasure every minute and die every time we say goodbye."

Susan couldn't believe what she was hearing. "But why don't you ever call me afterward? Why do you leave me lost and uncertain, waiting to hear from you?"

"That's the way I feel when we're together," he admitted dryly.

He held her tight, his chin resting on the top of her head. Susan wished she could look at him, watch him as he spoke.

"Later I realize you've probably got plenty of men wanting to date you."

"I don't," she murmured, and heaved a troubled sigh.

What would it take to convince Adam she wasn't turning away hordes of men to be with him?

"Well, if not, then there's something wrong with half the population of New York City."

"Oh, Adam."

"I wish I had a dime for every time I picked up the phone to call you or all the times I've found myself standing outside your apartment building. Then I stop and realize you'd be crazy to be interested in someone like me."

"I admit it then," she told him forcefully. "I'm crazy, because I'm interested in you, Adam Gallagher. I'm very interested. Now is that plain enough for you, or do you need more convincing?"

His soft chuckle mussed her hair. "That'll probably hold me until I get downstairs. I'm not the most secure person when it comes to romantic involvements. I don't know if that's a result of Gail or just being homely."

"I wish you'd stop saying that," she said, and released an angry breath. "You are not ugly! I find you so attractive, I don't know what to do or say to convince you."

"When you're in my arms, I don't need anything else. It comes after a long day at the office and I find that I want to share my day with you. Then I realize I can't bore someone like you with something so trivial."

"Yesterday I had an argument with an agent. The woman was wrong and unreasonable, and my afternoon was ruined. All I could think about afterward was how much I wanted to be with you. I probably wouldn't have said a word about her or the disagreement, but I needed you."

"Next weekend—"

"Yes," she interrupted with a small laugh. "Yes what?"

"I'll go, no matter what it is or where it's at. I want to be with you every weekend for a long time."

"Litchfield, Connecticut?"

"Timbuktu."

"Susan," he groaned, "I mean it."

"So do I," she whispered lovingly.

"Some friends of mine are getting together for the weekend. We'll be staying with my mother, who'll probably force you to look at baby pictures of me."

"I'll love it."

His grip tightened as his mouth moved roughly over her hair. "Do you want to meet again tomorrow morning?"

"You mean"—she swallowed tightly—"to run?"

"Sure."

Susan wasn't about to refuse.

"Only this time let's complete the full loop. We only went a mile today."

"Robe?" Rosemary called from the bedroom. "Check," Susan said with a happy laugh. "Toothbrush?"

"Got it."

"Is there anything you haven't got?"

"Not lately," Susan admitted with a contented sigh. Rosemary glanced over at the two pieces of luggage sitting beside the door. "Are you sure you're just going for the weekend? I've seen you pack less for a six-day conference."

"I know." Susan smiled ruefully. "But Adam said something about dinner and dancing Saturday night, and I couldn't decide what to wear so I packed three outfits."

Not for the first time that week, Susan noted the distant look in her friend's eyes. "Is everything all right, Rosie?"

"Sure," she replied flippantly, and turned away. "Are you sure there isn't something wrong between you and Carl?"

"Nothing's right between us," she returned flatly.

"I'm sorry." Susan's look was sympathetic. She couldn't help feeling her friend's unhappiness, but she wasn't all that surprised. Almost from the beginning Susan had thought that Rosemary's and Carl's personalities didn't mesh.

"Well, at least one of us is happy," Rosemary added with a meaningful shrug.

There hadn't been a time in her life when Susan was more pleased with the way her life was going. Every morning she met Adam and somehow, by the grace of God, managed the two-and-a-half-mile run. Usually they jogged at a much slower pace than Adam would have elected. But he was content to be at her side no matter how slowly she ran. Twice he'd phoned her for no particular reason other than to chat. And Thursday they met after work for a drink. After the lonely weeks of waiting for Adam to contact her, the last one had been heaven. Susan couldn't have been more excited about the weekend trip to Litchfield if she had been going on her honeymoon.

Adam was equally elated as he tucked her suitcases under his arm and leaned over to lightly brush his mouth over her lips. "Ready?"

"I think so." Her eyes smiled warmly into his. Turning, she flashed Rosemary a smile. "Take care. I probably won't be back until late Sunday."

"No problem," Rosemary said, and waved. "Have a good time, you two."

"We plan on it," Adam answered for them both.

This was the first time Susan had seen Adam's car, a year-old station wagon.

"To haul the soccer team," he explained when she arched a delicate brow questioningly.

The drive to Adam's hometown took almost four hours; they had stopped for dinner and leisurely prolonged the journey, waiting until the heavy weekend traffic thinned out.

"You'll like my mother," Adam told her, his free hand cupping hers as they headed back onto the freeway from the restaurant.

"I know I'll love her." *How can I help it when I already love her son?* Susan added silently. Her gaze fell on Adam as he drove, his profile illuminated by the headlights of oncoming cars. The beams flickered over the uneven planes of his face, blunt, hard features that looked as if someone had carved him out of wood. Facial contours that did little to reveal the gentle character of this wonderful man. Watching him, Susan's heart swelled with pride and a love so strong it stole her breath.

Apparently Adam felt her close study. He turned and

gave her a smile that caused her heart to leap. "Happy?" he questioned as his hand squeezed hers gently.

"Oh, yes."

"I think I should warn you. My mother's bound to ask us a lot of embarrassing questions. She's a true romantic and would like to see me married and giving her a passel of grandchildren to spoil."

Susan's heartbeat raced to double time. If Adam proposed, she'd accept without a second's hesitation. "I think I can handle that; don't worry about it." She hoped her voice didn't relay the path her thoughts had taken. In the past she had chased after Adam embarrassingly, but when it came to a proposal of marriage, it would have to come from him. She didn't want him teasing their children someday about... Their children. The thought came so quickly, so naturally, that it put a halt to everything else. Her sight, hearing, breathing— the thought of being a wife and mother hurled her right out of reality. It took her a moment to realize Adam was talking and she hadn't heard a word he'd said.

"I'm sorry, I didn't catch that," she mumbled, looking over at him.

"I was just saying that I didn't doubt you could handle my mother's curiosity. If you can deal with pesky agents and finicky authors, my mother will be a snap."

Susan clenched her hands together tightly when Adam exited from the freeway and entered a residential district of middle-class homes. No sooner had he parked the wagon in front of large two-story house with a huge porch than the front door flew open.

"Ready?" Adam whispered.

"I think so." One look told Susan she was going to like Adam's mother. There was no difficulty identifying the two as family. Each possessed the same wide forehead and the long, narrow face. Adam's mother was tall; her hair was completely white and pinned at the base of her neck in a small bun. Her dark eyes twinkled delightedly as her gaze fell from Adam to Susan.

"Mom's going to love you," he said, and gave her arm a reassuring squeeze before opening the car door and climbing out. He held a hand to Susan, who scooted out his side. Immediately he pulled her to him as if making an unspoken statement about their relationship.

Gently he hugged his mother, then curved an arm around Susan's shoulders. "Mom, I'd like you to meet Susan Mackenzie. We're good friends."

The white-haired woman pushed her glasses to the end of her nose and beamed Susan a warm smile. "Anytime my son brings a girl home to meet his mother, she's more than a friend. Welcome to Litchfield, Susan."

"Thank you."

With one arm around Susan and another around his mother's thick waist, Adam escorted them both into the house. The front door opened to a wide hallway. The living room was to the right and had a fire crackling in the fireplace. The stairway was to their immediate left, and the homey kitchen directly in front of them.

"I imagine you're starved," Adam's mother said, tucking a stray hair into the small bun. "Adam, why don't you bring in the luggage. Susan can have your sister's room. And Susan, you come with me so we can get to know one another."

Adam gave her a reassuring smile and winked. Dutifully she followed his mother into the kitchen, which was surprisingly large. A round oak table with claw feet was set in the middle with a freshly pressed linen cloth.

"You have a lovely home, Mrs. Gallagher."

"Olivia," she corrected gently. "I suppose I should think about selling out and moving into one of those fancy condominiums. But this has been home almost forty years now, and I can't see myself living anywhere else."

"My mom and dad are the same way."

After taking down mugs from the polished cupboards, Olivia turned and gestured toward the table. "Sit down and make yourself at home. I baked Adam's favorite deep-dish apple pie, which he'll manage to eat up in the time he's here. Would you like a piece?"

Susan was about to refuse. It had only been a short time since dinner. "Yes, please," she found herself agreeing. "Can I help?"

"No. You just make yourself comfortable. I'll join you in a minute."

Adam sauntered into the kitchen and kissed his mother on the cheek. "The luggage is safely delivered. Is there anyplace else you'd like me to disappear to so you can barrage Susan with questions?"

Keeping a straight face, his mother turned. "Get the ice cream out of the basement freezer, would you please, Adam?"

"I don't like ice cream on my pie," he protested. "I know, but I do. Now be away with you."

The minute Adam was out the back door, Olivia

turned and shared a conspiratorial smile with Susan. "I really am pleased you've come. He needs someone."

"I like him very much."

"How'd you meet?" she questioned as she set coffee mugs and apple pie on the table. She pulled out a chair and sat beside Susan.

"At a party," Adam came in and answered for her. "You remember Ralph Jordan, don't you, Mother?"

"Ralph Jordan, Ralph Jordan." Olivia Gallagher repeated the name as if turning it over and over in her mind. "Of course, that college friend of yours. He's in publishing, isn't he?"

"Literary agent. He recently opened his own agency. He gave a party to celebrate. That's where Susan and I met; she's an editor."

"Associate editor," Susan corrected between swallows. "This pie is great." She dipped her fork into the flaky crust and leaned forward slightly to take another bite.

A pleased smile tugged at the corners of Olivia's mouth, denting crescent-shaped grooves along the side of her face. "I'll give you the recipe if you like," she offered.

"I would," Susan accepted, and noticed the shocked look in Adam's eyes. He opened his mouth and closed it, giving his mother a perplexed look.

"You're meeting Lenny, Burt and Gary tomorrow night?" his mother asked. "This get-together is coming to be an annual thing with you four, isn't it?"

"Unless we make the time, we'll never see one another."

Adam had explained they were meeting his best high-school friends when he asked her to accompany him. From what she could remember, Lenny was a used-car salesman, Burt an electrician, and Gary a lawyer. The four had gone all the way through school together, and Gary on to college with Adam. Susan didn't need to be told that Adam was the kind of man who took friendship seriously. He didn't easily oblige himself to others, but when he did that commitment was total. If only she could find a way to explain to him that it was this kind dedication that made him so special to her. She was tired of dating self-centered, self-satisfying men who never looked past her face.

The three didn't move beyond the kitchen until it was late. Susan enjoyed the teasing banter exchanged between mother and son and nearly laughed out loud as Olivia brought out the family picture album as Adam had threatened she would.

"Mother," he admonished sharply, "Susan isn't interested in seeing that."

"Yes, I am," she contradicted, and flashed Adam a cheeky grin. "I know darn good and well that when you meet my parents, my mother is going to do the same thing." Her voice had dipped slightly; she hoped to convey the message that she planned on introducing him to her family. It wasn't a question of "if" but "when."

"Next thing I know, Mom will have you reading all those silly books she treasures," Adam returned, and he gave a short derisive snort.

"Do you read romances?" Olivia studied Susan. "All the time." When she'd first met Adam, Susan hadn't told him who employed her. All Adam knew was that she was an associate editor. He had no idea she worked for Silhouette.

"I knew a sweet girl like you would read romance novels."

Adam mumbled something under his breath that Susan couldn't make out.

"Mom's addicted to those things. I think she belongs to two or three of those book clubs."

"And what harm does it do?" his mother shot back defensively. "I can sit down and throw away the problems of the world and feel young again."

"Hogwash."

Enjoying this all the more, Susan hid a smile. "Do you enjoy Silhouettes?"

"I love them," Olivia returned enthusiastically. "I get the Romances and the Special Editions."

"Susan, you don't honestly read those things, do you?" Adam regarded her seriously. His eyes narrowed, forcing crinkling lines about his eyes and mouth as his expression developed into a troubled frown.

"Of course I do," she said with a reassuring smile. "I work for Silhouette."

"You're an editor for Silhouette?" he echoed disbelievingly, and rammed a hand through his hair. "A romance editor?" He murmured the question. "Why didn't you say something before now?"

"It never came up."

"A romance editor from Silhouette. Well, I'll be." Olivia looked at Susan as if she were sitting next to a famous movie star. "You must know all the authors."

"We have a wonderful group of authors, all excellent writers in addition to being wonderful people." Her mind wasn't on what she was saying to Olivia, but on the strange look that had come over Adam. She watched as the color drained from his face, his look remote, disturbed.

He excused himself a few minutes later. Susan's eyes followed him as he left the kitchen. What was wrong? What had she said that had upset him so much?

Olivia's gaze followed Susan's. "You love my son, don't you?"

"Very much," she told her honestly.

"He's been hurt," the older woman explained.

Dropping her gaze, Susan cupped the empty mug with both hands. "He told me about Gail. I know how much she meant to him."

"You'd never do that to him," Olivia said knowingly. "I knew the minute you climbed out of the car how you two felt about one another. Has he told you he's in love with you?"

"Not yet," she whispered achingly.

A hand reached across and gave Susan a reassuring squeeze. "He will; just be patient."

A sad smile touched her eyes. "Patience is one thing Adam's teaching me. I knew how I felt about him almost from the beginning, but he's unsure. It's been only in the last week that we've been seeing one another regularly."

"He's not unsure," his mother countered. "Only cautious. Once burned, twice shy."

"But I'm not Gail."

"Deep down he knows that. It'll take some time for

him to openly admit how he feels. After he does he'll never give you reason to doubt again."

Susan's worried expression softened. "I'm not giving up on him, not by a long shot. That guy is stuck with me whether he likes it or not."

They talked for a few minutes longer, and Susan helped Olivia clear off the table. Adam wasn't in the living room and Susan assumed he'd gone up to bed. Feeling frustrated and a little hurt, she sat and chatted with his mother for another hour. When Olivia yawned, Susan made the pretense of being tired herself. Olivia led her up the stairs to the room where Susan would be sleeping. The door opposite hers was closed. Olivia glanced at it, frowned and gestured with one hand.

"I thought I'd taught my son better manners than this."

"Please don't be angry. I'm sure he's very tired."

"I won't have company making excuses for my son. If he was ten years younger, I'd take him over my knee and spank him good and proper."

The mental picture produced a weak smile. "Good night, Olivia, and thank you." She hesitated momentarily. "When we drove up to the house tonight, Adam told me I was going to like you. He was right." Impulsively, she gave the woman a small hug.

It was no use sleeping. Susan changed into her long silk gown and pulled on the pink velvet robe and matching slippers. Sitting on top of the single bed, she couldn't help wonder what had gone wrong. What had she said? The only thing she could possibly attribute his anger to was the fact that she was a romance editor. But why should that upset him? It didn't make sense. Nothing did with Adam. Would she ever understand him? They'd been so happy. Dear God, she prayed, don't let it be ruined. Not when she'd come this far.

A half hour later Susan heard a noise downstairs. She sat up, uncertain. Both she and Olivia had assumed Adam had gone to bed because the wagon was parked outside. But had he?

Gently laying aside her covers, she climbed out of the bed and stuck her feet into the slippers. Tying the sash of her housecoat, she carefully opened the bedroom door. A dim light illuminated the stairway. Noiselessly, Susan moved down the stairs. Halfway down she paused.

Adam was sitting in the living room, slumped forward, his face buried in his hands. He looked as if a great weariness had settled over him and he was friendless and discouraged. A sadness possessed him, a hurt he would never share. As if aware someone was watching him, he straightened and turned his head. Their eyes met and locked. Susan's stomach knotted into a ball of pain at the look she had come to recognize in Adam. He was blocking her out, shoving her away as forcefully as if it were physical. With silent steps, Susan made her way down the stairs.

"Adam, what's wrong?" she questioned softly. His face twisted into a scowl. "Nothing."

"Obviously something's bothering you." She sat opposite him so that he couldn't avoid her.

"Have you ever thought about what a plain name Adam is?" he asked, and sighed heavily.

The faint odor of alcohol shocked Susan; she'd never

known Adam to have more than one drink, two at the most. "Mine isn't exactly one of the more exotic ones," she offered, noting his impassive expression.

He ignored the comment, reaching instead for a stack of Silhouette romances on the table beside the chair. Opening one, he gave a short, humorless laugh. "Honestly, how many men do you know named Remington?"

"Well, there's that one on television," Susan returned.

Angrily he tossed the book aside and opened another. "How about Jefferson, Tate or Thornton?"

"What difference does it make what the names are?" Susan couldn't understand what was troubling him. If Adam was hurt and confused, she was doubly so.

"It makes one hell of a difference." Forcefully he expelled a harsh breath. Despair flickered across his face and he paused to run a hand over his eyes. "Have you taken a good look at the jackets of these books lately?"

"Of course I have. Silhouette's proud of the quality of their covers."

"They use real macho men for the models, don't they?"

"Some women think of them that way." Her voice faltered slightly. "Adam, I don't understand what any of this has to do with us."

"Susan, look at me. Look real good." His dark eyes probed hers. "They'd never use me on the cover of one of these books."

"Me neither! What does it matter?" Her eyes pleaded with him.

"You're on every one of them," he shouted. The back

of his hand lashed out, knocking a stack of paperbacks onto the floor.

Susan gave a small gasp. "Adam! Won't you please tell me what's wrong!"

"There is no happy-ever-after, Susan," he murmured dejectedly. His brow was furrowed in a deep frown.

"You're not making any sense." She watched him with a sad, pleading expression.

The hard look in his eyes softened. "I know I'm not. Go up to bed and get some rest. We'll talk in the morning."

"I'm not going to sleep until this thing is cleared up. It's the fact that I'm a romance editor that disturbs you so much, isn't it?"

His eyes didn't leave hers. "I wish I'd known that from the beginning. It would have saved us both a lot of trouble."

"But why?" She almost shouted the question.

"Go upstairs. Please." He glanced away, refusing to bring his gaze to hers.

Talking wasn't doing any good. Whatever was troubling Adam had to be settled in his own mind. Bending, she reached down and straightened the books into a neat stack. "Good night, Adam."

"Good night," he mumbled. He looked at her sightlessly, his expression stoic.

Halfway up the stairs, Susan stopped to glance back on the dejected figure, yearning to answer his doubts and know his love, desperately afraid she never would.

Susan changed in and out of the three outfits so many times that her stomach had coiled into a tight ball. She'd hardly seen Adam all day. His mother had taken her out for some sight-seeing, but neither was really interested in what they were doing. Releasing a slow, painful breath, Susan decided to wear a fisherman knit sweater and tweed pants, knowing she looked lean and leggy. Her hair was styled softly on top of her head with short wisps framing her forehead and temples.

"Oh, Susan, you look lovely," Adam's mother said as she descended the stairs.

Adam stood and came forward to meet her. His mouth quirked derisively. "She always looks beautiful." The words weren't meant as a compliment, and Susan unconsciously winced at the pain that seared her heart.

They barely spoke as Adam drove them across Litchfield. As he brought her into the restaurant, he paused, glancing over the crowded room. Susan heard someone shout his name, and Adam gave an abrupt nod. Cupping her elbow, he led her into the dining room.

Susan couldn't remember being more nervous.

Meeting Adam's mother had been less traumatic.

Adam made the introductions, and Susan shook hands with Lenny and his wife, Pam, who returned her smile. Next was Burt, a balding man with a prominent moustache, and his wife, Linda. Lastly, Gary, the tall and good-looking attorney Susan had heard the most about, and his date, Michelle, a sleek blond. Space was cleared for them, and Lenny waved to the waitress, telling her they'd like to order cocktails.

Two rounds of drinks followed before Susan saw the menu. If anyone noticed that Adam was especially quiet, they didn't comment, nor did they attempt to draw

Susan into the inconsequential chatter. When Gary tried to bring her into the conversation, she answered his questions with one-word responses and smiled, but the look didn't reach her eyes.

Their meal arrived and Susan did little more than sample the dinner. For all she was aware, the food might as well have been sawdust; everything she swallowed seemed to stick in her throat.

One look confirmed that Adam wasn't enjoying himself any more than she. When the dishes were cleared away, the small party moved into a cocktail lounge for an after-dinner drink. Although Susan was seated beside Adam, they could have been across the room from one another.

The evening was quickly becoming an ordeal, and Susan didn't know how much more of it she could take. When the band began playing, the other couples rose to their feet, leaving Susan and Adam alone. The air between them was heavy and thick, and Susan hung her head, pretending an inordinate interest in her drink.

When Adam reached across and took her hand, she brought her face up and met the weary look in his eyes. "I've been acting like a pig all night," he said. "Why do you put up with me?"

For a second the words confirming her love nearly slipped from her mouth. "We all have an off day now and then," she told him softly. She wasn't looking for excuses. All Susan wanted was to have things right between them.

"Would you like to dance?" His invitation was issued on a husky murmur. He stood, offering her his hand.

Susan rolled back the chair and gracefully rose to her feet.

They'd never danced before, and she was amazed how perfectly they fit together, their steps matching one another's. For the first few minutes Adam held her stiffly, but gradually he relaxed, bringing her as close as possible. "Oh, Susan," he whispered in her ear. "You deserve so much better."

"That could be," she teased. Already the healing power of his touch soothed the pain of his earlier rejection. "But I only want you."

Groaning, he tightened his hold and gently kissed her temple.

When the band stopped playing, they came apart reluctantly and walked back to their table. Lenny came from behind and slapped Adam across the shoulders.

"You must be doing better than we thought," Adam's friend joked loudly. "Otherwise, what would a beauty like Susan be doing with you? Come on, good-looking, let's dance."

Before Susan could protest, she was jerked back onto the dance floor and into the eager man's arms.

Six

Shock and anger froze Susan until Lenny had reached the dance floor. When he skillfully twirled her into his arms, she made a small, protesting sound.

"You okay, little lady?"

"No," she murmured, but she felt like shouting at him. Lenny's unkind words could ruin everything. "How dare you say anything like that to Adam? How dare you?" She held herself unyielding and stiff against him.

The wide, friendly smile on Lenny's face relaxed. "No need to take offense. Adam knows I was teasing. Why, we've been friends since grade school. I know him better than you."

"I doubt that," she seethed. "I doubt that very much. Now if you don't mind, I'd rather sit this one out."

Lenny seemed relieved to be rid of her. Laughing, he grabbed his wife's arm and returned to the populated floor.

Adam's look was anxious. Susan noted how his eyes

followed her as she weaved a path between the other dancers and around chairs.

"Lenny didn't try anything, did he?" Adam stood to meet her, and the question was issued in a deceptively calm voice. The hard set of Adam's mouth told her how angry he was.

"No." She shook her head, her eyes pleading with him, giving him her hand in silent invitation, she whispered, "There's no one I want to dance with except you."

Adam hesitated before curving an arm around her waist and leading her back onto the floor. Automatically her arms went around his neck as she fit her body to his.

His fingers moved against the small of her back, molding her to him, arching her closer.

When he didn't say anything, Susan decided she must. "Are you angry?" She didn't need to clarify the question.

"No. Lenny only said what everyone's thinking."

"Oh, Adam," she moaned softly, "that's not true."

He squeezed her, his strong hands cutting deeply into her waist. "It's the most honest statement I've heard all night."

"Adam, Adam, Adam," she murmured, her voice weak and low. Gently she raised her head and kissed the harsh lines of his jaw. "Didn't your mother ever tell you beauty is in the eye of the beholder? And I behold you as my Prince Channing. Please don't let a few unkind words ruin our night. It got off to a shaky enough start as it is."

She could feel him smile against her temple and relaxed. Everything was going to be all right. Whatever had been bothering him had apparently been settled. Adam had answered the questions that troubled him. Once Gary interrupted them, asking for a dance, but Adam laughed his friend off. "I'm not letting the prettiest girl here out of my arms. Find yourself another partner."

Gary looked surprised but agreed good-naturedly. "You don't mind, do you?" Adam tipped his head back to watch her.

"I'd have minded a lot more if you'd let him take me."

Lifting her hand to his lips, Adam moved his mouth sensuously over the smooth skin of her palm. Susan felt her knees go weak at the potency of his touch.

"Two can play that game," she whispered, her teeth taking little nipping bites at his earlobe. Satisfaction came as she felt him shudder.

"Susan," he groaned, gathering her intimately close. "Let's get out of here."

"Okay," she agreed, shocked at how unnatural her voice sounded.

Adam's arms tightened around her. "Lord, I'm hungry. I don't know about you, but I didn't eat a bite of dinner."

"I nibble your earlobe and you start talking about food?" Susan sighed mockingly. "Where's the romance?"

Adam stiffened and nearly missed a step. "I'm not a romantic man," he returned in a tight voice.

Her hand caressed his angular jawline as she laid her head upon his chest. The ragged beat of his heart sounded in her ear. "I was only teasing," she whispered apologetically.

Capturing her hand, he kissed her fingers. "I know, I'm sorry."

"Now that you mention it," she said with a low laugh, "I am hungry."

"Ready to go?"

"More than ready."

They made their excuses and were out the door within ten minutes.

Two hours later Adam parked the station wagon in front of his mother's house. Coming around to her side, he opened the door and helped her out. Immediately he took her in his arms and kissed her hard and long, stealing her breath.

"What was that for?" Her feet still hadn't touched the ground. Even speaking coherently was difficult.

"My mother," he whispered, and chuckled. "She's staring out the upstairs window, and I wanted her to know everything's all right."

"So you kissed me for show, is that it?"

"That, and because I couldn't keep my hands off you another minute."

"Good, I didn't know if I could stand it much longer myself." Sliding her arms around his neck, she stood on the tips of her toes, her mouth teasing his with short kisses that promised more than satisfied.

"Susan," he groaned, "you're playing with fire."

"I know," she whispered seductively.

In response, Adam draped an arm over her shoulders and lead her toward the house. A light had been left on in the kitchen. Susan waited at the bottom of the stairs while Adam turned it off. Immediately the room was cast in darkness. The only light came from the flickering shadows of the moon as they played across the room.

Standing on the first stair, Susan waited for Adam to come to her. "Adam," she whispered, as he located her in the dark and slipped his arms around her waist. "Oh, Adam," she said softly.

He buried his face in her neck, holding her as if she was the most precious gift he would ever receive. Together they stood, neither speaking, in a world that seemed to be created for them, for this minute.

When his mouth found hers, Susan thought she'd die with longing. He didn't stop; he couldn't seem to get enough of her as his mouth lazily sought her eyes, her forehead, her cheeks and chin. Impatient fingers entwined with her hair, pulling out the pins that contained it. When it tumbled down like a thick brown curtain, he drew in a deep, shuddering breath and claimed her lips in a fierce, devouring kiss that left her weak and willing.

Susan could hear the wild, pounding beat of her heart echoing in her ears. She didn't protest when Adam coaxed her off the step and led her into the living room, lowering her onto the sofa. Her arms reached out to him as he brought her back into his embrace. Unerringly his mouth found hers, deepening the contact. His hands slid under the bulky sweater, caressing her back, slowly moving around to cup her full breasts. Intimately his thumb slid over the lacy outline until her nipples peaked and hardened.

"Susan, oh, Susan." An all-consuming fire had been ignited between them, but it wasn't right. Not here in his mother's home. Not now. She understood what he was saying without the words.

Weaving her fingers into the hair at the side of his head, she expelled a long, choppy breath and pulled him to her breast.

Adam held her for a long time, until his breathing was controlled and even. He helped her stand and loosely wrapped a hand around her waist to guide her up the stairs. Outside her bedroom door, he kissed her again. Lightly, sweetly, gently.

Susan didn't sleep for a long time afterward, knowing the only obstacles that separated her from Adam were two thin doors.

Olivia Gallagher hugged Susan as Adam slid the suitcases into the back end of the wagon. "Now don't make strangers of yourselves, you hear."

"We won't, Mother," Adam answered for both of them. Coming around to the side of the vehicle, he kissed his mother firmly on the cheek.

"Got the pie recipe?" Olivia quizzed, tucking a wisp of white hair back into place.

"Right here." Susan patted her purse. "I'll let you know how it turns out."

"Just remember to use Jonathan apples. That's the secret."

"I promise."

"Mother," Adam objected impatiently. "It's already three hours later than I'd planned on heading out."

Giving them each another quick kiss, Olivia stepped back and Adam helped Susan inside. He came around and started the engine. After a quick wave they were off.

The day had been beautiful. Church in the morning and then an early Thanksgiving dinner with Adam's sister, Theresa, and her family afterward. Adam had said something that morning about making it back to New York before dark. But already dusk was beginning to set.

Susan settled back comfortably and almost instantly fell asleep. Adam woke her outside her apartment.

"We're back already?" Susan asked on a yawn as she sat up and stretched, raising her arms high above her head.

Inserting her key into the apartment lock, Susan pushed open the door and stopped abruptly. Something was wrong. She couldn't immediately say what it was, but something was definitely different.

"What's the matter?" Adam asked from behind her.

"I don't know. Rosemary," she called out softly. Hurried strides carried her across the small apartment to the lone bedroom. Opening the door, Susan stopped and gasped.

"She's gone," she cried, trying to keep the panic out of her voice.

"Who's gone?"

"Rosemary," she shouted unreasonably. "All her things are missing. That's what's different. Rosemary's gone." Her voice wobbled uncontrollably. "Someone kidnapped my roommate. Oh, Adam, what can I do?"

Running a hand over his face, he stood, his brow wrinkled in thick lines. "It's unlikely that a kidnapper would move her things."

A noise outside the apartment drew their attention. With a smile of happiness, Rosemary floated into the apartment.

"Rosemary," Susan cried, returning to the living room. "What's going on?"

Susan's roommate all but danced across the floor. "I got married." Proudly she held out her hand. The ring finger sparkled with a tiny diamond.

"Carl?" Susan asked in disbelief. "Not Carl, silly. Fred."

"Fred," Susan gasped, and slowly lowered herself onto the couch. "Who's Fred?"

"The guy from the health-food store. You know Fred."

"Oh, that Fred."

"Will someone please tell me what's going on here?" Adam inquired in measured tones.

Susan ignored him. "Isn't this rather sudden?"

"You know me," Rosemary answered, laughing off her friend's concern. "Once I make up my mind about something, I don't like to sit on it. Fred felt the same way. Aren't you going to congratulate me?"

"You idiot," Susan said, and sniffled. "You crazy fool, I'm going to miss you terribly."

"I know." Rosemary laughed gaily. "I thought about that for a long time, but our tiny bedroom simply isn't big enough for the three of us."

It felt strange to live alone, but Susan decided not to

get another roommate. That meant a tight budget and watching her pennies, but she knew she could manage it.

Monday morning Susan was at the park expecting to meet Adam for their usual run. When he didn't show up, Susan assumed he was extra busy or had forgotten. When he wasn't there Tuesday or Wednesday, she felt hurt and disappointed. Was he playing games with her again? He'd given her more trouble than any ten men she had dated previously. Well, she could play some games of her own. For the rest of the week she didn't bother to go to the park. But when the weekend arrived, she couldn't stand it any longer.

Against her better judgment, against everything she wanted to prove in this relationship, she called him.

The phone rang five times before he answered. "Yes," he snapped.

"It's Susan." Her resolve nearly wavered with the unwelcome note in his voice.

The pause was almost indiscernible, but enough for her to notice. "I've been meaning to phone. I've had a hectic week." His voice softened somewhat.

"I thought you probably had." Silence.

"You're closing me out again, aren't you?"

"No." He was lying and they both knew it. "I've just been busy, that's all."

"Too busy to run? You love to jog."

"Maybe next week. Listen, Susan, I'd like to chat but I've got something going on here. I'll give you a call next week."

"Sure," she whispered through the hurt. "Sure, Adam, I'll talk to you later."

True to his word, he did phone the following week, but the conversation was short and stilted. More than once Susan had to bite her tongue to keep from screaming at him. She was certain he'd given up running because he didn't want to meet her. Before they hung up, she told him that her schedule had been changed and she wasn't going to be able to jog anymore. It was a half-truth, but she didn't want to deprive him of something he enjoyed. Although Adam didn't comment, Susan felt confident he knew what she was saying.

Another week passed without hearing from him. Whatever was troubling Adam had to be settled in his own way. Susan didn't know what more she could do. Adam couldn't hold her and kiss her as he had, then turn away so abruptly. Obviously there were problems he needed to work out. And she had her pride, too. In the past she had been the one to pursue him. Perhaps if she backed off and gave Adam breathing room, he could settle this within himself. When he was ready, she'd be waiting.

Because she was lonely, Susan began dating again. No one special and never the same man for more than a few times. Casual dates with friends. She threw herself into her work, often staying until six or seven so that she'd be so tired she wouldn't stop to answer the nagging doubts. Or give in to the impulse to contact him.

Adam continued to phone, usually when she least expected it. He didn't ask her out again, or suggest that they meet, and Susan didn't prod.

At Christmas she spent hours searching for a special card that would say exactly how she felt, deciding in the end that she'd never find one. She ended up mailing the same one that she had sent to all her family and friends. Adam mailed her a card with his name scribbled at the bottom. There was no written message. Susan wondered if he had searched for the perfect card as she had. She doubted it.

A few days before Christmas he phoned. Again when she had least expected him to call—early on a Saturday morning.

"Hello, Susan, I'm not interrupting anything, am I?"

"No, of course not." Didn't he know by now that he was the most important person in her life?

"I just wanted to wish you a Merry Christmas."

"You too, Adam." She paused and an awkward silence followed.

"Are you going home for the holidays?"

"Yes, I'm flying out the twenty-third and will be back the twenty-sixth." She couldn't afford it, but her parents had paid part of the air fare. Susan was sure her mother knew something was wrong, although Susan hadn't written anything about Adam or their relationship. She wondered what her family would think if she confessed she was in love with a man who didn't love her. Probably disbelief.

"You're not staying long, are you?" It was more a statement than a question.

"I can't spare the time from the office."

Another silence.

"Are you driving to your mother's?" Susan asked.

"Yes. She sent her love, by the way." His mother's love, but not his.

"Tell her Merry Christmas for me. Theresa and her family too."

"I will." He hesitated. "Well, I suppose I should be going. I didn't want to disturb you."

"You're not."

"Are you jogging these days?"

"All the time," she lied cheerfully, anything to keep the conversation going. She didn't want to hang up, not when she hadn't talked to him in days. "I…was thinking about going this morning, in fact."

"I won't keep you then. Good-bye, Susan, have a nice holiday."

For a long time after the line was disconnected, she held on to the receiver. She hadn't seen him since before Thanksgiving and was starving for the sight of him. Maybe he'd been hinting that he'd be at the park. Even the slightest possibility of running into him was enough for her to dig through her drawers and pull out the turquoise sweatsuit she had once treasured so highly.

Shivering, Susan briskly walked the two-and-a-half-mile course, desperately clinging to the hope of seeing Adam. When he hadn't shown by the time she'd finished the full circle, tears of frustration and disappointment filled her eyes. Tilting her head back, she took in huge breaths to quell their flow. She sat down on a bench where she used to meet Adam in the mornings. Sniffling, she stood, knowing how silly she must look walking around Central Park at Christmas time with tears in her eyes. Her throat hurt with the effort of suppressing the flow.

What was the matter with her? Was she so obtuse that she didn't understand that Adam didn't want to see her again? Hadn't he made himself crystal clear? For whatever his reasons, she mused, to ignore her or not to ignore her was his prerogative.

Was she so weak that her ego couldn't withstand the rejection? Maybe if she didn't love him so much, it would have been easier. This was just the kind of thing her authors weaved novels about. Wasn't it Adam who had told her: "There is no happy-ever-after." The time had come for her to accept that.

A chilly breeze caused her to shiver. A tear escaped and made a wet track down her pale face. Quickly she wiped it aside and pressed an index finger under each eye to stop others from escaping.

Dejected, defeated, discouraged, she returned to her apartment and took a warm bath.

"Karen would like to see you in her office," the receptionist, Dana Milton, told Susan when she walked into the office the second Monday in January. Christmas with her family had been wonderful. Wrapped securely in their love, Susan had returned to New York feeling relaxed and refreshed.

Stopping off at her small office, Susan hung up her coat and placed her purse in the bottom drawer of her desk. The telephone was already ringing, but Susan ignored it. On her way past the receptionist, she asked Dana to hold all her calls.

In the last part of the month she was scheduled to fly to Texas and speak at a writers' conference. She liked to travel and get the opportunity to meet authors. The conference was probably what Karen wanted to talk to her about.

It wasn't. The first thing that came into her mind as she went back to her office was that she'd need to have new business cards printed. How silly her thoughts had come to be lately. She was now a full editor and no longer an associate.

The first person she called was Adam. She'd never phoned his office, and hadn't talked to him since before Christmas.

"Dr. Gallagher's office." His receptionist sounded young and pretty and Susan immediately fought back the hot waves of jealousy.

"Hello," the voice repeated.

"I'm sorry." Susan breathed in sharply. "This is Susan Mackenzie. Would it be possible to speak with Dr. Gallagher?"

"I'm sorry, Dr. Gallagher's with a patient."

"Please tell him it's me, I'll hold."

She didn't know if he'd come to the phone or not. An inordinate amount of time seemed to pass before the receptionist came back on the line.

"He'll be right with you."

"Thank you." Susan sighed gratefully.

Not more than a minute later and the phone was connected again. "Susan, are you all right?"

"Yes, I'm sorry. I know I shouldn't call you like this, but I had some news. Some good news," she amended, "and you were the first person I wanted to tell. I got a promotion. I'm a full-fledged editor now."

"Congratulations. I'm sure you deserve it." The genuine pleasure in his voice created a warm glow within her.

"At least it means I'll be able to keep the apartment. Although I hate to see the entire amount of my raise go toward the rent, I've discovered I like living alone. I don't think I could find anyone else who'd put up with me the way Rosemary did."

His chuckle was warm and friendly. "I'm very pleased for you, Susan." It was the most they'd said to one another in weeks.

"I won't keep you. I know this is an awful time to phone, but I was so excited I wanted to tell someone."

"I'm glad you did." He didn't tell her he'd talk to her soon, or again, or anything. But she didn't notice it at the time, only later. Much later.

An hour after their conversation, a dozen red roses were delivered to her office. Beautiful roses. The sender's card bore only one word: "Adam."

With the promotion came new responsibilities, and Susan threw herself into the task eagerly. Not until another week had passed did Susan realize she hadn't heard from Adam. Nothing since before Christmas. Only the roses. Had he given up phoning her too?

Five days later, Susan nervously dialed his phone number. Her hand shook as she lifted the receiver to her ear. Nothing had ever seemed more difficult.

He answered on the third ring. "Hello."

"Hello, Adam, I haven't heard from you in a long

time." She forced a cheerful note into her voice, aware she wasn't fooling him. "Did you get my card?"

"It arrived last week. There wasn't any need to thank me."

"Of course there was," she contradicted softly. "The reason I phoned was to let you know there's going to be a small party celebrating my promotion at Rosemary and Fred's next Friday night."

He hesitated, and the taut silence vibrated in her ears. "I'll have to check my calendar."

"Go ahead, I can wait." If he declined, Susan didn't know how she'd react.

He didn't take more than a few minutes. "It looks like I've got hospital duty that night."

Disappointment washed over her. "I'll talk to Rosemary. I'm sure we can change the party to Saturday night without too much trouble."

She heard the irritation in his short sigh. "I don't want you to do that."

"But I'd like you to be there. I haven't seen you in months."

"I told you, I'm busy," he said gruffly.

"Adam." She forced herself not to plead. "This is important to me."

"You know the way I feel about parties."

Her laugh was short and derisive. "We met at a party! Are you saying that you'd accept an invitation from Ralph Jordan, but not from me?"

The line seemed to crackle with the tense silence. "I told you, I'm busy."

"Adam," she pleaded, angry with herself. "Please."

"Susan, no."

Never had any word sounded more hurtful or cruel. For a moment she closed her eyes as the pain of this final rejection seared her heart.

"I won't trouble you again," she whispered achingly, hating herself for the way her voice wavered.

"Good-bye, Susan." His voice had softened slightly, and she realized it wasn't her imagination when she heard the painful regret.

The next day Susan met Rosemary for lunch at a small deli in Rockefeller Center. Susan forced down soup and a sandwich, and Rosemary dug into a yogurt thick with nuts and fruit.

"Would you mind very much if we canceled the idea of a big party?" Susan asked casually. "Parties can be such a hassle, and I think I'd like it more if we all went to dinner at that new vegetarian restaurant you've been telling me about." Susan hoped her friends would forgive her.

"Great idea," Rosemary agreed instantly. "I'll make the arrangements and get back to you later."

"You don't need to do anything, you know that."

"Are you kidding," Rosemary teased. "Fred and I are looking for an event to announce that I'm pregnant."

Susan stopped eating, the sandwich lifted halfway to her mouth. "Rosemary," she whispered, her eyes round and happy, "that's wonderful."

"I know. Fred and I are really pleased. I wanted Adam to be my doctor. He understands my desire for proper diet. You don't mind, do you?"

"Of course not. Have you seen him yet?"

"Two days ago. He asked about you."

Susan hid her surprise; but then, it was only natural that he would make a polite inquiry. She didn't fool herself by making more out of it. That's all it was.

Thinking about her conversation with Rosemary later, Susan mentally marked February first on the calendar. That should be enough time for Adam to have sorted through his feelings. He might want her to believe he didn't love or need her, but she knew him too well. Adam Gallagher wasn't the kind of man who could hold her in his arms one day and be hurtful the next.

Setting a date in her mind served another purpose. It gave Susan a day to set her sights on, a day to hope for. If he hadn't contacted her by then, the solution was simple. She'd go to him. Turning her away would be far more difficult if he had to look her in the eyes.

The morning of February second she made an appointment with his receptionist. A few days later she sat nervously in one of his examination rooms, her teeth nibbling on the soft flesh of her lip. Several times she clenched and unclenched her fists. She prayed this was the right thing to do. Once again she was swallowing her pride and coming to him.

"Susan?" The disapproval in his voice did little to calm her. But when he glanced up from the chart, a gleam softened the hard look in his eyes. "You've cut your hair."

She'd forgotten he hadn't seen it. Her hand fingered the shoulder-length curls. "It's not as short as it looks. I had it styled is all. Do you like it?"

He ignored the question. "What's the problem?" He

made no move to examine her, instead he leaned against a chair on the opposite side of the room as if he wished to put as much distance between them as possible in the cramped quarters.

"Don't look so welcoming," she said with forced gaiety. "Don't you remember you said I could come see you if I was sick?"

"I remember." He didn't look pleased about it.

"I'm having a small pain," she continued, undaunted.

"Where?"

"On the left side of my chest, about the center."

"Your heart?" he questioned sarcastically.

Susan smiled weakly. Her idea hadn't been that creative.

"Let me listen," he returned crisply, and walked to the table where she was perched. Lifting up the back of her sweater, he placed the cold stethoscope on her sensitive flesh. "Take deep breaths."

Susan complied, drawing in several mouthfuls of air. This wasn't going well. What had she expected? It was all she could do not to reach out to him, touch him. The minute he'd walked into the room, she'd drunk in the virile sight of him. He looked tired, as if he was putting in long hours, but then so was she—immersing herself in work to forget.

"Everything sounds fine," he said flatly. His mouth moved into a forbidding line as he moved to the small desk and pulled out a pad.

"Adam," she whispered entreatingly. "I've waited three months to see you. At first you phoned me, now you don't even do that. Almost three months, Adam.

I thought by this time you would have worked things out. I need you. I'm miserable."

He ripped the sheet from the pad and stood handing it to her. "Have your druggist fill this."

"Are you listening to me at all?" She raised her voice, pleading with him.

His eyes refused to meet hers. "If you continue to have problems, I'd suggest you see a specialist. My practice is limited and I doubt that I'll be able to help you." His hand clenched the doorknob, and Susan noted that although his voice was cool and detached, his knuckles were white.

"Don't do this to us, please." She hung her head, the soft curls falling forward to shield her from the final embarrassment.

"That prescription should take care of any problems you have. Good-bye, Susan."

She didn't even bother to read it, knowing it was for placebos. Dejected, she stood and put on her coat. Grabbing her purse, she hurried out of the office. Not until she was seated in the taxi did Susan decide that this is what it must feel like to die. Her stomach was constricting into a tight ball of pain. Swallowing, breathing, talking were almost impossible.

The cab jerked in and out of traffic, speeding up only to have the driver slam on his brakes a minute later. Susan hardly noticed. Every New York cabdriver she'd ever ridden with drove in the same way.

Not until he yelled at her to hold on did Susan look up and see a bus racing out of control, heading directly for the passenger side of the cab. Only then did she let out a scream.

The terror in her own voice was the only thing she heard as metal slammed against metal and she was violently thrown against the door.

Seven

Deep, piercing pain filtered into the dark world in which Susan lay. Her head throbbed so hard and strong that she raised a tentative hand to feel what could be hurting so badly. Her fingers encountered a gauze wrapping. She tried to open her eyes, but they felt weighted as if someone were pressing to keep them shut. One refused to open; the other opened just enough for her to recognize that the bright overhead lights must be in a hospital.

A raised voice could be heard coming from the other side of the room. "I want a plastic surgeon brought in."

"I don't think she'll need—"

The first voice didn't get the chance to finish.

"I don't care what you think, I want one and I want one now. Is that understood?" His irritation seemed to vibrate across the room.

"Yes, doctor."

Adam. Adam's voice was the angry one. Susan had never heard him talk that way to anyone.

From the distance came the sound of soft moaning. Not until Adam moved to her side did Susan realize the groans were her own.

"So you're awake." The gentle quality she loved about him was back. "We were beginning to wonder how much longer you'd be out. How do you feel?"

For a moment her mouth refused to obey, and when she finally managed to speak, the words felt thick and heavy. "Don't ask."

"I'll have the nurse give you something for the pain." She tried to reach out and touch him, but his hand stopped hers, gripping her fingers. Slowly his thumb caressed the back of her wrist in a gentle, soothing movement.

"You've been in an accident," he explained in a soft, assuring tone. "The reason you can't open one eye is because it's swollen shut. The pain in your chest is from cracked ribs."

"My head?"

"I imagine it feels like it's split wide open. You've got a whopper of a concussion."

Even with only one eye opened just enough to see, Susan noted the twitch of a nerve in his hard, lean jaw as he looked down at her. Hadn't she heard him demanding that a plastic surgeon be called?

"My face?" Her voice quivered. What had happened to her that made Adam look at her like that?

"Luckily you put your hands up, which prevented your face from being cut anymore than it was. There are several scratches. Nothing major."

A weariness flooded her, waves of fatigue rippling

through her. Susan fought it as long as she could. Finally she succumbed to the overwhelming force as Adam whispered something about talking to her later. When she woke again there were no bright lights overhead. The railing on the bed assured her she was still in the hospital. Her mind buzzed with questions.

Why had Adam been in the emergency room? How had he known about the accident?

Her mouth felt thick, as if someone had stuffed it with cotton. She longed for a taste of cool water. Maybe she could ring the nurse. Although her hand fumbled around the bedside for a buzzer, she couldn't find one and eventually fell back to sleep.

The room was filled with light when Susan was stirred awake. She turned her head when a tall nurse opened the door and stepped into the room.

"Morning, I thought you'd be awake by now." The white-capped nurse moved to the side of the bed and stuck a thermometer in Susan's mouth. Fascinated, Susan watched as the digital readout showed her exact temperature. The nurse discarded the mouthpiece and checked the bottle and tubes connecting the I.V. in Susan's arm.

"When will Dr. Gallagher be in?" Susan questioned, following the woman's actions as the efficient nurse progressed around the bed.

"Dr. Gallagher?" she repeated. A frown marred her wide forehead as she removed the chart clipped at the end of the bed. "You've been assigned to Dr. Manson."

"But Dr. Gallagher saw me in the emergency room;

I'm sure he did." It hadn't been her imagination. She was positive Adam had been there.

"Dr. Gallagher examined you when you were admitted, but your chart shows Dr. Manson's name. You can ask about it later when Dr. Manson does his rounds." Susan didn't need to ask, she already knew. Adam had requested to be relieved of her case. It shouldn't have surprised her, but it did—almost as much as it hurt. When he'd rejected her so many times, how could she hope to believe he'd care now?

"Would you like something to drink?" the kind woman offered.

"Please," she mumbled. "And would it be possible, I mean…could I see a mirror?"

"There's one above the sink, but for right now I'm sure Dr. Manson would like you to stay in bed. I don't think we have a hand mirror available. If you'd like, I could ask."

"What do I look like?" Susan knew it was an unfair question, but she had to know.

"Let's put it this way," the nurse chuckled. "I wouldn't want to see the other guy. But you'll improve. Don't worry."

Dr. Manson was a short man with thinning gray hair and twinkling blue eyes. Susan liked him immediately.

"Good morning."

She offered him a weak smile. "Morning. When can I go home?" All she wanted to do was get out of there.

"Soon," he said, and laughed. "I swear, some people don't know when they've got it good. You're the third person this morning who would prefer other accommodations." Lifting her chart from the end of the bed, he skimmed over its contents and shook his head approvingly. "We were worried last night about internal injuries, but you seem to be doing fine. I imagine tomorrow we can release you if you like."

"I like," she stated emphatically.

"Don't do too much today. Get out of bed if you want. I've got you on a soft-food diet, and I'll check with you tomorrow morning."

"Thank you, doctor."

Breakfast arrived and Susan looked at it disparagingly. She managed to down the mushy applesauce and a small bowl of Jell-O. Afterward she was so weak she lay back and, before she knew it, was sound asleep.

A noise in the room woke her. When she opened her eyes, Adam was standing beside her bed.

"Shouldn't you be in your office?" she asked, surprised at how distant her voice sounded.

"I just finished delivering a baby and thought I'd check and see how you're doing."

Turning her head, she purposely looked away from him. "Fine," she mumbled.

"Dr. Manson says you'll be able to go home tomorrow. I'll take half the day off and pick you up about noon."

Susan jerked her head around, shocked at his offer, then winced at the pain that shot through her head. Hadn't he made it clear that he didn't want to see her again? What had altered his decision? Obviously the change of heart had been a sudden one. Only a few hours ago he had given her case to another doctor. Having her as a patient was more than he was willing to do.

Pride nearly erected its vindictive head as she began to insist she didn't need him, could find her own way home. But something stopped her. It didn't take her long to recognize that she was willing to accept the crumbs he offered. She didn't care what the reason was as long as Adam was there.

"You were in the emergency room last night, weren't you?"

Adam agreed with a blunt shake of his head. "They called me."

"But how? I didn't give anyone your name."

He glanced away, an uneasy look flickering across his face. "Apparently the prescription I gave you was clenched in your fist. The ambulance driver found it."

"Adam," she whispered imploringly. "Is my face bad? No one wants to tell me anything."

Again she noted how a nerve twitched in his jaw, but his eyes softened. "You've got a few cuts, but they'll heal quickly. Your eye's swollen, but quite a bit less than yesterday." He hesitated. "You're still the most beautiful woman I know."

"Oh, Adam." She sniffled as turbulent emotions engulfed her, nearly overtaking the delicate hold she had on her composure. To hide her reaction, she asked another question. "Do you know anything about the cabdriver? Was he hurt?"

"Cuts and bruises. From what I understand he was treated at the scene and released." He paused, and a finger lovingly traced her lips. "You really are beautiful."

His hand squeezed hers and she felt the moisture build in her eyes. Wiping a tear away, she tried to laugh. "Look at me. You tell me I'm pretty and I cry."

"I'm not going to convince you everything's fine until you've seen for yourself. Here, sit up." He reached behind her to the bed controller, pushing the button that folded the bed upright. "There's only a few scrapes and bruises, trust me."

Once he'd positioned the bed so that she was sitting upright, he opened the small closet beside the sink and took out her housecoat and slippers.

"How'd you get those?" She stared incredulously at her velvet robe and matching slippers.

Adam's look was almost boyish. "Yes…well, I took the liberty of opening your purse and taking out the key to your apartment. I brought some other things I thought you might need. You don't mind, do you?"

"No, of course not." Would this man ever stop amazing her?

"I also contacted the Silhouette offices and told them about the accident. Rosemary phoned me later and I assured her you were going to be fine. She said to tell you she'll be in later today. You're not to worry about a thing, everything's been taken care of."

Folding the covers back, Adam helped her to scoot her legs over the edge of the bed. Bending down on one knee, he placed her slippers on her feet, then helped her slip her arms into the robe.

"What about the I.V.?" Susan looked up anxiously. "Not to worry," he assured her, and wheeled the tall pole with the attached plastic bottle to the side of the bed.

"What is this stuff anyway?" She eyed the whole setup suspiciously.

"Sugar water with some antibiotics to ward off infection," he told her. Offering his hand, he smiled encouragingly. "You ready?"

"As I'll ever be." A small stool rested beside the bed, and Susan tentatively placed a foot on the grooved black surface. The hospital gown rode up to expose the top of her thigh and she moved quickly, then sucked in her breath at the sharp pain that pierced her ribs.

Adam wrapped an arm around her waist. "Hey, not so fast."

Guiding her with a protective hand, he led her to the mirror. One glimpse of her cut, ravaged face and she let out a gasp of dismay. Her left eye was grotesquely swollen, and deep purple color covered one side of her upper face extending as far down as her cheekbone. Tiny cuts and scrapes outlined the delicate curve of her jaw. White gauze was wrapped around her head, and she noted two butterfly bandages near her hairline.

"It's beauty and the beast all right," she whispered brokenly. "Only I'm the beast." A huge lump quickly formed in her throat as she buried her face in Adam's chest.

"It's not so bad," be whispered soothingly. "Within a month no one will know you were ever hurt."

"A month," she groaned.

"Honey, believe me, when I first saw you, I was afraid it was much worse."

Honey! The affectionate term rolled off his tongue as if he'd said it a thousand times. A silly weakness seemed to attack her legs and she swayed toward him. Quickly Adam's arm held her secure. "Let's get you back into bed. Rest today. I'll be back tonight to help you walk."

"Yes, doctor," she retorted primly.

A crooked smile slanted across his mouth. His lips lightly brushed her cheek as he helped her back to bed.

"I'll see you later," he promised.

Susan leaned against the pillow and sighed. Immediately her ribs protested, and she released a quivering breath until the pain subsided.

Rosemary stuck her head in the door at lunchtime. "Susan," she cried, unable to hide her shock. "Oh my goodness."

"I know, it's awful, isn't it?"

Her friend moved tentatively into the room. "Here, Fred and I wanted you to have this." She set a bushy plant on the table beside the bed. "It's an aloe vera plant. They're wonderful for all sorts of medicinal purposes. I brought along a booklet for you to read…only you probably shouldn't with that eye. At least not right away."

"Thanks, Rosie. I'll keep it in the medicine cabinet."

"Now I know you're going to be all right," Rosemary said, and gave an approvingly look. "When you can tease, then you must almost be back to normal." She walked to the window. "Not a bad view."

"Honestly, for what this room's costing me, I could be vacationing on the Mediterranean."

Rosemary agreed and glanced at her watch. "I gotta get back to the salt mines. Are you sure there isn't anything I can do for you?"

"Smuggle me in a pastrami on rye and hold the mayo," she shot back hopefully.

"Are you nuts!" Rosemary's round eyes widened with disbelief. "You're asking the wrong person. Adam would have my head. Do you have any idea how bad pastrami is for you?"

A flick of Susan's wrist dismissed the advice. "I don't want to know. All I care about is something that doesn't swim in my mouth when I swallow."

"Tofu on—" Rosemary offered sincerely.

"Forget it, Rosie, I'll eat cherry flavored gelatin."

"The hospital is filling you with that junk!" Bright brown eyes burned with outrage. "Boy, they better not try it when I'm here." Patting the slight swell of her tummy, she gave a determined look. "Baby and I are only interested in good food."

"I'm sure Adam will make the proper arrangements," Susan assured her, silently questioning Rosemary's definition of good food.

The indignation dissipated. "If you need anything, let me know. Okay?"

"I will." She smiled softly. "Thanks for coming." Her head had begun to throb again and her ribs ached. Settling back, she flipped the switch to the television and ran through a variety of stations. Finding nothing to interest her, she took another nap.

After dinner Adam returned, helping her out of bed and walking at her side as they strolled the hallway several times. One band was linked with Adam's while the other pushed the portable I.V. pole. Two beautiful floral bouquets had arrived that afternoon. One was from

Adam and another from her co-workers at Silhouette. Adam didn't look at either one, nor at the plant Rosemary had brought. The thought passed through Susan's mind that he didn't want to know if another man had sent her flowers. For a time she tried to think of a natural way to assure him that he was the only one, but she abandoned the idea because he would know exactly what she was doing.

"How long will it be before I can go back to work?" she quizzed as they made their last round and headed back to her room.

"I think a week should do it."

"A week," she cried, her voice high with consternation. "I can't miss that much time." Already her mind was racing toward a writers' conference she was scheduled to speak at in Florida in the middle of March.

"Sure you can," he contradicted.

"But, Adam," she continued the protest, "I'll go crazy sitting in that apartment every day all by myself."

"After the first couple of days, I don't see why you couldn't go in for a few hours in the mornings. But not any more than that," he warned.

Susan lay for a long time thinking after Adam had kissed her good night. A light kiss against her forehead. Just the day before, he had forcefully pushed her from his life. The accident was the only reason he was back. But for how long? Should she prepare herself for another separation? She had never been this close to a man, this vulnerable. The power he had to hurt her was beyond even her own understanding. Caring this deeply for someone had called for risks, and she had been the one to step forward. Not Adam. Just when she was sure she'd lost him forever, he was back. That frightened her more than losing him.

Adam stopped in briefly early the next morning with the reminder that she should be ready to leave about noon. Later, when Susan checked the closet, she found a set of loose-fitting clothes and marveled at how Adam seemed to think of everything.

Dr. Manson gave his smiling approval when he checked on her shortly after Adam left. He stood chatting with her for several minutes after completing a thorough examination and signing the release papers. "So, you're Adam Gallagher's girl. I must admit I've never seen him lose his cool the way he did after they brought you into the emergency room."

At Susan's shocked look, Manson continued. "Most doctors agree it's better not to treat family members, or those we love. The difficulty is in keeping ourselves detached enough not to react emotionally. It only took me two seconds to see Adam cared deeply for you."

Susan wanted to argue that she was sure he was mistaken. But was he? Did Adam truly love her? If so, what could have prompted him to act as he had these last months? One thing she did know—she couldn't take any more hurt and rejection. Adam was back; she didn't question why or for how long. Gladly she accepted what he offered. But when he chose to leave, and Susan was sure he would, then she would allow him to go freely. For three miserable months she'd hung on to the hope, the dream of his love. But no more.

As he'd promised, Adam sauntered into her room at noon, pushing a wheelchair as though it were a grocery cart. He twirled it around a couple of times, making her smile.

"Show off," she admonished gently.

A hand under her elbow helped her off the bed. "Ready?"

"Am I ever! Does everyone feel this way?"

"What way?"

"Eager to get home. Everyone's been wonderful, and even the food, what there was of it, wasn't half-bad. But I'm so ready to go home."

"Almost everyone," he assured her. Slowly he lowered his gaze to the rapid pulse hammering at the base of her throat. Mentally Susan chastised herself for not having more control over her response. One slow, appraising look and she crumpled at his feet. His dark eyes roamed her face, the sensual tension building until her stomach tightened. Angrily she jerked her head aside. What was the use? She was only setting herself up for more hurt.

During the ride home, Adam worked hard to lighten the mood and tear down the tension between them. Joking, he carried her things into the apartment, set her on the sofa and fluffed up the pillows.

Susan tried her hardest to throw herself into his happy mood but failed miserably. When Adam insisted on cooking their dinner, she watched with amazement as he set the table and brought out an expensive bottle of wine.

As much as Susan wanted and needed him, she

couldn't let this continue. She knew his motives. "Adam," she whispered, "the accident wasn't your fault."

His high spirits were lost as he expelled his breath forcefully. "I know that."

"Then why are you doing this? I don't know how to react when you're kind to me. I'm afraid." To her horror, large tears filled her eyes and spilled down her colorless cheeks.

Adam ripped the apron from his waist in one angry movement and tossed it across the room. "Damn it, Susan. Don't cry. I can't stand to see you cry."

"Then just leave." Her voice wobbled ridiculously as she pointed a finger at the front door.

Frozen, Adam stared back at her as if a tug-of-war were pulling him from both sides. Finally he reacted, grabbing his jacket from the back of the chair.

"Don't you dare leave me," she shouted, and hiccupped ingloriously.

He got as far as the front door, his hand on the knob. His back was to her and she watched as a shudder went through him.

"I need you," she whispered, her voice so low it was almost inaudible. She wasn't referring to the accident, and they both knew it.

When he turned, a tumult of emotions played over his strong face. Pride, indecision, pain and something she couldn't recognize.

Of its own volition, her hand reached out to him. The action seemed to break something within him and he hurried to her side, falling to his knees and wrapping his arms around her. Even in his urgency he was conscious of her ribs and the pain his hold could inflict. "Susan, dear God." He murmured her name over and over again, rubbing his chin against her hair. "I saw you in that room, blood everywhere, and I died a thousand deaths. If I lost you…" He didn't finish.

Her hands roamed his back, loving the feel of him as she buried her face in the wide expanse of his chest. "Oh, Adam," she cried, tears streaming down her face. "I've missed you so much. You sent me away and I wanted to die."

Gently he broke the contact. His large hands framed her face as he lovingly spread kisses over her lips and cheeks and forehead, as if to kiss away the pain of his rejection.

"Adam." His name slipped from her lips in a half pleading cry.

A tense groan was muffled as he found her mouth and savored again and again the softness of her lips.

Her hand left his shoulder and lovingly explored the line of his jaw before curving into the thick dark hair. The kiss hardened, demanding and relentless, drawing from Susan her heart, and touching the softness of her soul.

When he pulled away, his breathing was hoarse and uneven. "Susan, we've got to stop," he groaned.

"I know," she agreed, and unbuttoned his shirt, desperate for the feel of his bare skin. When her fingers encountered the cloud of dark hair, Susan became incapable of coherent thought. Right or wrong, she hadn't the power to reason anymore. The potent masculine feel of him enveloped her senses until they cried out at fever pitch.

When Adam's hands opened her blouse and cupped her unrestrained breasts, he gently kneaded their fullness and she grew weak with desire. Lost in a mindless whirlpool, Susan groaned softly, encouragingly, as his head bent to kiss the swelling curve.

He pressed her back against the couch, and Susan drew in a sharp breath as pain pierced her ribs.

Adam hesitated, then pulled away. Still within the circle of his embrace, she could feel his aching regret. "I'm sorry, love," he whispered in a quivering breath.

"Sorry?" she repeated. A shudder wracked her shoulders, and Adam kissed her softly as if the action would absorb her pain.

His mouth twisted wryly as he lifted his head. "Those ribs must be hurting like hell," he muttered thickly.

"Not as much as…" She paused, biting off the words. He already knew how much sending her away had hurt. At the time, Susan hadn't been aware of how acutely he'd shared that pain.

"Are you ready for a glass of wine?" His jaw was set in a determined line as he battled his need and desire. Gently he tugged her arms from his neck. He kissed her fingertips and then the bridge of her nose before helping her fasten her blouse. She hadn't worn a bra intentionally. The restraining fabric would have cut into her ribs, hurting the tender area.

"I… I didn't know you had a hairy chest." Her voice was incredibly weak.

"You never asked." His voice didn't sound any less affected. Standing, he moved into the kitchen and returned with two glasses of wine, handing her one.

"Do you always keep dead flowers?" he quizzed, sitting opposite her.

Susan smiled softly to herself, aware that he had purposely taken a seat across from her so as not to be tempted. "Dead what?"

"Looks like roses, or what used to be roses." He picked a long stem from the vase resting beside the chair on the end table.

"Oh, those. I didn't have the heart to throw them out."

A coldness frosted his eyes as he lifted the wineglass to his lips and took a drink. "Someone special must have given them to you, for you to keep them this long," he commented with light pretense as his eyes avoided hers.

"Someone very special did," she returned.

"Who?" His voice was rough in demand. Vaulting to his feet, he stalked to the other side of the room. "No, don't answer that. I don't have any right to know."

"The next time you send a lady roses, the least you can do is remember it."

"Me?" He swiveled around sharply, a shocked look on his face. "When?"

"You honestly don't remember?" she teased. It was obvious he didn't. "When I was promoted."

Wearily Adam slouched back into the chair. "That long? You kept them that long?"

Lowering her gaze, she rubbed a finger around the

edge of the crystal glass. "It was all I had," she said into the cup, not intending him to hear. Forcing herself to smile, Susan looked up. "What's for dinner? I'm starved." She wasn't, but was desperately seeking to change the subject.

"Crepes stuffed with shrimp and fresh mushrooms."

"Adam." Surprise caused her to blink twice. "You can cook like that?"

"Well," he hedged, "not quite, but I do an excellent job of placing something in the oven and setting the timer."

"Oh, Adam," she said happily. "We have so much in common."

They played a game of Monopoly after dinner. Adam won, but Susan's interest wasn't on the board. Adam waited until she'd changed into her pajamas before kissing her good night. The kiss was almost brotherly.

"Miser," she complained.

"Troublemaker," he countered, bringing her back into his arms and kissing her soundly. But he didn't allow it to deepen into passion.

Locking the door after him, Susan leaned against the solid frame and swallowed a happy lump.

Adam was hers.

A half hour later the phone rang and she struggled out of bed, pressing a hand to her ribs as she rose.

"Hello."

"Susan, are you all tight?" It was Adam.

"I was until I had to answer the stupid phone," she objected strongly.

"Sorry." His apology was filled with barely contained amusement. "I forgot to tell you not to fix lunch tomorrow."

"Good, why?"

"I'm bringing over something special."

"You mean something more than you."

"That was dumb."

"No dumber than calling me in the middle of the night to talk about lunch."

He chuckled, and Susan was lost in the deep, rich sound of his laughter. "You're right, but I had to hear your voice one more time before I went to bed."

"Oh, Adam." It was one of the most beautiful things he'd ever said to her.

That night was the first of many they spent together as the week progressed. Adam couldn't have been more gentle or loving. He kissed and touched her often. He made excuses to be with her. But he never allowed their lovemaking to rage out of control as it had that first night.

When she was able to return to work, he met her two and sometimes three nights a week. Occasionally they dined out, other times cooking for themselves, or as Adam said, setting the timer. Afterward, she sat at his side reading manuscripts while he looped an arm over her shoulder and worked brainteasers. Susan had never been happier. But late at night, alone, she couldn't push the troubled doubts aside. How much longer would this last before Adam pulled away? Could she bear to let him go?

Three weeks after the accident and it was difficult to tell that anything had happened. Her face had healed beautifully, as Adam repeatedly told her.

Humming happily, she set the table, anticipating Adam's arrival. She placed a candle in the middle of the fresh linen cloth and popped a tuna casserole into the oven. She wasn't much of a cook, but made a humble attempt now and then.

Adam knocked, and when she let him into the apartment, he carelessly tossed his coat over the chair. Surprised at the restrained anger that seemed to exude from him, Susan didn't comment.

She wiped her hands on the apron and kissed him on the cheek. "Have a bad day?"

"No worse than usual."

"I tried my hand at a new recipe and whipped up a tuna casserole."

His razor-sharp gaze sliced into her as he stared at the table. "What's the candle for?"

"No reason," she said, and shrugged. "I thought it might add a little romance to our meal."

"Romance," he spat, viciously throwing the word back at her. "You live and breathe that garbage, don't you?"

Stunned, Susan said nothing for a minute. "If you don't like the candle, then I'll take it away."

"I hate tuna," he shouted at her unreasonably. "I've hated it since I was a kid. If you'd bothered to ask, you might have known that."

"I'm sorry, I… I guess I should have."

"Do you have to apologize for every little thing? Don't you ever get tired of groveling?"

Eight

Susan breathed in sharply in an effort to control her temper. Wordlessly, she walked across the room, took Adam's jacket off the chair and handed it to him.

"It's obvious you've had a rotten day. I'm sorry about that. But I think it would be better for both of us if you left now before you end up wearing the tuna casserole."

"Threats, Susan?" Thick brows arched arrogantly as he issued the question in a calm voice that belied his anger.

Susan wasn't fooled. "We'll have dinner another night." She stalked purposefully across the room and held open the door.

"There won't be another night," he informed her casually. "I should never have let things go this far. The whole situation between us should never have happened. I knew the minute I saw you at Ralph Jordan's that you spelled trouble." He jerked his arm into the jacket. "This is it, Susan."

Did he expect her to cry and beg? She wouldn't,

not anymore. If Adam Gallagher could walk out of her life, then she could stand by and let him go. That was the decision she'd made in the hospital and she meant to stick with it.

"Threats, Adam?" She returned his own words.

His shirt was stretched across his broad chest, and Susan directed her gaze to the rippling muscles rather than meet his eyes. Her pulse drummed to an erratic tempo, and she cursed herself for the telltale tremble in her voice.

"Good-bye, Adam," she whispered softly.

He paused as if he wanted to add something, then clamped his mouth tightly shut and stormed out the door.

Gently, Susan closed it, then turned the lock before leaning against the solid wood, needing its support. Her knees felt weak, but with a determined set to her shoulders, she returned to the kitchen, removed one place setting, lit the candle and dished up her dinner. "My, this is delicious," she spoke out loud. The casserole tasted of overcooked noodles and dried tuna, but she managed to down every bite until her plate was empty.

After washing the dishes she took a long, hot shower and curled up on the sofa to watch television. Her mind was only half on the situation comedy, but she refused to answer the nagging doubts that repeatedly demanded her attention. "No," she whispered forcefully.

"If Adam says we're through then so be it." Hadn't she mentally prepared herself for this? Hadn't she accepted and known from the beginning it would happen?

The accident and the closeness they had shared afterward was only a reprieve.

Two miserable days later Susan flew to Florida for
the writers' conference. The Boeing 747 took off during a thundering rainstorm and descended from blue
skies. This was her first trip to the Sunshine State, and
she marveled at the beauty. Although her free time was
limited, the conference organizers saw to it that she was
given the opportunity to see some of the local sights.
Susan only wished her mind had been more on what
was happening around her.

She arrived home late Friday afternoon. Absently,
she sorted through mail and tossed the bills and junk
pieces on the tabletop before carrying her suitcase into
the bedroom. Usually home offered a feeling of welcome, peace, a solace that came from things familiar.
But not today. She didn't allow her mind to follow its
natural course. What was lacking was Adam. Closing
her eyes to the hurt, she mentally shook herself. How
easily she'd become accustomed to chatting with him,
sharing the minor details of her life, that easy camaraderie. Within a space of time he had become her best
friend. But admitting the source of the problem did little to lessen the pain of his absence.

Saturday morning, rather than face the day staring
at the walls alone, Susan rose early and walked to the
office to catch up with the workload that must have
reached mountainous proportions on her desk. With
her hands stuck deep into her pockets as she strolled,
Susan thought how much Rosemary would approve if
she could see her now. The walk, although she hated

to admit it, was pleasant. Block after block the exercise helped stir her blood and quicken her heartbeat. At least now she felt alive and not half-dead as she had since Adam left.

Letting herself into her small office, the first thing she noticed was a bouquet of flowers. She glanced at them quizzically, unpinning the attached card. It read: "I deserve to wear that casserole. I'm sorry. Meet me at Tastings Thursday. Love, Adam."

Thursday! The flowers must have arrived when she was away. What must he be thinking? Grabbing her coat, she flew out of the office, impatiently tapping her foot on the elevator ride down. Once on the street, she madly waved her arms until she was able to attract the attention of a taxi. The driver steered haphazardly across two lanes of traffic. With a grimace, Susan climbed inside and breathlessly relayed Adam's address.

She almost threw the fare at the astonished man as she leaped from the back seat and raced inside the apartment building. Too impatient for the elevator, she took the stairs, bounding up them two steps at a time until she arrived at the fourth floor and staggered into the hallway.

She was leaning against the wall taking in giant breaths when Adam casually opened the door.

"Adam." Throwing herself into his arms, she hugged him fiercely.

"Susan, are you all right?"

"Yes…," she gasped. "I mean…no. Oh, Adam, I was in Florida."

He sat her down on one of the two wing-backed

chairs that dominated his living room and left her for
a moment while he went into the kitchen.

If her legs hadn't felt like cooked noodles, she would
have gone after him. "Adam," she pleaded.

"Here." He handed her a glass of water and knelt in
front of her.

She set the water aside, and with eyes sparkling with
happiness, she placed her hands on his shoulders. "I've
missed you so much." Closing her eyes, she leaned forward until their foreheads touched. Lovingly her hands
traced his jaw.

His fingers stopped hers and brought them to his
lips. "You idiot," he groaned, and hugged her. "There
was no need to half kill yourself to get to me. I already
knew you were in Florida. When you didn't show, I
called your office and asked—"

"You called?" she asked incredulously.

"What's so unusual about that? I call you all the time."

"I know, but never after a fight. Never!"

"We don't argue," he contradicted, a cooked smile
tugging up the edges of his mouth.

"Adam, for heaven's sake, would you stop being so
obtuse! I can't stand it."

Her happy gaze met his as he kissed her hungrily.
Every minute of their separation, each second apart,
was worth the thrill of Adam's touch.

"Were you miserable?" she asked him.

"Yes," he replied on a forceful note.

"I love it," she cried cheerfully, but her heart repeated
that it was Adam she really loved. "But if you were so
down and out, why didn't you meet me at the airport?"

"I was planning on it. You weren't due in until this afternoon."

"That's right," she murmured, more pleased than she could remember being about anything. "I was able to connect with a flight yesterday afternoon and opted to come home early," she whispered in a rush, and threw her arms around him a second time. "Oh, Adam." She swallowed the lump of joy that blocked her throat. "I'm so pleased to be home."

He took her to the Palm Court at the Plaza Hotel, and they lunched on luscious salads. Not until the meal was finished did Susan notice the pinched look about Adam's mouth.

"I've been talking fifty miles an hour and hardly giving you time to say a word."

Adam swirled the wineglass, and the imported Soave sloshed over the edge. "What do you want me to say?" The smile didn't reach his eyes.

"I could think of several wonderful lines," she whispered. Like "I love you, Susan Mackenzie," her mind added.

"I'm sure you can." His eyes avoided hers.

Sighing softly, she reached across the table for his hand. "Adam, what's wrong?"

Wearily he rubbed his face. "It's been one of those weeks. I've been miserable without you, Susan."

He needed her, but he wouldn't admit as much.

Something deep and dark was troubling him. He couldn't hide it from her; she knew him too well. Perhaps that bothered him more.

"Didn't you say something about picking up some work at your office?"

Susan nodded. "Do you want to meet me back at my place later? I'll cook us dinner." Looking at the leftover food on her plate, she added, "Something light."

"Fine." He took his wallet from inside his coat. "I've got a few errands to do. I'll see you tonight."

As it turned out it was much later. When Adam hadn't shown up by eight, she frowned and dialed his number. The phone rang ten times before she replaced the receiver. Perplexed, she sat on the sofa, feet crossed, as she read over book proposals she'd brought home from the office. Nothing held her concentration as her gaze swung to her watch every five minutes. Where was Adam?

When the doorbell chimed she nearly leaped off the couch. "Hi," she said, and didn't mention how late he was or ask why.

Again his smile didn't reach his eyes. "Sorry, I didn't mean to take this long." He didn't offer any information or excuses.

"No problem. I wasn't hungry. Do you want me to fix you something?"

"Sure," he agreed.

Susan suspected he only wanted dinner so she'd be kept busy in the kitchen and wouldn't ask questions. When he barely touched the scrambled eggs and bacon, she knew she was right.

He wrapped his arms around her later when they sat on the sofa. Again she noted the sadness in his eyes as he laid his head against the back cushion.

"Adam?" she questioned softly. "What's wrong?"

"Nothing," he denied a second time. He closed his eyes and released a deep sigh. Susan watched him, all the more troubled.

"Let me massage your temples. You look like you've got a headache." Standing behind him, she gently pressed her fingertips in a rotating movement against the sides of his head. Gradually she worked her way down his neck to his shoulders. The muscles were tense and corded as if every inch of him were prepared to spring into action.

"That feels good." His head began to move in a circular action, keeping rhythm with her hands. "Want me to do you?"

"No," she answered, and gently laid her lips along the side of his neck. "Mmmm, you smell good. What is that?"

He chuckled and it was the first time she'd heard his laugh since that morning. "Antiseptic."

"It isn't either," she insisted, and gave a shout of surprise as he tumbled her over the back of the sofa into his arms and kissed her long and hard. In the past his kisses had been deep, but now there was a punishing quality to the way his mouth ground over hers. Weakly, she submitted, knowing he needed her and was using her. She gave him what she could.

When he released her, Adam's gaze narrowed briefly at her swollen lips. "Did I hurt you?"

"No," she lied in an attempt to assure him she didn't mind.

His thumb traced her throbbing mouth in a gentle, soothing movement. "Did I mention that Joey Williams was back in the hospital?" He said it so casually that for a moment she didn't recognize the significance.

"No." She breathed in deeply. "No you didn't." So that was it. Joey. The little boy Adam loved. "How... how's he doing?"

Adam didn't respond immediately. Instead he picked up one of her manuscripts and leafed through the neatly typed pages. She knew what he was thinking as clearly as if he had shouted the words. The books she edited were filled with the light side of life, fantasy, happy-ever-after. But not for Joey. And not in the world in which Adam lived and worked.

"Not good," Adam answered at last. "What happens when someone submits a manuscript?" He was purposely changing the subject. He gathered her in his arms, holding her head against his chest.

She spoke because she knew that was what he wanted. "Did you know Silhouette receives seven hundred manuscripts a month, far more than a handful of editors can deal with?"

"Seven hundred," he repeated. "I knew these books were popular, if my mother is anything to go by, but seven hundred hopefuls every month? My goodness!"

Susan smiled softly. "If someone submits a full manuscript instead of a proposal—"

"What's a proposal?"

"Three chapters and an outline."

She felt his nod against the top of her head. The slow drum of his heart sounded reassuring in her ear.

"What happens then?"

"A full manuscript goes to a freelance reader, who

reads the book and writes a report on it before an editor looks it over."

"What about the proposals?"

"The editors divide the workload and get to them as quickly as possible."

"That's what you're reading now?"

She nodded. "I enjoy it. Some of our best writers were discovered in the slush pile."

"Where does an agent play into this?"

Susan laughed lightly. "You'll have to ask Ralph that one. He does a good job of sticking material under my nose whenever he gets the chance."

"Okay, suppose you want to buy someone's book."

"It's called acquiring. Then I either talk to that person's agent or directly to them. We agree on an advance and I send the order through to the managing editor in the contracts department. That's where Rosemary works, by the way."

A hand smoothed a curl away from her neck as his fingers toyed with her hair. Susan was sure he was only half listening.

"After the author signs and returns the contract, some of the advance is issued. I put through another payment request for the second half when the manuscript is completed and any revisions needed are done. Then the book is scheduled. With twenty-eight books released each month, this is more difficult than most people realize. For instance, we don't want five books coming out all located in Kansas City. And titles can be a hassle."

"I bet they are," he mumbled.

"Adam," she admonished gently, "you haven't heard a word I said."

"Sure I did."

Rather than argue, Susan straightened. "Want to play cribbage?" They had played the card game several times in the past. Their skill was equally matched, but when she won three games running, she realized Adam's mind wasn't in it.

Adam helped her pick up the board and cards. "Walk me to the door," he requested lightly.

Susan did as he asked, then slipped her arms around his neck, anticipating his kiss. Slowly his eyes lowered to look into hers. His troubled features mirrored all the turbulent emotions he had stored inside his heart.

The hand at the back of her neck tightened, urging her mouth to his Susan's lips parted in eager welcome as his mouth consumed hers.

"Adam." She released his name on a rush of air. Desperately she longed to share his burden. Compulsively she molded her body to his, as if to bring him as close as physically possible. Was there anything so insurmountable that they couldn't face and conquer it together? "I'll see you…"

"You'll see me." He released her and kissed her forehead. "I don't know when."

"It's okay. I understand."

His brilliant dark eyes narrowed. "Do you, Susan?"

"Yes." She nodded, emphasizing that she did.

"I don't want to hurt you again. I hate myself afterward."

"You aren't going to hurt me," she countered softly. "I'm a big girl."

He kissed her again lightly before letting himself out.

Susan didn't hear from him until Tuesday of the following week. He phoned late one night.

"Hi, honey, how's your week going?"

"Fine, and you?"

"Great." The word was emitted in a flippant tone, and Susan wanted to shout at him that it wasn't necessary for him to lie to her.

"Any news?" She didn't need to clarify about whom.

"Nothing," he responded in the same tone. "What about you?"

"One of the editors is sick and it looks like I'll be traveling to Texas soon."

"Another conference? Do you usually travel this much?"

"We all do our share, but it usually isn't more than a couple of times a year." Was Adam suggesting that he didn't want her to go, that he may need her? She broached the subject carefully. "Is there a problem? I mean, I'm sure one of the other editors wouldn't mind."

"It's no problem for me," Adam returned. "Why should I care?"

Indeed! Susan bristled. They spoke for a few minutes longer, but the conversation was unsatisfactory and left Susan deflated and angry.

They met for dinner early the next week. Susan was several minutes late and found Adam already seated and studying the menu when she arrived.

"Sorry, but I got held up in traffic," she said in a slightly breathless tone as she slid into the seat opposite him and shrugged off her coat.

Adam looked up, but only said, "Are you ready to order?"

"Order?" she asked. "I've barely caught my breath. Adam, you wouldn't believe the day I've had. First I got stuck on the phone with an agent who was making the most unreasonable demands. And just before I left an author called wanting to go over the editorial changes I'd made on her manuscript. Over the phone, mind you. It just seemed to be one thing right after the other."

He offered her a poor facsimile of a smile.

"I'm sorry, Adam," she said sincerely. "I didn't even ask about your day."

"Nothing unusual. Mine certainly can't compete with a popular romance editor's day."

Susan decided to ignore the sarcastic tone. "Ralph Jordan called today. He's giving another party. Are we going?"

"We?" He raised one thick brow.

Deliberately, Susan laid the menu beside her plate. "Adam, what is wrong with you? You haven't said a civil word since I arrived."

"Not for lack of trying, I assure you." His face was buried in the menu, blocking her out. "With you chattering away with inanities, it's difficult to speak at all." Susan expelled a slow, measured breath, trying with great difficulty to maintain her limited patience. "Is it Joey?"

He slammed the menu on the table, the commotion

attracting the attention of others. "Joey's home; are you satisfied?" He was nearly shouting, his voice biting and bitter.

Unbelievably hurt, Susan closed her eyes to a rush of pain. She never would have believed Adam could talk to her that way.

"Don't tell me you're going to cry. I can't stand women who cry."

For a long minute Susan said nothing. "I used to think you were the gentlest man I'd ever known. Something's wrong, Adam. It's obvious you don't want to share it with me, and that's your prerogative. But something's got to be done. Over the last couple of weeks I find it difficult to even like you."

"Maybe that's the way I want it."

"Then why invite me to dinner? Why phone me? Certainly you're not enjoying this any more than I am?"

His eyes were sad and haunted. "For the first time all night, you're talking sense. Why are we here? What the hell do we have in common? You're the beautiful romance editor who lives in never-never land among the happily-ever-afters."

"I think I've heard enough." Scooting out of the booth, she stood beside him and hurriedly placed her arms inside her coat sleeves. "When you've settled whatever's troubling you, then give me a call. I'll be waiting."

He started to say something, but Susan didn't wait to listen. Instead she hurried out of the restaurant and hailed a taxi before he had the opportunity to follow. Another week passed before she heard from Adam again. He called to apologize, but he didn't suggest they meet and she didn't ask.

Ralph Jordan's dinner party came and went. She didn't attend and assumed Adam hadn't either.

Susan couldn't recall a more frustrating time. Adam was not the same man she'd met. Examining the two sides of his personality was like seeing two entirely different people. She felt helpless and lost, cold and empty. Even Rosemary noticed things weren't right.

"You don't look good. I don't think you're getting enough vitamin A."

"Honestly, Rosemary, I'm fine."

"I'm serious," her friend returned. "Vitamin A as in Adam."

Susan grinned. "No, I suppose I'm not. I haven't seen him in almost two weeks, one day and"—she lifted her arm to examine her wristwatch—"eighteen hours. Not that I care."

"I noticed," her friend murmured. "You know what the problem is, don't you?"

Interested now, Susan had a difficult time containing a smile. "No, tell me."

"You know one another too well."

Susan gave a good-natured laugh. Some days she didn't think she knew Adam at all. Certainly not these last weeks.

"Fred and I knew in one day…"

"How'd you know?" Susan asked seriously, the amusement slowly dissipating.

"Well we'd gone out to dinner and the fortune cookie said—"

"You mean to tell me," Susan interrupted, "that you and Fred got married on the sound advice of a fortune cookie? Rosemary Thomas Bradly, I am shocked."

Rosemary had the good grace to blush. "You mean because we were married so soon?"

"No, silly," Susan said, "that's romantic. I'm shocked that the two of you were eating Chinese food with all the MSG and heart-bending toxicants."

Later, when Susan lay in bed staring at the ceiling, it wasn't as easy to put on a smile and tease. There were only the darkness and the doubts. How could a man who was gentle and kind one minute turn into a snarling, unreasonable bear the next? Maybe she was totally wrong about him. Maybe the time had come for her to…

The doorbell interrupted her thoughts.

Susan sat up and threw back her bedcovers. A quick look at the clock assured her it was well past midnight. Who could it possibly be at this time of night? After tying the sash to her robe, she turned on the light switch in the living room.

The bell sounded again.

Peeking out the small hole in her door, Susan saw no one. "Who is it?" she called.

For a moment there was nothing.

"Adam."

Nine

"Adam," Susan said softly as she unlocked the door.

He hesitated, searching her face as if desperate for the sight of her. "I woke you."

"No," she told him. "I'd gone to bed, but I wasn't asleep. Come in."

"I don't think…" He paused and looked past her into the dimly lit room. "A cup of coffee would help."

"I'll put some on right away." Her eyes didn't leave him as he came into the apartment and slowly lowered himself onto the sofa. He looked terrible. Susan couldn't remember seeing anyone so pale.

Moving quickly, she poured water into the tea kettle. As she worked, Susan glanced into the room at Adam. He was leaning forward, elbows on his knees with his face buried in his palms. For the first time she noticed the bloody knuckles on one hand. Adam had been fighting? She couldn't believe it.

He must have felt her scrutiny because he dropped his arms and sat up. Never had Susan seen a look more filled with pain. A torment so deep it reached all the way to his soul.

After setting the kettle on the stove, she moved to his side, kneeling in front of him. "Adam," she whispered, all the love in her heart shining through her eyes. "What is it? Won't you tell me?"

Although he looked directly at her, Susan was sure he was hardly aware she was there. "Joey Williams died tonight."

A soft protesting moan came from deep within her throat. "Oh, Adam," she whispered, her voice shaking, "I'm so sorry." Sliding her arms around his stomach, she rested her face on his chest and started to cry. "You loved him so much." Sobs shook her.

Adam resisted and tried to push her away, but she wouldn't let him, tightening her grip around this man she loved. He held himself stiff and unyielding until something seemed to snap within him.

He shuddered against her and released a deep, mournful cry like that of an animal caught in a trap, facing death. Fiercely he hauled her into his arms, hugging her so close that for a moment Susan was afraid he would crush her. Huge sobs wracked his body as he buried his face in her neck and wept.

"His mother wanted him to die at home," Adam told her with a sobbing breath. "I knew he wouldn't last much longer, and tonight she had me lift him into her arms. He died there two hours ago."

"Adam," Susan cried, wanting so badly to comfort him.

"All the years I studied and there wasn't a damn thing I could do. Never have I felt so damn helpless."

"You did everything you could," she whispered soothingly.

"Not enough, not near enough."

She couldn't understand anything more he said, his words muffled in her hair and by his tears. She didn't know how long he held her. As the shuddering sobs subsided, she heard the brittle whistle from the kettle on the stove.

Briefly Adam raised his head, noting the source of the distraction. Reluctantly he released her.

Before she left, Susan lifted his hand and kissed his bloody knuckles. She walked to the kitchen and wiped her face dry, then poured them each a steaming cup and returned to Adam.

His eyes remained red and haunted, and his gaze avoided hers as he took the coffee. "Thank you," he murmured.

Susan knew he wasn't referring to the drink. Neither spoke. They didn't need words. The closeness between them was beyond expression.

After a few sips of steaming liquid, Susan placed her cup aside. Adam curved an arm around her shoulder, bringing her close. She rested against him while his hand tenderly stroked the length of her arm.

When the soothing action stopped, Susan lifted her head and noticed that Adam was asleep.

Carefully, so not to wake him, she slipped from his embrace. He was exhausted, mentally and physically.

When his head dropped to one side, she brought out a pillow and blanket from her bedroom. With only a minimum of encouragement she was able to ease his head onto the feathery softness. After removing his shoes, she lifted his feet onto the sofa and covered him with a blanket.

Even in sleep, his look remained troubled. Susan stood and watched him for a long time. He had come to her in his grief, and that meant more to her than the finest gifts. Because what he had given her, his trust and love, was beyond price.

Flipping the switch to the lamp cast the room into darkness. Susan paused, standing above Adam. Gently she bent down, lovingly brushed the thick hair from his forehead and kissed him.

When she woke the next morning Adam was gone. A scribbled note left on the kitchen table briefly thanked her and stated the date and time of the funeral. With her morning coffee cupped in her hands, Susan fingered the plain piece of paper. Joey's death explained so much of Adam's behavior these past weeks. Why hadn't he said something? She expelled a frustrated sigh when she recalled that he'd tried the day he told her Joey was back in the hospital. Perhaps she should have pressed him more. But at the time she didn't feel she could. Adam had known then that there was nothing he could do for the child and had carried the burden all these weeks.

She remembered the day she'd met Joey, the twinkling, happy eyes and the love and admiration the boy had had for Adam. Later when she'd asked Adam if Joey was going to make it, Adam had answered her with an emphatic yes as if he had infused his own fierce determination into the child, lending the boy a part of himself. With Joey's death, that part of Adam had died.

Susan didn't see Adam until the day of the funeral. She slipped into the pew beside him and listened to the comforting words of the beautiful service. Her hand was tightly clenched in his.

Afterward the Williams family came over to Adam. Mrs. Williams, tears glistening in her proud eyes, hugged him.

"We owe you more than words can ever express," she said. "Thank you for making it possible for Joey to come home those last days."

Mr. Williams, pale and drawn, shook Adam's hand, and Mrs. Williams smiled weakly at Susan.

"You must be Miss Mackenzie. Joey mentioned how pretty you are." She inclined her head toward Adam. "Hold on to this man," she whispered. "There aren't many as wonderful as Dr. Gallagher."

"I know that," Susan agreed.

"In the end he hardly left Joey's side. The Lord knows when he slept. Our family will never forget him."

Susan nodded because the lump in her throat had grown so large it was impossible to speak.

"Honestly, Rosemary, I don't know how I let you talk me into these things," Susan complained under her breath as she moved her body in rhythm to the fast-paced music that filled the gym.

"You love it and you know it," Rosemary returned, only slightly breathless.

"Well darn it, if we're going to do this aerobics thing, the least you can do is sweat. I'm wringing wet."

"If you were in better—"

"Don't say it," Susan warned. "Besides, pregnant women aren't supposed to be able to do this kind of thing."

"Jane Fonda does."

It was becoming increasingly difficult to talk, and Susan wondered what Jane Fonda had to do with this. Her feelings toward the talented actress were decidedly unpleasant at the moment. Weakly, Susan motioned with her hand that she'd had enough. Panting, she leaned against the wall of the gymnasium, waiting until Rosemary had finished the routine. Rosemary leaped enthusiastically with each beat of the music. The only evidence that her friend was pregnant was the gentle swell of Rosemary's abdomen. Susan watched her, longing for the day she could have a child. Adam's child. Already she knew a boy would be named Joey, although she'd never discussed it with Adam.

Within a few minutes Rosemary joined Susan. "You were smart to stop when you did since this is your first session."

"My body knows when it's had enough."

"There's a word for that," Rosemary murmured, pinching her bottom lip with two fingers as she thought.

"It's called wisdom."

Rosemary poked her with an elbow. "Know-it-all! Come on, let's go have some carrot juice."

Susan shook her head. "No thanks, I brought my own drink."

"Diet soda?" Rosemary asked in a whisper. Susan nodded.

"Well for heaven's sake, don't let anyone around here see you drinking it. You'll be railroaded out of the place."

"I'll have the carrot juice," she grumbled.

Round white enameled tables were set in a sun room with a refreshment bar. Susan located a vacant table while Rosemary brought back their drinks. The place was packed. Susan couldn't understand how so many women could torture themselves this way for thinner thighs. As far as she was concerned, it was all genetic anyway.

One sip of the orange-colored juice and Susan grimaced.

Rosemary laughed softly. "I had them spice it up a little."

"With what?" Susan demanded, then abruptly shook her hand. "Never mind, I don't want to know."

Dark expressive eyes sparkled cheerfully as Rosemary took another sip from the straw. "It's probably best you don't."

"That did it." Hurriedly Susan pushed the drink aside.

"I was teasing. It's just carrot juice."

"Sure," Susan murmured, and bent down to pull up her leg warmers, which had slipped ingloriously around her ankles.

"Have you seen much of Adam lately?" Apparently Rosemary had thought it best to change the subject.

"Quite regularly."

"Honestly, you two should get married. What are you waiting for?"

"A proposal."

"Well, that's silly, you—"

"It's not silly at all. If we're going to get married, I think it's only right that Adam do the asking. I was the one who asked him out the first time. And he refused; that still rankles."

"Has he said he loves you?" Rosemary looked worried.

"A thousand times," Susan confirmed, and sighed heavily. "But never with words."

"Perhaps he needs a little prompting?"

"Not from me," she stated emphatically. "For once I'm going to keep my mouth shut."

Taking a sip of her drink, Rosemary mumbled, "For you that must be difficult."

"Have you got everything?" Adam questioned as he lifted her suitcase.

"I think so." Susan did a quick survey of her bedroom. Everything looked neatly in place. The items she needed were carefully packed in her suitcases.

"I'm ready." Adam was driving her to the airport. After dinner she would be flying to Boston for a promotional tour with several authors. The tour would be five days of interviews, talks and traveling. Susan always enjoyed working with the publicity department. But now she almost regretted having agreed to go. Something was happening with Adam, but she had no idea what.

"That look is in your eyes again," she told him as they sat in the cozy restaurant not far from the airport.

"What look?" He glanced up, his fingers busy, gently twirling the wineglass.

"The one in your eyes," she repeated. "Since we've arrived, you've toyed with your napkin, fiddled with your fork, and done everything possible not to look at me."

"That's because every time I stare into those gorgeous eyes of yours I'm tempted to toss good manners out the window and pull you into my arms."

"That sounds interesting," she teased, but Adam ignored her, pretending he hadn't heard. Susan knew differently.

Even his kisses had been different lately, almost polite yet wonderful and gentle. She didn't know how to explain it. But now wasn't the time to discuss it.

When it came time to board her flight, Susan couldn't fault his kiss then. He found a quiet corner that offered as much privacy as possible and unhurriedly drew her into his embrace. Susan studied the strong, uneven lines of his face. Adam Gallagher was a vital, compelling man although he insisted he was "plain looking." Even if it was true, Susan was no longer aware of that aspect of Adam. She saw the man, as she had that first night when she'd only guessed at the vibrancy within him that made her heart sing.

"I'm going to miss you." His voice was a caress, husky and warm.

"Good, because you know how I feel." Adam had never verbalized the words, but neither had she. A thousand times she was forced to swallow back the natural flow of her love. From the first time they'd met, it had always been her. Adam's mother had told her to be patient, and for now she would be content, although it grew more difficult as each week passed. He loved her. She knew it without the words. When he told her, it would be from his heart and so much more meaningful than if she prompted him.

"Yes, I do."

She heard the taut pain in his voice and narrowed her gaze, perplexed.

"Yes, I do," he repeated, as he lowered his mouth to savor the softness of hers. The kiss was slow and exploring, his tongue outlining her lips, coaxing her mouth open. Gladly Susan succumbed to the sweet tide of longing that swept through her.

Time away from New York helped put her relationship with Adam into perspective, but it didn't offer the answer to the doubts that plagued her. Several times she toyed with the idea of phoning with one excuse or another, knowing she only needed to hear his voice. Usually late at night when she knew he'd be asleep. Or early in the morning when he'd be busy. As much as she hated to admit it, calling him probably wasn't the best thing.

When the plane touched down at Kennedy, she eagerly anticipated their meeting.

He waved when he saw her, and Susan had to restrain herself from running into his arms. Adam looked wonderful. The color was back in his face; his eyes were warm and excited. It'd been so long since she'd seen him this happy.

"Welcome home." He looped an arm around her waist, took her hand baggage and kissed her cheek.

"You look marvelous."

"I am. How was the trip?"

"Great," she said, and sighed. "But I must admit it's good to be home."

He squeezed her close. "It's good to have you back. I've got some fantastic news."

"What?" She stopped walking so she could watch him.

"I've accepted a position in Seattle, Washington, at the Fred Hutchinson Cancer Research Center. I'm moving next week."

Ten

"Seattle, Washington?" The words went through her like a bolt of lightning and she paused, stunned, as the shock hit her full force.

"It's the opportunity of a lifetime," Adam continued, undaunted by her obvious surprise. "I can't tell you how pleased and excited I am."

He didn't need to tell her; it was there for her to see. "Congratulations," she murmured, a breathless quiver to her voice.

"Honey, I think you'll understand that I've got a hundred and one things that need to be done. Meeting you tonight was important and I did want to tell you my good news. But I've got to get back to my office right away. You understand, don't you?"

"Oh, sure. Of course I do." Fixing a smile on her face, she wondered if he detected the forced quality in in her voice. Numbly she followed him to the baggage claim area, barely aware of where they were going.

When he carried her suitcases into the apartment, she

stepped aside, a determined lift to her chin. He kissed her at the door. A brotherly kiss.

"Be happy for me." His voice vibrated with the depth of his feeling.

"I'm thrilled," she lied. I'm dying, her heart answered.

He hesitated, his gaze playing over her profile.

"I appreciate that you came to the airport, but it really wasn't necessary." A weary sigh escaped and she looked away.

"I wanted to, Susan." He glanced at his wristwatch. "Go," she commanded, fighting to keep the sarcasm out of her voice. "I understand."

She understood all too well. Adam was running. Running from New York, running from the memories of the little boy he couldn't save. But most of all he was running from her love. Her suitcases were just inside the door, and Susan looked around with a feeling of desolation. Within days she would be losing Adam, the most important person in her life. A heavy weight settled over her heart.

She barely slept. Just when she felt herself drifting off, the pain would return and she'd jerk awake.

Because she couldn't tolerate the thought of staying in the apartment on a Saturday morning, she dressed and walked to the park. Hands buried deep in her pockets, Susan sauntered around the soccer field. The season was over and the chalk line that bordered the playing area had faded long ago. But the happy thoughts the area evoked were fresh and potent.

"Are you going to let him do this?" her voice asked.

Yes, her heart answered, knowing there was nothing she could do to stop him.

Hating herself for being weak, she phoned him when she got back to the apartment.

"Hello." He sounded preoccupied, busy. "Morning," she said on a falsely cheerful note.

"Have you had breakfast?"

"No time, I'm sorting through my things, deciding what I want to take and what I'm going to store at my mother's. It's shocking how much stuff I've accumulated in the last few years."

"Let me help you. I'll stop by the bakery on my way over and bring some croissants."

The pause was only momentary. "Sure."

"I'll stay afterward and help you pack books and stuff."

"There's no need," Adam answered unevenly.

I'm not letting you go that easily, her mind shouted. "I want to help."

"If you like." He didn't sound as if he did. "I want to," she repeated.

The flaky croissants were still warm from the oven, but neither Susan nor Adam seemed to have much appetite. Carrying the paper plates into the kitchen, she dumped the leftovers in the garbage. With a shaky smile, she pushed up the sleeves of her sweatshirt.

"I'm ready. Where would you like me to start?" Boxes littered the living room. Most of the furniture was pushed to one side of the room. Bookcases filled with leather-bound books stood against one wall.

"Go ahead and pack up those."

He left her alone, and went to work in his den. Susan recognized that the move was intentional. He didn't want to be with her, was avoiding her as much as possible.

Lovingly she ran her hand over a worn copy of The Citadel by A. J. Cronin. In some ways Adam was like this frustrated, unhappy doctor.

As she carefully placed the books inside the boxes, she examined each one with the knowledge that she was learning more and more about Adam. From the things he treasured, he gave away a part of himself.

Susan could hear his movements in the other room. After a half hour of silence she called to him.

"Do you want a cup of coffee?"

"Sounds great. I could do with a break."

She poured them each a cup and sat on the plush carpet drinking hers. Adam didn't seem to want to stop working and continued going through his desk drawers. "There's a chance I'll be in Seattle sometime in June." She didn't add that was when her vacation was scheduled. Purposely she let him think it was business related.

"Wonderful." He didn't sound as if he meant it. "My parents live in Oregon."

He stopped what he was doing and looked up. "I'd forgotten that."

Of course he had. Washington State was as far away from her as he could get, and without knowing it he'd placed himself in her home territory. She watched as a frown worked its way across his face.

"But I think I should warn you, my schedule is very tight," he explained.

Susan didn't know how much more of this she could take. He was saying that if she did come, he'd make excuses not to see her. Cradling her knees, she stared into the dark coffee. Usually she drank it thick and dark. Today she added several teaspoons of sugar, knowing she needed energy. Rosemary would have been aghast. A sad smile touched her face.

"What's so funny?" Adam asked. "My thoughts, I guess."

The natural question would have been to ask her what she was thinking, but Adam didn't. Perhaps he was afraid of what she'd say.

"I'll finish packing the books," she said, and stood. "Susan." Her name was issued on a soft, anguish filled tone.

She turned around. "Yes?" Her eyes pleaded with him, but he shook his head and looked away. "Your desk must be piled high. I've never known you not to go to the office on a Saturday after a business trip."

"There's nothing pressing," she told him casually. No, she wasn't going to make this easy for him. Not one bit. He was going to have to shove her away. It didn't matter if he pushed her so hard that she stumbled and fell backward. Because somehow, some way, she would pick herself up again. She was a survivor, if nothing else.

Two boxes were already filled and Susan scooted them aside. She pulled a third cardboard case across the carpet, then carefully slid out the bottom row of books.

As she did, several Christmas cards fell onto the floor. One was a flowery, romantic one that immediately attracted her attention with its huge red poinsettia and the bold words calligraphed across the top: "TO THE WOMAN I LOVE." Another was a humorous one, identical to one that Susan had read that Christmas while looking for a special card for Adam.

Sharply she sucked in her breath. Four cards had spilled onto the carpet, each one fresh and unsigned. Adam had bought these cards for her. He'd deny it vehemently if she were fool enough to confront him. But she knew. Because she had done the same thing.

Acid tears stung the back of her eyes, burning for release.

"Susan, would you mind..." Adam came into the room and paused when he found her posed with the cards in her hands. "Throw that stuff away. They're just some old cards that must have fallen back there from Christmas."

"They're unsigned." One tear weaved a path down her face.

"Yes, well, just throw them away."

Another tear joined the first, followed by several more. "I don't understand you, Adam Gallagher."

He rammed a hand along the side of his head. "Damn it. I knew this was going to happen. You know how I feel about tears."

With all the frustration and anger burning inside, Susan hurled the cards at him. "You have no idea, do you?"

"Idea?" He stared at her blankly.

"I ate tofu on a cracker for you," she shouted, nearly choking on her tears. "I practically killed myself just for the pleasure of running with you. I could barely make it over speed bumps and I was cheerfully jogging miles and miles just to be near you."

"Susan, stop it," he demanded. "You're not making any sense."

"I'm making perfect sense," she shouted unreasonably, waving her arms.

"Susan, please."

"I swallowed my pride so many times I nearly gagged on it." Sobbing uncontrollably, she stormed from one room to another, finally locating some tissues with which to blow her nose.

Stunned, Adam stood in the hallway looking dumbfounded.

"You know what your problem is?" She pointed a finger at him. "You don't need to answer that because I'm going to tell you. Adam Gallagher, you're a coward." She noticed a muscle move against the side of his jaw, but it didn't stop her. Bending down, she picked up the card with the poinsettia. "Just who were you intending to give this to? Your mother?"

"No." He glared at her. "Gail."

The anger drained out of her as she stared back at him speechlessly. Somehow she never believed he'd resort to lying.

"Okay, Adam." Her voice caught on a sob. "You won't say it, so I will. I love you. I'll love you all my life. Move to Washington! Have a good life! But I swear I'm going to haunt you. When you look into another

woman's eyes it'll be my face you'll see. When you run
in the mornings it'll be my footsteps you'll hear behind
you. And…when you look into some little boy's face,
you'll see the son you wouldn't give me." Tears were
streaming uncontrollably down her cheeks now. Wiping
them aside, she looked at him one last time. He stood
proud, defensive, stubborn…and insecure. "Good-bye,
Adam." The words were issued softly, belying the inner
turmoil. Taking her jacket, she stepped out of his apartment and out of his life.

She walked when she wanted to run, swallowed back
the sobs when her heart was breaking. By the time she
was on the street, the tears had abated and the weight
in her heart seemed to press harder and heavier.

Before she was aware of her destination, Susan found
herself in Central Park. Her eyes were dry now, but
she sniffled as she strolled along the footpath. For old
times, she told herself.

She paused at the bench where they'd met in the
mornings, and ran a hand longingly over the painted
wood surface. Those few short days were the happiest of
her life. Dejected and miserable, she sat, leaned against
the back of the bench, stretched out her legs and crossed
them at the ankles. Her chin was buried in her jacket.

She'd done it again—made a fool of herself in front
of Adam. Fool or no fool, how could he leave her when
she loved him so much?

Someone sat at the other end of the bench. Susan
took it to be a stranger until he assumed the same position as she, crossing his feet at the ankles. Those shoes
were lovingly familiar. Adam's shoes. He didn't say a

word. She didn't either. Forcing herself to stare directly ahead of her, she didn't move, hardly breathed.

"I have to go away," he said in a controlled voice that seemed devoid of emotion.

Susan said nothing.

"I'm so much in love with you that I can't hide it anymore."

She didn't move, the words paralyzing her.

"When we first met I couldn't believe someone as beautiful as you could be interested in a nobody like me."

The argument was old. She was sick of it and refused to be drawn into it again.

"Later, when I learned you were a romance editor," he continued, "I knew it would never work. But I already loved you, and as much as I tried to force myself to leave you alone, sever our relationship, I couldn't."

"Why?" The one word came out high and uneven. "Because I can never be like the men in those books. The man every woman dreams about, the kind of man you deserve. I'm not rich, dark or handsome. I'm a weak man. The night Joey died, I proved to you just how weak I am. A man crying. That must be a first for you. I'll never be the strong and silent type."

"What makes you think I want that?" Still she didn't turn or look at him.

"It would be impossible for you to read and not compare me with the hero in those books. Maybe not at first, but eventually; and when the comparison came, I'd fall short. With Gail I made the mistake of believing a woman could love me in spite of my plainness. I don't want to make that mistake again."

"Don't compare me to Gail," she hissed.

"It's not only that," he murmured. "You work with beautiful people and unreal situations. I deal with reality."

"I love you, Adam," she told him, hands clenched in her pockets. "You, Dr. Adam Gallagher, not some insensitive, conceited male whose interests revolve around himself. I'm flesh and blood and capable of distinguishing between fantasy and reality."

"You were right when you said I'm a coward. I'm more of one than you know. I was in the park watching you last Christmas. Hiding."

"Hiding? When?" For the first time she turned her head to look at him. He was pale, his mouth tight, the eyes dark but brilliant.

"I called you and purposely mentioned something about running, hoping you'd come to the park. Yet when you did, I stood in the distance, unable to come to you. Afraid that when I saw you again, I wouldn't be able to hide my love."

She released a shuddering breath. "You know, Adam, I was the one who introduced myself to you. I asked you to kiss me that first time. I followed you, made excuses to see you. Nearly killed myself to become physically fit to run with you. Made an utter fool of myself so many times I've lost count. I even had to be the one to tell you I was in love first. But so help me, if I end up proposing, I'll never forgive you."

"Will this help?" He took something out of his pocket, flipped open the velvet top and handed it to her.

Susan sat up shocked. A diamond engagement ring from Tiffany's. Her mouth dropped open, but words refused to come. "When? How?"

"I got the ring after the accident. I knew then I couldn't live without you."

"Why has it taken you so long?" she asked in a painful gasp.

Adam took the ring from the case and slipped it on her finger. A smile of immense pleasure turned up the edges of his mouth. "I was just waiting for the right moment."

"Oh, Adam!" She smiled and threw herself into his arms.

* * * * *